The
Crossed
Keys

DAVID DEMSKI

The Crossed Keys

Concerning the cover photo... you wouldn't believe how many fog-less mornings the author had to suffer through waiting for a shot dreary enough to use.

This is a work of fiction. Names, characters, places, and incidents either are products of the author's imagination or are used fictitiously. Any resemblance to actual events or locales or persons, living or dead, is entirely coincidental. Basically, the author is saying he made this shit up. Because he did.

Having said the above, the M1868 Papal States Remington is a very real weapon. Google it. It's interesting.

First printing December 2020 – Yes that 2020

ISBN-13: 978-1727590364
ISBN-10: 1727590368

If you are so inclined, you can write the author at:
crossedkeysbook@gmail.com

To my wife, my daughter, and my son.

I love you all so very much.
Be wary when you make your way out into the forest.

To my mom.

Thanks for teaching me to enjoy reading.

The Crossed Keys

Coffee, tea, or noodle soup?

Even from a short distance, the flickering flames of the small campfire could barely be seen through the dense wall of waxy evergreen branches. A thick circular stand of long established holly, pine, and hemlock formed a barrier that sheltered the camp in which the fire burned. For well over a century those trees parted the cold wind that rushed down through the valley, not unlike the rocks that parted the water in the many streams nearby. Tents, canoes, and other supplies were stored safely in the tall but twisted growth. The relative stillness of the air made the camp feel little warmer than if it had been set in the barren deciduous forest just feet away. At the far end of the stand, the sky opened wide as it reached a dark still lake which spread out among the deep places between the wooded hills. Places carved from granite by ice age glaciers which were later filled with frigid clear water. If one stood in just the right spot the peak of Mount Washington could be seen across the lake and far off in the distance. It was a cold late October night in northern New Hampshire.

The modest fire had burned long enough to create a hot base of glowing coals in the bottom of the blackened stone circle, stones that were piled and re-piled time and time again. The rounded river rocks had long since split into jagged angular shapes after frequent heatings had cracked them along unseen faults. The site was very old, often forgotten, but occasionally rediscovered throughout the years. Having just stumbled upon it the autumn before, the man tending the fire was only the latest in a long line to shelter there.

Andy had been back for at least a half of an hour, which in turn was at least an hour after the sun had started to sink below the western hills. He had no idea what time it was, and that didn't matter to him at all. The rising and setting of the sun were his only points of concern while he was hunting. Andy had just returned from the icy edge of the nearby lake where he finished field dressing and cleaning two large rabbits. Rabbits he opportunistically shot while finding his way back from where he hunted that day. Unexpected situations like finding those hares were justification enough for him to always carry his little Henry survival twenty-two. Unfortunately for him the moose he was actually seeking, through the distant marshes and brush around the lakes and ponds, had avoided his stalking so far. He still had three more days to hunt and his hopes were high. Andy was in the right part of the forest and had seen enough game signs to reasonably believe that at least one big bull was in the area.

With the sun decidedly gone for the day leaving just the stars and waning quarter moon the only natural light, Kent, another hunter was making his way back to the same camp. He confidently walked through the darkness, finding his way by differentiating between the black and almost black shapes he passed. Though he always carried a good flashlight, GPS, and a compass, his well-honed woodsmen skills were enough to guide him to his friend without needing any of the devices. Once he made it into the general area of their camp, being downwind, Kent followed the welcoming smell of wood smoke the last several hundred yards until he saw the fire. Not concerned with finding game after the sun set he had made good time heedlessly pushing through the underbrush as he hiked from the distant hills where he had spent the day hunting.

Andy heard the sounds of Kent's uncaring footfalls, stopped what he was doing, and looked up to see his friend coming out of the shadows.

"I guess you've managed to find some Sherpas somewhere around here. Huh? Are they carrying back that moose you bagged? I figure you must have gotten some assistance, because you didn't fire any signal shots for me to come and help ya." Andy called out while Kent was still fifteen yards away. "Or maybe I just didn't hear 'em, since there's no way an expert marksman like *YOU* would come back empty handed *TWO* days in a row."

Kent's mind immediately began imagining the majestic towering peaks of the snowcapped Himalayas and the people who called it home. He knew that not all Sherpas hauled supplies up and down mountains for wealthy climbers, however, that fact wasn't something he'd mention to his companion. Details just weren't what Andy was interested in. Instead, the only reply offered was a gloved middle finger and a halfhearted grin.

Kent knew where Andy's barb had come from. The night before, sitting around the fire recounting the day's events, Kent told Andy of his hunt and how he decided to pass on a smaller bull he could have taken. Twenty four hours later, and Andy was still picking on him for what he saw as an unforgivable missed opportunity. What it boiled down to was just two different hunting philosophies. Both men, now in their late thirties and early forties had known each other for nearly a decade. Hunting always brought out the boasting, as well as the taunting. They wouldn't have it any other way.

Finally in camp, Kent was close enough to notice the two rabbits being forced on to hastily carved wooden spits. He decided it was his turn.

"Uh huh. Look who's talking. We didn't hike and canoe into the absolute middle of nowhere for you to go rabbit hunting!" He laughed. "Some big game hunter you turned out to be. You know you could have gotten those rabbits about ten feet out of your back door."

"Really? You're going to give me shit? Over this? Over shooting us some dinner?"

Kent had no intention of letting Andy off so easily.

"Yeah, actually think I will, I think maybe you should have just stayed at home to shot rabbits. Since I doubt you'll even get to see a moose this year. You could have saved yourself a lot of time, money, and effort by just sitting in your backyard." Kent chuckled before continuing. "You know, if you did practice some of your elite hunting skills a little more, you might have been able to defend your vegetable garden this summer. You know, you might have even had some actual produce this year."

"Whatever, Kent. Coming from you, that's pretty damn low. No need to pick on a man's vegetable garden. I never claimed to be a farmer. As you know I'm certainly an elite hunter. You may have also heard that I'm quite the lover. And, in some circles I'm even known as an adventure seeking son of a bitch. But a vegetable gardener? Well, gardener not so much so. Though some of the pepper plants survived, and I had my share of cherry tomatoes this year." Andy finished in a mumble before giving up on any real defense with a unenthusiastic shrug. "Anyway, I was done for the day and was walking back. It was mostly dark. No real chance in that kind of light for a long range shot at a moose. So, when I came to a clearing full of these guys, I took a couple shots. Let me tell you, huge warren, I haven't seen so many rabbits in one place... Well, ever... Anyway, got us a pair before they all holed up. I figured some fresh meat roasting over the fire tonight would make a nice addition to what we brought. Plus, you know me. After spending the last couple days walking around armed I needed to shoot at something. So *BAM*, instant dinner for two."

"Well as long as you keep *BAMMING* and making all that noise on your side of the mountain, have at it. You can scare anything you want towards me. I'd appreciate the help. But yeah, a nice brace of rabbit will be… uh… nice." He paused in thought and then loudly enough for Andy to hear, but mostly to himself he said "I was wondering who was popping off all those rounds. If those shots were yours... well... I guess we really are alone up here."

At the edge of the camp Kent sat down on the ground and leaned against a loose pile of large stones that looked as if it could have once been part of a larger, now long abandoned, structure. In doing so he took the weight of his frame pack off his shoulders for the first time in hours. He wiggled out of the straps and once his arms were completely free he just sat there on the soft loam. The relief was just what he needed. Exhaling deeply the strain and tension from the hike drained from his body.

Kent rested for several minutes until something occurred to him.

"Hey. Andy. Hold up a second. You know, I heard at least five shots out there and only see, one, two... yeah only two rabbits. As a hard adventuring hunter lover, or whatever it is you are, I can't imagine you'd miss, so...?"

Smiling, his friend stopped what he was doing and purposely turned to face Kent. This time it was Andy who slowly raised his hand and flipped Kent the bird.

"Open sights. In the dark," was all he said.

After a while, once the cold ground became uncomfortable, Kent decided it was time to move. He checked the open bolt on his rifle again, put the weapon in its case, and propped it up against another case leaning on one of the two canoes. Kent then made his way around the camp, preparing for the night. With each shift in the slight breeze the comforting smell of meat roasting over the open fire spread throughout the clearing reminding the men of just how hungry they were. Deliberate and practiced in their motions, little was said while they enjoyed the quiet sounds of the forest and the simple pleasures of being outside. In turn they each finished their separate tasks before making their way to improvised log seats on opposite sides of the small fire. Warming themselves while silently waiting for the game to finish roasting.

When the rabbits were cooked, the spits were removed, and each man took one. Andy started immediately on the steaming hot food with his knife, cutting the lean rabbit into quarters. The first section he grabbed was tossed from hand to hand, searching for something cool enough to hold. Kent delayed his meal only long enough to offer a short and silent prayer of thanks. Once finished he too quickly followed Andy's lead, scorched fingers and all.

The roasted game, once it was just barely cool enough to swallow, didn't last long.

"Darn, that rabbit was really good," Kent said, tossing the last of the bones into the hottest part of the fire. "Darn good, and sure beats the heck out of the trail food I was planning to eat tonight. Thank ya Andy."

"You're welcome. I thought you'd appreciate it." Still seated Andy gave Kent a mock formal bow with a goofy smile.

It had been a long active day with both men out of their tents and on the trails before sunrise. They were tired and enjoyed the opportunity to relax, gazing into the glowing coals and taking turns squinting as the smoke alternated drifting between them.

As the night continued to deepen, the bitterly cold wind they were generally protected from slightly picked up, enough to be noticed as it pushed on and through the trees that sheltered them. Branches creaked and groaned, swaying almost invisibly in the darkness above. The night turned darker still when the soft glow of the partial moon dipped out of sight behind the surrounding rocky hills. Not that they could see it through the trees but a frosty haze covered the sky and dimmed what remained of the stars. For the hunters, the campfire was the only source of light anywhere to be seen.

Inactive long enough, and deciding it was almost time to turn in for the night, Kent got up first and started looking around for a nearby patch of snow. An early winter storm came heavily a week before, but as it often does in autumn on the East coast, the weather warmed up immediately after. Much of the snow had melted, but just before the men headed off on their five day hunting trip, the temperature dropped again. Small white drifts from the storm only still lingered in the shadows and hollows, but the snow that remained wasn't going to melt any time soon.

A dozen or so steps away Kent found what he was looking for. Just outside the fire's circle of light and beside a tree, he reached down for a handful of snow that hadn't yet turned into solid ice. Rubbing the clean but painfully cold slush between his hands, he washed away the last remnants of the rabbit dinner.

As Kent was about to turn back towards the fire, a loud *CRACK* shattered the relative silence they'd grown accustomed to. A branch snapped.

Different than most any other sound in the forest, the acuteness of it did more than just stand out. It was like an alarm, and like any alarm, the noise they heard wasn't the concern. As loud as it was, they knew it was a branch of substantial size and was broken by something of equally large proportions. Something that big was something that could be a concern. Without saying a word Andy immediately stood up looking around for the source. Kent remained where he was but made the familiar reach to his hip, grabbing for his "bear repellant." His hand wrapped around the large handle of a Smith & Wessen 460V, a big bored, brightly polished revolver.

Looking away from the fire the men's eyes struggled to adjust to the darkness with no immediate avail. The world outside the camp looked like nothing more than a black void. As far as their eyes could tell nothing existed beyond the firelight. Both remained silent and strained their ears trying to hear anything. Anything that could be used to identify whatever it was that sounded to be just out of view.

Two flickering specks appeared first, faintly glowing like red and yellow flames, moving with gentle sways. Those were followed by the soft sounds of footfalls on pine needles, accented by the muffled crackles of smaller twigs and dried brittle holly leaves. The men quickly and fully turned towards the sight. Focusing first on the twin points of light, within seconds the men started to be able to make out something else. Something that was less dark than the rest of the night, something which developed into the rough shape of a man. A shape of a man that continued to make its way closer. A shape of a man... that was... waving its arm at them. Within another second or two the floating fire lights morphed and became a pair of oversized round glasses reflecting the campfire back at them, the man shape, became an actual man.

"Hello?" The person approaching called out. "Um, excuse me. Hello there?"

Having made his way close enough to the campfire, the shadows ultimately parted to resolve the vague man shape into an actual man. A tall but thin mousy man who looked fairly abused and disheveled. His khaki pants were wet and muddy to the knees as were his light blue jacket sleeves to his elbows. He was obviously cold and obviously out of place.

"Hello? Hi, um, sorry to be a bother, but I really could use some assistance from you gentlemen. That is, if doing so would not be too much of a bother?" The stranger asked in a formal manner and with a New England accent that seemed just a little unusual to the men.

With no immediate objection from the bewildered Kent or Andy, the man promptly made his way to the fire and thrust his hands out greedily over the flames. Kent slowly walked his way back into camp. He tried to relax, but didn't take his eyes off of the out of place and unexpected visitor. The new comer wasn't a bear, wasn't a coyote or wolf, and to Kent he didn't appear to be any other kind of threat. Hesitantly he removed his hand from the sidearm still in its holster and tried to shake off the uneasy feeling the encounter had given him.

"I am very thankful. I am so cold right now and… and… I am so glad I came upon your camp, gentleman. And cold." he stammered through his chattering teeth.

"Cold? No wonder" Andy started, a little reluctant at first, as if unsure where to begin. "Wearing just, just a Goddamn a windbreaker? And your shoes are... crap, and soaking wet. What the hell man, what are you doing all the way out here?"

Both campers made their way closer to the visitor.

"He's wearing some North Face gear Kent, he must go on a lot of adventures," joked Andy in a whisper as he walked past Kent to reach the shivering man. He then half kicked and half rolled an additional log into position to use as a seat for the nearly frozen stranger.

Kent, unsure of what else to do, decided to also make himself useful. He put on one of his gloves and grabbed the pot that was heating over the fire.

"Have a seat, friend. Let's pour you a cup of this hot water. We can make it into coffee, tea, or noodle soup. Your choice, I believe we still have all three left."

"Thank you, um, soup if you will. It's been a very long day, I could use the... um... nourishment." The man said sheepishly. "I really do thank you."

"Yeah, yeah. No worries. Now, seriously." Andy continued pressingly. "What the hell are you doing all the way out here? There's nothing around here. Nothing at all."

"Um, I'm not certain where I should begin." He just left the comment hang, and nervously glanced around the camp until his eyes finally glazed over and settled on the canoes off towards the end of camp. His facial expression froze and he appeared to be lost in thought or confused.

In less than a minute Kent was nearly finished making the soup. Having collected what he needed, he poured steaming water into a collapsible bowl that held the contents of a packet of dry soup mix. Once offered the bowl and Spork the professor re-engaged. Both were taken cautiously and a little clumsily. Kent lightly brushed against the skinny man's hand during the transfer. His fingers were ice cold.

"Wrap your hands around that bowl. It will help you warm up. Just be careful though, the soup is nearly boiling. Believe it or not, you can burn yourself before you even feel it with hands as numb as yours. Got it? Ok, so? Like Andy asked, what were you doing out there? But I guess first things are first. You hurt? Is there anyone else out there with you we should be looking for?"

"Well… um… I'm fine. Just displaced, I guess you could say. Was, hiking. Nature. Getting in shape, alone. Just me. I'm alone, well, not alone. I'm now here with you, but no one else. No one else I know is out there. Does that answer your questions?" He replied in fragments before loudly slurping his first mouthful of soup. He didn't appear to care that the dry egg noodles hadn't had a chance to soften in the hot broth yet or that the water was still nearly scalding. Clouds of steam rose from the bowl and partially hid his face. "I left this morning to go on a little day hike, walk through the aphyllous forest, ascend a few hillocks. Get my heart rate up. Then everything went… um… well… not everything went according to my original plans. I only scheduled a few hours in the morning for this activity. To only be on the trails for a few… I um."

Andy started to feel sorry for the man. He looked pathetic and sounded addled and distracted. It was clear he wasn't an outdoorsman, or even athletic. Andy thought being lost in the forest all day must have taken its toll on him.

"Look. You're alright now, just take it easy. Between me and Kent here, we've got enough gear to share and we'll get everything sorted out for you in the morning. I'm Andy Warren by the way, and that sad looking son of a bitch over there is Kent Williams. And you are…"

"Professor West…" He paused. Andy and Kent gave each other a glance. The man still to seemed confused. "Um, Herb West. I don't know why I just said that. History. Professor of. Um, Herb. Hopefully one day Doctor West, but that doesn't matter at the moment. Thank you, again. Both of you. I have to admit I came to your fire with the intention of only getting directions and warming up just enough to dry my feet. Now I'm a little hesitant to head back into the forest. Though, I'm sure I can't be too far from the trail…"

The professor fruitlessly looked around as if somehow, just then, he would spot the path that would lead him out of the forest.

"No, actually. No you really are too far from the trail. Seriously, there isn't a trail to anyplace you need to go that's anywhere around here. Plus, it is just too darn dangerous for you to be heading out in the dark. Especially with how you're dressed." Kent stated as if it wasn't up for debate. "Where did you even come in at, or park? You say you have been wandering around since this morning, Professor? You could have, and most likely have, put miles behind you in all that time. Most likely in the wrong direction. No, I strongly suggest you consider staying here with us until first light. We're really pretty far out in the sticks and you're just not prepared for that type of a trek. Listen, you can't be out there and not be properly equipped. Did you even bring a compass, a map, heck, even a flashlight?"

Kent immediately regretted his tone, which was a little harsh and judgmental compared to the polite demeanor he normally displayed around those he just met, but watching people act in dangerously moronic ways had always been a sore point for him. He thought of them as the "there ought to be a law" crowd. Kent hated how stupid people hurt themselves doing something stupid and then blamed their stupidity on the legality of the act and not themselves. In the end their dumb actions and lack of accountability result in new laws which just limit everyone else's ability to enjoy life.

To answer Kent, meekly and with reluctance, Professor Herb shrugged his shoulders halfway to his ears. "I've, um... Well, if you must know, I have an App for all of that."

Then with a little more confidence, he quietly said, "Or I did, until I slipped and dropped my phone. I unsuccessfully attempted to transverse a small brook. Instinctively I tried to brace my fall, to keep my face from striking the rocks, at that point I let go of the device. The now inoperable screen was the result."

He reached into his pocket and pulled out an older, dark, and lifeless iPhone. The phone, coupled with the look on the professor's face, was just too much for the hunters. Kent shook his head smiling while Andy let out a belly laugh large enough to cause a giant cloud of breath to nearly obscure his entire head. A moment later he fell back down into his cut log seat.

"You were relying on your PHONE! A fucking god damn iPhone!" he continued while laughing. "Man, you really are as lucky as shit to be alive. Seriously, you've made too many mistakes for one day. This is not your neighborhood park. What did you plan on doing with that thing? You don't need driving directions to Whole Foods out here. This is nature. Real honest to God nature. People die out here. Truly, literally, die! Hell, it was just last summer two hikers were never found again after setting out in these hills. You know what? There's a hell of a lot more than just a good chance you wouldn't have been alive tomorrow if you hadn't run into us. Shit, that in itself was one in a million. Needle in a haystack kinda deal. Damn. With how wet you are, and how cold it is, I can't believe you don't already have hyperthermia."

Humbled but thankful, West replied, "Yes, yes. I began to realize some of that just before the sun set. I didn't know what else to do so I just kept going forward. Although I'm glad I did, even with all my mistakes. I made it here. I now know how fortuitous it was stumbling upon this camp site. You are the only people I've seen all day."

"Hey. It's alright, don't worry about it." Kent interjected, attempting to quiet Andy down a bit. "Things happen. Out here though, you really do need the right tools for the job. Next time you'll know better."

Andy took the hint and stopped grinning before he chimed in.

"Yeah. No worries though, you'll be all right now. Um. Let's see, I guess we're just about four miles or so from the nearest real road. From what I recall, that is. By hiking though, it could be more than that. Actually how far of a walk depends on if you can find trails that don't meander too much. I'm not sure how bad that will be, that's not the way Kent and I came in. But still, we'll point you in the direction of the shortest way out and you won't need a canoe like we did to go that way either. The hike will take you a good bit of the morning. In the sunlight, we'll break out one of our maps. The directions shouldn't be…well, I don't know." Andy doubted himself. "What do you think

17

Kent? I'm of the mind that to be safe, one of us should take 'em out in the morning. Professor, you really don't want to get lost again, there isn't anyone else you're likely going to run into if you make another mistake."

Andy looked to Kent questioningly. He continued when he received an uncertain but affirmative shrug.

"We'll get you to the road. From there it should be easy enough to flag down a car. Our phones don't work here either, where we are now, but they might once we get you out of this valley. You'll be able to call someone and have 'em met you. Tonight though, we'll just build up the fire a little more than normal and you can use my emergency blanket. If it gets much colder, I guess we can let you climb into one of our tents with us."

Glancing over to look at the two tiny one man tents set up a few feet away, Kent fake coughed "Not mine," while covering his mouth.

Andy continued unfazed.

"It'll be a tight fit, but it's more than possible and you'll be warm. Just relax and rest up. Big hike in the morning. You're safe and if you wanna look at the bright side, now you've got a good story to tell at the next facility meeting. You'll make it out of this adventure a little uncomfortable but still alive."

"Thank you for your... um... kindness. Yes, indeed. Leaving here alive would be... pleasant." West replied.

The professor remained seated in front of the fire while the hunters collected items from around camp. Kent found a dry pair of socks, a pair of gloves, and a scarf. West changed into those. Andy took out his Mylar emergency blanket and also handed it over to the professor. Both hunters gave him a quick lesson on how to hold the blanket open so that heat reflected from the fire back onto his body.

After everyone wrapped up what they were doing the professor began to recount his journey. Before too long he became side-tracked and was sharing a brief history of jewelry. Once comfortable and thawed out, it was obvious the Professor enjoyed lecturing and he quickly wandered between a wide variety of disparate subjects. The disjointed speech he used when the hunters first met him slowly transitioned into a flowing, comfortable, almost sing song cadence. While topically somewhat interesting, the rhythmic manner in which his story was delivered began lulling the men into a state where they came very close to dozing off. Both hunters soon found they had trouble keeping their eyes open.

"... and that is why Kennedy failed the Cuban people at the Bay of Pigs and ..." West was interrupted mid-sentence.

Forcefully resisting the strong urge to give into sleep, Kent stood up and briskly shook his head in an attempt to wake himself.

"Sorry to cut in like this," Kent said after clearing his throat. "But I think I could use a cup of coffee. You want something else warm to drink, Herb?"

"If you are fixing some for yourself, yes. The same. Please, and thank you. Though if you are tired we could just resume this discussion in the morning. I wouldn't mind. You can both turn in, I'm warm enough now. I can manage by myself just sitting here next to the fire."

"Na, soon maybe, but I'm good for a bit longer. Just needed to stretch is all. One slightly smoky cup of hot water coming right up. Sorry though, I should have mentioned it before I offered, but we didn't bring any sugar or cream." Kent apologized as he left the warmth of the fire to lower the food bag that was dangling from a rope several feet above their heads.

"Oh, um... Black is fine for me. I really would just like something that's warm. I'm sure the caffeine will also be a pleasant addition. For all of us."

The disruption of the lecture and spontaneous change of topics also caused Andy to stir. He stood and stretched as well, but then headed away from the fire. As he walked off he became just a dark silhouette behind his bright flashlight beam. Seconds later, a loud zipping sound ripped through the silence.

"I think I've also got something we might all want," his voice called out, somewhat dampened from inside the little one man shelter which was filled with his thick sleeping bag. The tent was roughly the size and shape of a coffin and the flashlight made the deep red fabric brightly glow. The shadows created by the ruby light danced on the nearby trees in the pitch black evening.

It didn't take long for Kent to make himself and the professor a cup of instant coffee. While two of them took their first sips at their mugs, Andy had made his way back into the firelight and produced an oversized metal flask. He held the stainless steel container proudly in the air, opened it, and took a large swig.

"Damn that's fine," Andy grunted out loudly with a cough. In the frigid air clouds of steam exploded from his mouth before disappearing into fleeting white wisps. He passed the flask to the professor, who smiled as he fumbled awkwardly one handed to reopen it.

"Thank you." He said before taking a mouthful of the drink. After a generous swig he gave Andy a quick head nod then held the flask out, passing it towards Kent. The professor's response to the beverage was uninspired. "The drink was… very… um… warming."

Kent didn't reach out towards West or his offering. Instead he held up his hand.

"Naaa, thanks. I don't drink all that much. At least not out here. Not while hunting." Kent said, shaking his head while he eyed the container suspiciously. He then looked back at Andy with a quick flick of his head indicating that's where the flask should go next.

"*JESUS H. CHRIST!*" Andy yelled from out of nowhere, abruptly disrupting the hushed atmosphere. The professor recoiled visibly from the outburst. "Just have a drink you pussy. It's not going to fucking kill you, every once in a while you can act a little social and let loose. Seriously man, lighten up. Besides, it's Maker's Mark which is fairly decent bourbon."

At that stage in the evening, Kent wasn't in the mood for a lengthy debate with Andy over something as meaningless as a sip of whisky. Giving in was the path of least resistance, so he decided to take a drink. He wasn't happy about it. Annoyed Kent snatched the flask from the professor's still outstretched arm. He opened it, gave Andy a "screw you" kind of a look, took a swig, and … coughed. He coughed twice more while handing the flask back to Andy, who was chuckling loudly to himself.

"Well, maybe it's, uh… not Maker's Mark. I actually don't recall what I put in there, but damn. It sure isn't very smooth, is it?" Andy laughed.

"That's enough for me" Kent said wiping his mouth with the back of his hand. The harsh shot made his eyes water. He looked directly at Andy and gave him a scowl.

Andy didn't appreciate the attitude and said "I swear, sometimes I think you are the whiniest little bitch I've ever met. I sure do hope you packed enough tampons for the rest of the trip."

"Forget you Andy. You know I don't really drink whiskey all that much, that doesn't make me what you called me," Kent shot back.

Sometimes Andy went too far for Kent. He wasn't really angry but he felt he couldn't let a taunting like that go without a reply. Unfortunately, his reply actually *DID* make Kent feel whiny at the very least, but despite knowing better he continued on with his defense.

"Out here, what it means is that I'm smarter than you are. How much does that flask weigh? We fight to save every single ounce hiking out to this place and you go ahead and bring useless gear!"

"I, um… appreciated the beverage," the professor chimed in. He then immediately looked as though he wished he hadn't.

Ignoring the professor completely, Kent continued.

"You didn't want to bring that extra box of twenty rounds because it was too heavy, but you'll bring that big ole flask! Ammunition, in the middle of nowhere, is way more useful than that bourbon is."

"Whoa whoa whoa whoa *WHOA*! First of all, it's my pack and it's on my back. I'll carry in it whatever the fuck I want. And second, let's not forget that whiskey is a disinfectant, a pain reliever, a water purifier, and at times it has even been used as currency. It's all around just good shit to have. Third, easy up there Mr. I live in a big ass glass house and like throwing big ass rocks. Let's talk about that extra fucking rifle you drag around *EVERYWHERE* and *NEVER* even take out of its fucking case. How much does that bitch weigh? Pounds versus my ounces. A lot of Goddamn pounds! Smarter than I am my hairy ass." Everyone was quiet for several seconds, and just focused on the campfire.

"As you said, it's my pack, just like that's your pack. I don't care what you bring. I just don't like being called a bitch, is all."

"Yeah, yeah. I know." Was all that Andy replied. There was a hint of embarrassment in his tone.

Fights like that, while not actually common, were also not completely unknown between the two men. Kent usually handled Andy better but at that moment he let the taunts get to him. Neither was really mad at the other. The heated feelings dissipated as soon as the words were spoken and both hunters felt a little guilty for how they acted. Neither one would, or needed to, apologize; nor would either hold a grudge. All it would take was a few moments of silence for the tension to pass. In the meantime the Professor just sat on his log awkwardly staring at his feet which were propped up on a rock next to the fire.

A few moments did pass. The fire continued to crackle. The wind continued to blow. The trees continued to creak and moan. Otherwise, all else was quiet. After a while Andy threw another piece of wood into the fire, momentarily pushing back the shadows and temporarily illuminating a little more of their surroundings.

The professor, who had spent the last couple minutes with a puzzled look on his face, was the first to break the silence and put an end to the stubborn standoff.

"I, um... I can understand the purpose of the whiskey, *NOT* to take sides. You understand, yes? Um. But why, why carry with you another gun if it is never used? I see you have a pistol on your hip. And over there I see two gun cases, with what I assume contain big and heavy guns. That's three guns just for yourself? To me, that seems like more firepower than is strictly necessary. Well, I don't see the need for anyone to ever own guns, but I don't believe now is the time to enter into that discussion. Is it some typical hunting practice I haven't been able to grasp? Andy says you never shoot it, if that is indeed the case, then carrying it all the way out here seems even more redundant and unnecessary. Why then, if you don't mind, the extra gun?"

"Well, you might have heard the expression that 'one is none and two are one,' but it's more than that with Kent and his rifle. Professor, it be best to just give up on that line of questioning though. I wouldn't even bother trying unless you plan on begging." Andy sarcastically tossed out with a grin.

Herb West, having asked his question, reset the atmosphere around the camp. Both Kent and Andy were thankful for it and the mood mostly returned to normal. Andy continued.

"All you'll ever get from Kent is 'right tool for the job – right tool for the job.' I've asked him about it a bunch of times. He's a fucking retarded parrot when it comes to that rifle of his. Right tool for the job, bwwwak. Kent wants a cracker."

Something about West's interest and expression caught Kent's eye. He focused on him for a few seconds and then into the fire for a few more before he finally shifted his gaze towards Andy.

"No Andy. No, I think I will tell you about it tonight. With West being a history professor and all, he may, well you both may... appreciate the story." He paused for a moment, something obviously on his mind.

The lull grew and Kent remained deep in thought, unresponsive to the glances from Andy and the professor.

"Anyone at home? Hello, McFly? Story time?" Andy mocked before breaking into a chuckle.

"Alright, give me a second. Let me finish collecting my thoughts. I'll tell you, however..." Kent continued forcefully. He looked between both men sitting at the fire, but stopped to really bore into Andy. "You have to let me tell the whole story. Start to finish. Alright?"

"Yeah, sure." Andy replied immediately. His curiosity had been piqued by both Kent's seriousness and the possibility of finally learning about the rifle. Something did bother him though. He looked back and forth between Kent and the Professor. "But, um... Why now? Not that I'm complaining, but you know I've asked you about that damn rifle before. Hell, I know I've asked you about it at least a dozen times. Thought maybe you were some kind of weird sexual gun deviant or some shit. Do you stroke it at night, Kent? Does she have a name? Are you two in love?"

Kent ignored the taunts and turned back to gazing deep into the fire.

"Seriously Andy. It's gonna be a long story, and I either tell all of it, my way, without your bull crap jokes, or I just don't tell it. I'm serious."

"Lighten up I said I would let ya. I'm curious. I've only ever caught glimpses of that thing. I wanna know about it. Seems important to you. I'll be good. Promise. I'll pinky swear if that's what it'll take.

That is what you and your sorority sisters did? Right? Pinky swears in between all the pillow fights in the old phi alpha house?" He said with a full toothy smile trying to antagonize Kent again.

The bait, however, wasn't taken. Kent, with his eyes still focusing deep into the pulsating red and blue coals, quietly began speaking.

A shallow trash filled depression

Well, I think I need to start at the very beginning. I grew up in West Virginia, a bit south of Morgantown and a few miles outside of a small town called Bucksburg. A tiny little place by any standard. It didn't even have a McDonald's back then. I think maybe there was a pair of traffic lights by the train tracks and another one on Main Street. Think small town. My parents and I lived neighbor free in a secluded house halfway up the side of a mountain. A place that doesn't look all that different from where we are now. At the very least the trees, plants, and hills remind me of it. I guess the Appalachians are the Appalachians a good bit of their length from Georgia to Maine. You know, they're the oldest mountain range in the world, or so I've heard.

Anyway.

We were poor, but not as poor as I'm sure you're imagining. I wore shoes. Never went hungry. I got what I needed, but my parents still struggled here and there. As a kid you couldn't help noticing that sometimes your family was just broke. I saw the stress and worry on my parent's faces and overheard it in their conversations. Overall though, life wasn't too bad for us. It probably helped that most everyone else I knew were pretty darn poor as well. To get by my parents put in a lot of hours. Extra shifts to get the bills paid on time. Dad worked at the mine, mom at the grocery store. They were gone a lot, but I didn't mind the time alone. Living out there, in the country, there was just so much for me to do.

I took full advantage of growing up deep in the woods. Hiking, hunting, building treehouses and forts. During the summer you'd find me splashing around in a stream, fishing or catching crawdads. I think they'd be called crayfish up here, professor. In the winter it was sledding, snow forts, and then sitting in front of the fireplace drying off and warming up. Staring into a fire, like we're doing now. Generally I was always doing something. Weather permitting, more often than not I was doing that something outside. When I didn't have school, I'd see my parents for breakfast and then not again until it was dark outside and time for dinner.

Thinking back, you might call me unusual but I even liked school. Not the classes so much, but because of the other kids. Living so far away from one another, school was where I got to spend time with anyone else my age. There was a group of three, and then later, four of us that were inseparable. Best friends. We also had another half dozen or so other kids that often floated in and out of our little clique as well. My friends and I always seemed to be finding ourselves in trouble at school. Nothing all that bad by today's standards, but when we entertained ourselves, the teachers always disapproved.

We caused enough disruptions that some the exasperated educators began to call us "the Monsters" and it was a name we all embraced. Having that moniker was like our friendship was more than just a casual clique, it was official. Like some special club whose charter was confirmed by adults. We wore that mantle with pride. The type of fierce pride only a first grader could muster. Of course when word of our antics at school made their way back home, well, that was something mom tried to discourage. Even after the all notes and the phone calls, I still don't recall ever being punished too harshly.

Even at that age I recognized that I was lucky.

Lucky I lived in such a wonderful place for a boy to grow up.

Lucky I grew up during a time that was a really great time for a boy to grow up in.

Everything was magic back then, a warm comforting kind of magic. A magic that made you feel safe and happy.

It's a shame it didn't last.

Anyway. If you are wondering, I lost what little accent I had after my dad died. After the funeral my mom and I moved to Philly, I was about eleven at the time. She had grown up there, and after my dad's accident she needed the comfort and support of her family. We moved in with my grandparents for a while. Eventually mom got an apartment of her own and once again life began to normalize. I eventually liked living there too, but it took some time. As you can imagine city life just wasn't the same. Not for a boy who grew up among the oaks and the rocks. Not for a kid without his dad to guide him and to lend him strength and support. For a while it was a hard time for me, though I'm sure it was harder for my mom. Maybe all that difficulty built character. If it did I couldn't tell you, but that's just the way it was.

As I said, things got better. I got less sad and less angry. I made new friends, though never as many and few as close as those I had before. I spent a lot more time alone, something I still do. I changed my hobbies. I learned to fit in. Still, I always missed the mountains. Maybe I missed my father and confused the two. I don't know. What I do know is that some of my fondest memories are from the side of that little green mountain.

Anyway, time went on. I grew up. Went to college. Graduated. Got a job. Standard stuff. I moved on with my life.

Eventually I found a job out of state and moved down to Washington D.C. for it. For the first time since I was eleven I lived close enough to easily visit my home state of West Virginia, and I did. My trips started out as just the occasional Sunday drives out to Harpers Ferry. Hike a little, find a restaurant and grab dinner, then head home. Those trips grew to weekend camping east of Morgantown and into the mountains of Western Maryland. It got to the point where I was leaving the city just about one out of every three or four weekends. Some of it was because I really dislike D.C. as a city, but the rest of it was because I just wanted be to where I felt I belonged.

But, I never went back.

I never went back to *MY* mountain.

I don't really know why I avoided it. Maybe I was scared to see it all again through an adult's eyes. Eyes unable to capture the childhood enchantment I remembered. I don't know. Maybe I was scared to find that the hills were smaller, the streams more shallow, and the trees less green than I remembered. Maybe I was just trying to protect all the good memories I had relied on. Memories I cherished and used when times were tough.

For whatever the reason, I just didn't go. I lived a little more than a four hour drive away, and never went back. That was just the way of it.

I guess a couple years before I met you, Andy, I was dating someone named Crystal. There isn't much to say about her, as we didn't date long. We had fun together but in the end it was just one of those things where we didn't really completely click.

Anyway, I met Crystal in the district, but she was originally from Pittsburgh and still had a lot of friends and family there. We decided to drive up early one Sunday morning to watch the Ravens play the

Steelers at Heinz Field. I may have put away a few extra beers at that game. Yes, joker, before you interrupt I did and still do drink occasionally.

After the game we had planned to have dinner with some of Crystal's friends and then get a room for the night. The timing and communication were off and our dinner plans fell apart. Crystal was still sober, so we decided to drive home a day early. Once in the car, I completely neglected the most sacred duty of a passenger on a road trip. I promptly fell asleep.

"It's about freaking time!" Crashed through my dreams.

I jumped awake dazed and disoriented. I felt the car rapidly decelerating and Crystal was loudly cursing at herself. We had been heading South on 79 instead of East on 70. Crystal drove for the better part of two hours before noticing her mistake. At the moment she yelled she had just found an exit where we could turn around. I looked out the windows, and even being confused and in the dark, I could tell she was turning around on *MY* old exit. The very same exit someone took if they wanted to visit where my parents and I lived. At that moment I was just a twenty minute drive from the home where I grew up.

I was shocked by the sudden revelation.

A couple seconds after I had realized where we were, we were once again back on the highway and driving away. Crystal was explaining to me something about maybe not completely backtracking and looking for another highway east. Or something. I wasn't paying attention. I was looking out the windows, seeing as much of the surroundings as I could before it all shrank away into the distance and darkness.

We drove on, but my mind lingered on that ramp. The signs, the overpass, the guard rail, even the litter on the side of the road looked nearly identical to how I remembered. Correcting that one missed turn was all it took for nostalgia to take over my thoughts.

We made our way back to the Capitol in near silence. My mind drifted through old childhood memories. I was overwhelmed. When required, I responded to all of Crystal's friendly queries but her attempts at conversation ended with short one or two word replies from me. I tried not to be rude. I just couldn't focus on anything other than my own thoughts. I needed to hold onto whatever it was I was rediscovering in myself. I wasn't ready to let those feelings and memories slip away. With just that one familiar section of road, less than a minute actually there, I couldn't get my head past the sense of longing that assaulted me.

Later that night, lying awake in bed, I made a decision… I'd go back.

I went back a week later and found myself standing next to the shallow trash filled depression which was once my beloved childhood home.

The house, to be blunt, the house simply wasn't there anymore. From what I could tell, it hadn't been there for quite some time. It was just a hole filled with rusting and rotting trash, vines, small trees, bushes, and leaves. You could see the basic outline of where it was by the few sections of foundation that still existed. In a corner, a couple pipes stuck out of what remained of a concrete slab. The sidewalk and driveway were still there, though showing their age and neglect by crumbling away. A plant covered, chest high, pile of charred rubble was pushed off to the side which contained whatever else was left of the structure.

Everything just looked so depressing to me. The weeds that grew out of the cracks appeared sickly, barely holding on, and ready to die. The leaves on the bushes were brown and a decaying yellow green. What pleasant hues that did remain in the yard, the gloomy overcast sky sucked the color from those. Nothing looked like it could thrive there. It was a world of junk, thrown away, discarded, and forgotten. The house had been burned, demolished, and scrapped from the face of the earth. I didn't know what I was expecting to find, but that morose looking hole certainly wasn't it.

Funny thing was that I was sad, but surprisingly, not terribly so. More disappointed than anything else. At least the garbage hole had saved me from presenting the awkward speech I had practiced on the drive there. I had planned to ask the new owners if I could look around and for them not to shoot me for trespassing. I was glad I was spared at least that small uncomfortable indignity.

With no one around to stop me, I walked the length and width of the lightly wooded lot. I searched the area but was unable to find much that I remembered still intact. A large boulder sticking out of the ground that I once played on, pretending it was a desert island. A tiny creek bed I used to jump over that only had water in the spring or after it rained. I walked the only level spot on the whole properly large enough to play any team sports on. Those things, they were still there, but that was all. Even the trees I once played on and under were gone. The towering oaks and maples I leaned against on lazy summer days were lumbered out years before. In their place grew scrawny, thorn covered black locust trees.

I guess you really can't ever go back home.

The whole experience was a letdown. A letdown and a terrible use of a Saturday afternoon. I felt silly for being so excited at the idea of coming back. I chalked those lost hopes up to yet another example of the dangers of over consuming alcohol. Clear headed, the world was as bleak as ever.

Disappointed, I symbolically lashed out against the cruelty of fate by kicking one of the many empty beer cans that littered the yard. I watched the sun faded container sail through the air and felt silly at my tantrum. That in turn irritated me. I bitterly walked back to the car, and focused on the long drive back to Washington and the backyard party I turned down to go to West Virginia.

I opened the car door, but something made me stop.

Just before I sat down and drove off, almost as if I was going to say my final goodbye, I turned to face the yard once more. I knew the day was wasted, but I hated thinking my trip would end on such a negative note.

I needed something to be there. Anything at all. It wasn't easy but I pushed past what I saw and instead remembered some of my happiest memories.

At that moment the clouds parted.

Nothing monumental or biblical, it was just sunshine. However, that small break in the thick cover soaked me in a column of bright golden light. The sun's warm rays briefly blinded me. I was forced to look down and away. The radiance felt so good on my skin that I closed my eyes and raised my face back up to greet it. It was at that moment I realized that maybe I wasn't home, but I was close enough.

I got into my car with a lighter heart, a smile on my face, and started driving. Not back to the city. Not away from my past. Not even to anyplace in particular. Instead of giving in and heading out, I began taking every back road I could remember. All the while I looked for anything familiar.

With each turn the mountains and trees started to come alive for me. The more I drove the more everything changed, the more the world filled with color as the sky turned from grey to blue. I felt the disappointment slip away with every new mile. The more I looked, the more I saw that I *HAD* made it back home.

It wasn't just that my house had become a hole. Some things were different, and some things had changed, but not everything.

At the house I was wrong, I didn't need time to stop, nor should I have expected it to have done so. Enough of the countryside was still how I remembered, but more importantly, enough of it still *FELT* how I remembered. I didn't need to come back to cinder blocks and plywood. Paint and carpet. I didn't need to come back to things. I had focused too much on the ditch that once was my home. Yes it was the center of my young world, but it was just the center of a much larger universe. The whole area was my home.

The mountains hadn't changed. The rivers, the trees, the roads were all still there. The town was a little bigger and a little closer to the next one over. "Hey, look over there, that house that wasn't there before."

A billboard for a Walmart just fifteen miles ahead. One lane bridge, now a two lane bridge. Changes all, but not changes that destroy the heart of a place. Once I let myself see it, I knew there was something right about being back. Even the air began to smell familiar. Rich, earthy, and alive. The surroundings made me feel like I belonged and I did. I belonged back in those mountains again.

I accepted that I wasn't meant to exist in concrete and marble cities. Places where straight asphalt paths cutting between four trees and dead grass is considered a park. I no longer wanted to be surrounded by noisy indifferent people with the stink of pollution, trash, and unwashed bodies. I didn't need to hear traffic, and construction, and morons babbling beside me every single day of my life. I hated the thought of going back to my daily routine. Aggressively pushing my way through the crowds just for the privilege of waiting for a train that's always late. What I needed was soft soil and fallen leaves under my feet, the smell of the forest, flowers, and earth. Hearing the trees rustling and the only babbling I wanted was that of brooks.

Not for one day, not for one weekend, but for as long as I possibly could. It was a dream, I knew that, but it was a dream I desperately craved. A dream I knew I needed.

The weather might have had something to do with my dramatic change in disposition. By the afternoon, that dreary Saturday morning had turned into a perfect example of an Indian summer in West Virginia. The temperature was warm, just shy of being both too hot in the sun and being too cool in a shade. Essentially, it was perfect. It was what a day in the country should feel like. The bright aroma of fresh cut hay and the rich scents old forest soil hung in the air. A light haze and the golden autumn sun gently colored everything sepia. I spent the rest of the afternoon with my car windows down and loud classic rock on the stereo. It was just me and the winding roads. Roads that felt like deja vu was around every turn. I really couldn't have been more content. It was perfect. It was magical.

I drove down those twisty bumpy roads until after the sun had set, after the night air became too chilly to keep the windows down, and long after I realized I needed to head back.

While refilling my gas tank for the return to the mundane, something caught my eye. Even then I knew it was a crazy impulse. With the pump still filling my car, I ran over and grabbed a free real estate magazine from a rack outside the station. I knew I couldn't move out to the sticks, I knew I'd never find work. Or at least work that would pay me as much as I was making. I had a good job and too many student loans. I wasn't going to quit and there was no way I could make that commute. But, seeing what was available would be fun. Right?

Before noon that Sunday I must have read each entry twice before I broke out a red marker. The following day that I started to make calls.

By Halloween, I had my own summer cabin in West Virginia.

More of the old rot gut

"What the hell, Kent!?! You weren't shitting me when you said this was going to be long. You tell stories like a girl, heavy on feelings, light on action." Andy nearly shouted as he jumped up breaking the mood. "I gotta piss. Wait for me. I don't want to miss any of your tear jerking REAL ESTATE adventure! Maybe when I come back, you'll be able to get to the point. You know, that thing in the case."

Calmly Kent replied. "I told you, it's my way of telling it or no way. I mean it."

"Yeah, yeah, yeah. When you started, your story it reminded me of the beginning of that old Steve Martin movie, 'The Jerk.' It was never easy for me. I was born a poor black child. I remember the days, sittin' on the porch with my family, singin' and dancin' down in Mississippi." Andy recited as he and his words faded into the shadows.

Finally, completely out of sight he yelled "Well, I hope you get to something interesting before I fall asleep. Or die of old age. The way this story is going it's a fucking possibility. Hey, if we're good, maybe you could promise to tell us about your homeowner's insurance! I bet that be exciting. Hey, what's your deductible?"

Again, Kent didn't take the bait and remained silent.

"Well, personally, I've become engrossed." The Professor added. "It may surprise you, but I've never been to West Virginia. Actually, I've never been outside of New England. Maybe one day I'll find the means to make my way South. The state seems to have had an effect on you, if I may say so. I don't know where this tale of yours is going and what it has to do with your gun over there, but I'm paying attention to what..."

"Rifle" Kent interrupted absentmindedly. His eyes were fixed deep into the fire, his thoughts a decade and miles away. "Rifle. Not a gun. I guess it doesn't really matter much, but there's a difference."

"Um, ok. I stand corrected. As you may have observed, I don't have much experience with weapons. Thank you for educating me. Let me try again, what all of this has to do with your rifle over there..."

"Oh, you'll see." Kent said looking up from the fire for the first time since he started telling his story. "I'm just setting the time and place, that's all. Just feel like the whole story is needed, like a short version wouldn't do. Not tonight. The importance of the weapon is tied to the place and the time I got it. In fact, there wouldn't be a story in a different place or time. Patience. I think you'll agree with me by the time I'm finished."

"What's needed around here is another belt of whiskey." Andy loudly suggested as he materialized out of the darkness and sat back on his seat. Again he produced the flask, this time from inside his coat, and took a solid pull.

"Fucking hell!" He wheezed which turned into a laughing cough.

With the top still unscrewed he waved the whiskey over the fire between the Professor and Kent who were still facing one another. The professor looked away first.

"When in Rome, as I've heard them say."

West reached out and took the flask, thanked Andy with a simple nod, and then took a shot. He screwed the top back on the flask and offered it again to Kent.

Kent didn't respond to the offer at first. He hesitated. However, once his mind was made up, he nimbly snatched the bourbon from the Professor's outstretched hand.

"That's my boy!" Andy cheered. "I knew you had it in you!"

Instead of drinking straight from the flask, Kent poured two fingers into the expanding camp cup he had been drinking his coffee out of. He slightly dipped his head towards Andy in acknowledgement, then raised the cup to his lips, shot back the amber rot gut, and let out a suppressed cough after he swallowed. Without comment, he passed the flask full circle back to its owner.

When Andy leaned in to grab the booze he gave Kent a questioning look, which went ignored. The professor continued focusing on Kent, waiting. Andy wasn't sure, but to him it seemed like there was some type of change in everyone else's mood. Not his, of course. After a second or two Andy gave up trying to figure out what was going on and just smiled. The night was just getting late he decided. He was still enjoying himself, even if Kent turned somewhat serious for whatever reason.

The story teller, realizing the others were as settled in as they were going to get, kicked a mostly burnt log a little further into the fire which sent embers skyward.

Kent then continued his story.

The sad smell of lingering smoke

That fall, everything just came together. The property was exactly what I was looking for. While I liked the house, I loved the land. Far off the beaten path, fully wooded, and completely neighbor free. It was perfect.

I was excited about making the most of my first real stay there. I had plenty of vacation time saved and I used most of it on that trip. Three weeks was more than enough time to settle in and fix up the place. Afterwards, I figured I'd just relax. I didn't have any desire to do anything else, although I did spend the last couple of days in Philadelphia for Thanksgiving. Being in West Virginia alone was the whole reason for the cabin, and I used it.

I've been calling it a cabin, because that's how I treated it. While I was doing okay, I certainly didn't make the kind of money that someone who has multiple homes makes. I couldn't "winter in Miami" or whatever. A small summer cabin in the woods? Well, I figured I could afford one of those. If only just barely. I stretched my finances to their limits and blew through my savings to make it happen. Calling it a cabin versus a second home was really just semantics, but it was how I was able to justify the expense to myself.

In reality though, most people would say I bought a quaint little single family home. With two large bedrooms and one and a half bathrooms it wasn't as tiny or rustic as I always though a proper cabin should be. Luckily it also wasn't much of a "fixer-upper" either. If it were located almost anywhere else in the country there was no way I could have afforded it. In the inflated real estate market of D.C., the cabin would have cost me an order of magnitude more than the condo I was living in... which itself had cost twice as much as what I spent in West Virginia.

I made arrangements for the power and phone to be turned on before arrived. I guess I should point out that all of this happened long enough ago that I still needed a landline. In the late 90's, in Bucksburg, there was no chance of getting a signal. Even these days service is sporadic while driving through some of the deeper valleys. In addition to getting the basic utilities turned on, I also had someone stop by and service the heating and air conditioning. I guess my point is that although the house had been sitting empty for quite a while, and needed cleaning, it was livable from day one.

When I opened the door and looked in at those empty dusty rooms I beamed with pride. I was elated. I felt like I was actually where I belonged. It was my first real house with real land and it was all my own.

Within a day or two, packages I preordered began arriving. In the first week alone UPS must have delivered me a literal ton of boxes from IKEA. I became friends with hex keys and those little one use wrenches. Nearly everything in the house, while cheaply made, was brand new. Completely matching furniture filled the house, which was a first for me. With a little work it didn't take long before the cabin transitioned beyond simply being livable to actually being comfortable. It became "my" home instead of "the" house. After reaching that point I hesitated starting too many new projects. Sure there were still renovations to do, painting and what not. I didn't slack off completely, but I did stop putting in ten and twelve hour work days.

Instead I focused on becoming familiar with the surrounding hills, valleys, streams, and trees. I walked the property daily, just taking in all the sights. I would grill outside nearly every evening. Later, after the sun set, I would sit out beside the fire pit. I did some plinking and I became reacquainted with my old Ruger 10/22 carbine, which I hadn't shot in over a decade. I stacked firewood and raked leaves. I basically did all the things that people who move to the country do. I didn't realize how generally stressed I had become until I felt it all slipping away from me. I slept like a baby up there. Some of that honest and simple joy I once had as a kid had returned.

Some, but not all.

There was still something that wasn't quite right. While I was happy, the area just seemed a little darker than it was a month prior for Settlement.

By late November, the leaves were nearly all gone from the trees. Only the oaks were stubborn enough to hold on to their dry and brittle foliage. At first I wrote off the forlorn atmosphere as just what happens in mountains when you're alone and the weather turns cold. Living is just a little harder up there. However, I couldn't shake the feeling that it was more than just winter approaching. Like there was something holding me back from really finding the nostalgia I was looking for. Like the warm glow I had discovered was growing dim. Harder to see. It was still there and I still experienced some real joyful moments, I just noticed that the sensation wasn't as overwhelming and intoxicating as it had been earlier that year. Little things kept adding up.

One of those little things happened the first Sunday there. It was a cold and rainy morning. Despite promises of sunshine from the local TV weatherman, the sky had remained the same drearily claustrophobic overcast it had been for several days before. Everything outside was made up of grey shapes fading into the mist, the world seemed devoid of color.

Bleak.

I took an early excursion into Bucksburg proper to visit the local hardware store. I needed paint, trim, and nails for one of the two bathrooms I had almost finished remodeling. I'd been up at the cabin for about a week, but that was my first drive into town. Any shopping I needed prior, I drove in the opposite direction. It was further away, but out by the highway there were a pair of big chain hardware stores. Going there mostly ensured that I wouldn't have to drive to multiple places to find what I needed. However, taking that forty minute trip every day for week had become tedious. On top of that, driving down highways and shopping at chains didn't leave me with the same small town feeling that I moved out of the District to find. A feeling readily available in the unorganized, cluttered, and dusty local hardware store. While I couldn't be sure my paint was manufactured in the last decade or two, I did succeed in spending some time in "my town."

Bucksburg is a lot like most other towns in that part of Appalachia. Rich in history, poor in wealth. The double laned Main Street winds through a deep valley next to a wide but shallow river. Thick tree covered slopes flank either side of the road with houses fanning out and halfway up the steep sides. The twisting zigzagging roads that branched off Main street climb up the mountains and in between the old homes. Old brick and old stone. Asbestos shingles and dented aluminum siding, both faded. The same business signs from the fifties and sixties still hung off buildings. Dated artistic trappings and reminders of better times. Cast iron, chain linked, or wooden picket fences, all in need of paint, roped off small homes with small yards. The VFW hall had a new flag flying high above the bright green neatly cut lawn. The liquor store across the street was awash in neon glow and faded cardboard displays. At the bottom of the hill, next to the river, train tracks sliced through the town. The trains ran a lot less frequently than they once did, but were still in use. It was a town that had seen better days, but hadn't given up.

It was old and poor but proud.

After leaving the hardware store and driving down Main Street, which was the longer but more scenic way home, my eye were drawn to something unexpected.

One of the town churches had a large white party tent erected on its parking lot. The parishioners, sitting under it, were singing. Each in their Sunday best, the congregation filled less than half of the huge space. Warm white Christmas lights wrapped around each of the support columns and gave the whole structure a welcoming glow. The shelter seemed out of place in the damp chilly fog and drizzle. It looked delicate and almost fairy-like compared to the oppressive weight of the sky, mists, and mountains. Those under the tent were huddled together towards the front, seated on white plastic folding chairs under the vinyl roof. At one point my family used to park in that lot, back when my mother took me to church as a child. I hadn't thought of Saint Joseph's Catholic Church in years. Not since my father's funeral.

Looking off to the side and beyond the tent, instinct and memory told me the skyline wasn't quite right. I did a double take, and slowed down below the already timid speed limit. The church itself was just a black skeleton amid a pile of charred rubble. Brick, timber, and roofing piled high. Yellow caution tape surrounded it all. I watched rain water collect from the ruins, heavy and black with soot, slowly ooze down the street before disappearing underground down through a storm drain. The water stained black everything it touched.

I recalled earlier that week, in a checkout line at the grocery store, the local newspaper reported that the church had burned down. It happened a couple of days before I arrived. I saw the story, but didn't put two and two together until then.

"Arson" the paper's headline read. While possibly a ploy for higher circulation, the large bold font had settled any dispute concerning the cause of the destruction. However, the first paragraph of the article itself was honest enough to mention that the official report found it was likely started by a candle accidently knocked over in the rectory. The elderly resident priest, Father Merrin, had died in the blaze. I vaguely remembered him from when I attended mass all those years before. His death must have been a big loss for the community.

Normally, tragedies like that would have been a scene of sad remembrance, but also one of hope and perseverance. Of a community overcoming its adversity. A time when people came together and stronger bonds were formed. Fundraisers and reflection. Bake sales and prayers. To me it just felt sick and dark. Hopeless.

Even after several days of light rain and having driven with my windows closed, I could still smell the smoky stink from the fire a mile outside of town. It wasn't the honest smell of a wood stove or a campfire, but rather an almost rotten stench of burnt plastic.

However, as I said before, the sight only bothered me until I was out of town. Until I was once again driving down those bumpy country roads. I didn't consciously pay the scene much mind after that. It was a little sad, sure, but didn't directly affect me. I hardly went to church those days and not to that particular church since the funeral. I considered myself religious, but going to mass was only something I did to make my mother happy. It always brightened her day when I put forth even that little amount of effort for Christmas and Easter services.

As I said, my mind didn't linger on the church. I had that new wood trim to cut and install and I was impatient to get back and finish the room. However, in hindsight, I know that the burned out building did have a lasting effect on my perception of the town. Not a large one, but it contributed to a growing state of unease.

Weather, as it tends to do, changed. Later that week I had some
reasonably nice and unseasonably warm afternoons. Whole days with
comfortable temperatures and deep blue skies. It was as if nature tried
one last offensive push against the icy onslaught of the upcoming
winter. A seasonal Battle of the Bulge.

Hiking during that nice spell was a real joy. While there weren't many
state parks around, there was a great deal of undeveloped and un-
forested land that was available for me to explore and I had purchased
near a hundred acres right in the middle of a huge track of it. Even in
the winter, when there are basically no leaves on the trees, I could only
see three artificial lights cutting through the darkness far off in the
distance. There was a real sense of being alone with nature. When I
felt the need to stretch my legs I just left my porch and wandered off in
whichever direction I wanted.

One day after getting back from a particularly enjoyable morning hike,
my empty stomach and a practically empty refrigerator dictated that I
needed to head out for an early dinner. I didn't know what I wanted to
eat, but I knew I didn't have it in the house. While there were more
dining options by the highway, I wasn't in the mood for any of the
interchangeable chain restaurants I'd have found there. I challenge
anyone to be able to explain to me the differences between a Ruby

Tuesday, Applebee's, or a TGIF. I wanted something with a little more character and something that wasn't deep fried or microwaved. For that I needed something local. Something real.

After twenty or so minutes on the road I found myself back in town and looking at my options. Unfortunately, being an old and poor town, Bucksburg didn't really have all that many places to eat. I saw general store selling some baked goods, a small convenience store with a deli counter, something that may or may not have been a restaurant, and a dive bar or two. I had no idea what I would find in any of those places for lunch. I reached the edge of the town, where many of the buildings were abandoned and dilapidated, and realized there wasn't much likelihood of finding anything else. I turned around. On my second pass, almost in the dead center of Bucksburg, I found street parking in front of a place that I missed the first time through. It was simply called "The Inn."

The Inn was a small neighborhood restaurant and bar. Maybe once it offered rooms to rent, but I never saw any evidence of that. The plain brick structure was mostly devoid of exterior adornment and was sandwiched in-between a bank and an antique store. The businesses' name was long ago painted in a now chipped but still reflective gold paint on the large plate glass window facing the street. The Inn's painted blue brick walls were faded and looked about as old as the town. Where the paint wasn't faded, it was peeling. Where it wasn't faded or peeling, there was exposed red brick crumbling away. Despite the lack of frequent maintenance, the overall appearance wasn't of neglect or decay but rather of just age. Along with everything else on that section of Main Street it had a feeling of solemn dignity to it. It had stood the test of time.

The open parking space was too much of an invitation to pass up so the decision was essentially made for me. I went to the Inn.

Laden with the scents of roasted meats, baked bread, fried food, and rich beer the welcoming warm air rushed out of the front door to greet me. Once inside, it was difficult to ignore all the tempting aromas. The room felt warm and comfortable. It was in stark contrast to the cool thin weather outside. A long bar ran down one wall of the narrow but deep room. Where the bar ended there was an open double doorway with a single step up that lead to a small dining room. I couldn't see it but the kitchen must have been somewhere at the very back of the building. The Inn was basically empty, with only three other men sitting at the bar. Each patron was dressed nearly identically, in well-worn jeans, work boots, and heavy flannel lined canvas jackets. They all watched me come in, though no one bothered to turn around. Instead their curious gazes followed me through the mirrors mounted on wall in front of them. From their seats, reflections provided a view of the entire room. I continued past them towards the dining room. Each footfall on the well-worn floor was loud in the hushed establishment.

A quick glance through the doorway and I saw that the dining room was deserted. No one was seated at the any of the perfectly ordered tables. I paused, considered my options, and then went back the way I came. I slid out one of the last stools at the end of the dark stained wooden bar. I was never really comfortable eating alone at a table in a restaurant. The prospect of being alone at a table and alone in an empty dining room was even worse. Sitting at a bar always seemed different. Less pathetic. At that moment, I also realized I was feeling a little social. Not enough to sit by the locals, but social enough to join in a conversation if one presented itself. Maybe that was the real reason I ended up at The Inn. I had been alone in the house for nearly two weeks without interactions deeper than a few words with cashiers or delivery drivers.

I settled down on my stool and after my eyes adjusted to the dim lighting I had a better view of the woman working behind the bar. Once I did I couldn't believe she wasn't the first thing I noticed. She was a true vision. The bartender had an "I'm not trying to be attractive, but since I am attractive, I don't need to dress like it" look. Cute, I would call her, although I know how much most women hate that word. Nothing was exaggerated on her, no heavy handed makeup, no push up bra, no painted nails, or product in her hair. Just simple natural beauty. Or at least it came off that way to me. Hand on my chin, I found myself gazing intently at her across the dimly lit room. Crystal and I moved on by then and since I was single I thought I could enjoy the scenery a bit before the bartender noticed my eyes were on her.

Unfortunately, in the essentially empty bar noticing me didn't take all that long. She walked down to my end of the room, turned to face me with a cold steely and unimpressed expression, slid me a menu, and then tossed a coaster down on the bar.

"Can I start you off with something ta drink?"

"Call me Ishmael," it was not. Her first words to me were obviously nothing notable as opening lines go, but I still remember them and how they were said to me... with a bit of irritation.

It took me a second to shift my mental gears from admiring her figure to deciding on a beer. I had no idea what I wanted or even what they had. I tried to stall.

"I'll start with a water," I said with my most pleasant smile.

"And, anything else?"

I didn't get the extra time I needed, which caused just a tiny bit of trepidation. I hoped it didn't show. I looked down at my menu thinking that maybe I had missed a beer list. I did a hurried review while she waited, but still didn't see anything. I looked up and focused on the bartender's beautiful face. I tried to give her my most helpless questioning look. She slightly rolled her eyes at me and returned an expression I could only interpret as annoyance. Finally, with one hand clutching onto the bar for support, I leaned as far back as I could without falling off of my stool. I strained my eyes and with some difficulty I was barely able to make out some of the taps near the center of the bar. Relieved, I asked for the first one I saw that wasn't some variation of Budweiser.

When she walked away without saying a word I felt a little ashamed. I assumed she must have caught me checking her out and apparently didn't appreciate the staring. For that sin I was being punished with poor service. While I thought I was being subtle, I guess I wasn't subtle enough. She was a probably used to oglers, and probably sick of them.

In an attempt to redeem myself, and through sheer force of will, I concentrated on the menu and not the bartender's features. She came back a couple minutes later with a frosty pint glass, slide it towards me and without a word walked back to the locals at the end of the bar. She forgot my water.

The next time she came by, I was a little more prepared to speak as I didn't take my eyes from the menu the entire time she was away. I hoped the absence of unwanted appreciation was appreciated as I ordered. It's funny, can remember most everything about that day, but I have no recollection of what I ate.

"Around here I'm Gwen or sometimes Gwendy. If you need anything else, holler." She mechanically informed me. It was probably something she said countless times. Of course, that was just when I began to take a sip of my beer. Thinking back, she may have even timed it that way. With my pint still raised to my lips I managed to give her an awkward head nod in acknowledgment. My uncoordinated fumbling caused beer foam to splash up onto my nose and down the side of my face. Before she completely turned to walk away I caught a glimpse of a smile.

After three or four steps she stopped and her shoulders slumped as if in resignation. Gwendy then turned back to me with a bigger smile than the one she left with. The way her lips gently turned up and how her hair framed her face, well, it was one the most welcoming and warm looks I'd ever seen. She cocked her head a little to the side and put her hands on her perfect hips.

"I can't believe I'm going to be so cliché as to actually ask this, but, you're not from 'round these here parts, are ya?" She laughed at herself and purposefully put on a little extra, mocking, twang when she said "around these here parts."

"Nope, I'm not. What gave me away?" I returned with a testing chuckle.

"Oh, nothing particular. I generally just recognize everyone who makes their way up to the bar. I don't recall seeing you before. So, you know. I figured you must be just passing through."

"Good, that's a relief. I'm glad I'm not standing out too much. Thought maybe I may have been wearing the wrong gang colors for this side of town." I mentally cringed at how bad the joke was, still, Gwen gave me a slight smirk. I cleared my throat and continued, "Anyway, you're close though for government work. I haven't been here before but I'm not passing through. I sort of moved. More accurately I'm in the process of settling into a place about, I don't know, about maybe fifteen or so minutes north of here."

"How does somebody 'sort of move', Mr. Um..." She paused, waiting for me to complete my sentence.

"Oh, Mr. Williams. Kent. Just call me Kent. Nice to meet you Gwendy." I reached across the bar and shook the hand she offered. It was small, soft, and warm. It was also a little damp from washing glasses, but I didn't care.

As I was about to start speaking again, she raised her hand.

"Just a sec, let me take care of these other fellas. Hold that thought."
"I think I can probably handle that." I finished in a mumble to basically no one as she was halfway down the bar before I was through.

I had to squint to watch her go. The bright midday sun seemed blindingly fierce compared with the darkness inside. Contrasted against the large window facing the street she became just a silhouette. Though, as a silhouette she wasn't any less appealing to look at. Seeing her move was like watching the title sequence in an old James Bond film. The loose fitting shirt she wore was nearly transparent as the sunshine drove through it, leaving very little to my imagination. The way she moved in that bright light, leaning and stretching as she distributed drinks and silverware, gave me plenty of details to take in. Her shoulder length red hair seemed to glow. Seeing her in that backlight somehow elevated the simple beauty I first noticed into something almost exotic.

I again found myself focusing on her to the exclusion of everything else around me. I took in all the details I could. While in shape, she wasn't thin or overly muscular. Athletic I guess most would say. Height? Five foot eight was my initial guess. I also guessed that she couldn't have been much more than twenty five years old, a guess I later learned wasn't too far off.

It only took a few moments looking down the bar at her before I became smitten. It felt so juvenile, and I didn't care.

She spent some time with the other guests, eventually reaching into the cooler and pulling out a couple brown bottles of beer. My jaw almost hit the bar when she arched her back to pull a church key from her back pocket, opened the beers, and then slid it back in place. She then turned her head in my direction and we made eye contact. Contact I immediately broke. I heard her let out a quiet little laugh as she went back to talking to the guys at the end of the bar.

She eventually finished and with a satisfied smile on her face made her way back towards me. I actually felt nervous. Like a kid caught where he didn't belong, I hid away by pretending to be studying the design printed on my pint glass. Though I instantly looked up when she spoke to me.

"So, Mr. Williams, how does one sort of move?"

"Well, first off, it's Kent." I corrected her. "Secondly, there's really not much too it. I moved in, but at the same time I didn't also move out. I'm going to live here, but also where I, um… also live."

It wasn't a great start to an already unengaging story, but I pushed on. I told Gwen how I found the cabin. I told her that I always wanted to have a place 'to get away from it all'. I did so in such a way that I hoped didn't make me sound like I was belittling her town. I didn't mention to her I was originally from the area, but rather that I just stumbled upon the sale. I told her about my job and living in Washington. Her side of the conversation consisted of questioning my judgement and telling me how boring it was being stuck there. She told me how she wanted to do something bigger, but enjoyed bartending and made a decent amount of money doing it. We talked about choices and outcomes, obligations and opportunities, cabbages and kings. In the end though, it was mostly just me rambling on and on.

I wasn't sure but I somewhere during our discussion I thought that Gwen's simple curiosity and work boredom maybe transitioned into a little bit of actual interest. Or maybe she just liked asking pointed questions. Either way, I enjoyed talking to her and kept at it.

It was mid-day and mid-week. A few new patrons, mostly the old or unemployed, wandered in and found a seat. A couple of couples came in and chose the dining room. One of the three old guys at the front of the bar weighed anchor and left. A little while longer, so did some of the newer arrivals. While the restaurant never filled up, when I cared to look around, each time I noticed the faces changed. Equilibrium was mostly maintained, and those present were spread out along the bar with plenty of seats in between. Gwen professionally took care of all of them. However, she spent most of her down time with me, at my end of the bar.

Her company put me in an amazing mood and the time flew by.

A couple beers longer than I should have stayed, I realized how late it had become.

"Wow, where did the time go? I'm going to have to ask for my check Gwendy."

"So soon? You sure 'bout that? What am I supposed to do with the rest of my day?" She said with a pouty smile as she walked over to the point of sale screen.

"I'm sure you'll find someone else to pick on."

My wallet was in hand and open when the bill was slid across the bar to me with a smile. Gwen turned and went to help another patron. I looked down at the slip and at first thought there might have been a mistake. According to the bill, I only had lunch and one beer. She had comped me most of my drinks. I put down enough to cover what I really owed and then some, it be a nice tip for her. I pushed my money across with the receipt and waited around to say goodbye.

When I waved off any change, Gwen said "Well, thank you Mr. Kent Williams, it's been a true pleasure. Ya know, I work lunch all week. Stop on by if ya ain't too busy."

I said something to the effect that I would be back and made my way towards the exit with a grin on my face. I couldn't believe how well the afternoon had gone and it felt like I was walking on clouds. I wasn't looking for a relationship or even a quick fling. Not that I would turn her down, I just wasn't trying at that time. I didn't hit on Gwendy, though I might have very innocently flirted a little. The truth was that I just enjoyed the company and my time there. Plus I am sure the beer buzz didn't hurt my mood either.

I was almost to the door when I noticed that the seat at the opposite end of the bar, closest to the exit, held a skinny, unshaven, and unkempt man. A man who looked at me with a concentrated intensity that grew as I approached the door. With every step I took he spun more on his stool to face me. His stare truly unsettled me. The man wasn't there when I arrived, I was sure of that. If I had seen him at that point, it might have been enough for me to second guess my choice of eateries. My discomfort wasn't in that he was dressed shabbily, though he was, but rather there was something unclean about him. I respect not spending money on anything other than honest clothing. It's a trait I admire. However, there is a difference between poor or frugal and uncaring. This man looked like he had given up years before.

"Kent? Is that what Gwen just said? Kent Williams?" He accused. I was about to move past him when he stopped me. He leaned over and held his arm out, partially blocking my exit. Mentally I prepared myself to brush past him and to physically respond to anything he might do to restrain me. "Kent Williams, the Kent who killed a buzzard in mid-air with a BB, that Kent Williams?"

His statement stopped me more than his arm and I turned to face him. I studied the shady character. Dumbfounded, I couldn't do anything but analyze the man and try and figure out who he was.

While I didn't want to engage him, or for that matter anyone else who looked like that, I became nervously curious. For a time, that shot in third grade made me darn near famous. It happened in front of a small group of kids, and within a couple of days almost all the boys in elementary school were talking about it. It was a nearly impossible shot. I remember my father being so disappointed in me when he heard I had killed something for fun and not food. Twenty years later, it wasn't anything that anyone should have remembered. I barely remembered it. How could that man have known about it? He looked old. Worn out. I told myself there was no way he could have gone to school with me. Or could he have? From the wrinkles creasing his face to the yellow teeth in his mouth, if he were my age, he lived a lot harder than I had. Yet, if he didn't know me from childhood, I couldn't imagine any other way he could have known about my brief moment in the limelight.

"I... I didn't use a BB, it was a Crossman .177 hunting pellet." I cautiously said. Instantly I regretted opening my mouth, as I had all but explicitly confirmed to him that I was the person he thought I was.

"And, and you pumped up your gun all the way to twenty," he said excitedly. A new smile took over half his face. He, of course, referred to the number of times I pumped air into the weapon. Ten being the maximum the owner's manual recommended. Although it was bad for the gun and hurt accuracy I went twice that many pumps for serious shots, as did every other kid on the planet who owned a Crossman air rifle.

He finally took note of the look of confusion I wore, which only added to his visibly apparent agitation. He twitched a couple of times before he basically shouted

"Kent. It's me, John! Your ole pal John Smalls. We was best friends! You always stayed over at my house! 'Member? I was... Um, you know, uh shorter back then. Younger too. If that, um... You know... If it helps ya? It's ME!"

The more I looked, the more his face transitioned into one could have been somewhat familiar. I remembered the name, although only vaguely at first. It took a bit to place him. We weren't best friends, but near enough. He was in my elementary school clique, a Monster, though he wasn't one of the original four. There was no reason to think that he was lying to me, but I had trouble associating the face in front of me with the one of the kid I knew twenty years prior. The face I knew back then had been one full of life and promise. A constant lopsided smile on a boy who had found joy in everything.

The journey from childhood to an adult can lead a man down many different roads. The roads he had traveled must have been hard, as the tolls extorted were plainly evident. His face was one of a desperate and defeated man. He had a look in his eyes that reminded me of a starved dying animal. Hungry. Unpredictable. Shifty. Though when he looked at me his eyes still had a twinkle of excitement left in them. Whatever had happened to John, and I guessed drugs, it left him a man with nothing much left to lose.

The nostalgia only lasted for a second though. Realizing Johnny was the person I remembered made me angry. The meeting seemed like a mocking twist of fate. I went to West Virginia to get back to my childhood. To find that lost spirit of my youth or whatever it was I was missing. Then Johnny appeared in a form that was the opposite of what I wanted. Seeing him abused and worn out represented a perversion of that spirit. His weathered and hollowed out face was like a nightmare overwriting what was once a pleasant dream. Just another reminder of the corruption that had been eating away at the amazing feeling I had that first summer day I was back. I wanted to get away from him, like he was somehow contagious. Like his ill fortune could be transferred to me, or at the very least darken the refuge I was looking to create in the mountains. I unconsciously took a step back. I needed to get away, but I knew I had to at least say *SOMETHING*.

"John. Wow."

That was all I could come up with. Brilliant, I know. Yet he didn't seem to take notice or care. All those years spent acclimating into a polite society had suppressed the visceral urge I had to curse loudly and push past him. Instead I mostly stood my ground. I glanced back over my shoulder looking for a way out of the conversation, but didn't see anything particularly helpful. Gwen, however, was there. Watching. Smirking while she took notice of the exchange. Apparently with some mild interest.

"Yeah man. It's been like, forever. I saw you sitting there, and I knew, I mean I just *KNEW*, I knew you was someone I knew. Then Gwendolyn over there said your name and it all popped back to me. All of it man. All of it. Damn. You, you left us. Long time ago. Never were the same with you gone. Everything changed..." He continued with a touch of sadness in his voice. "You were the first, you know. You lead the way as always. First you. Then Dave. Then Tim went away too. Then... Then I turn around and fucking everyone was gone. Out of here. Left the fucking building, man. Know what I'm sayin'? Everyone. But hey. You're back now, is that what you just said over there?" He pointed to my old bar stool. "Right? You're back?"

He was excited enough, earnest enough, for me to believe he may very well have been glad to see me again. He was just hoping I would answer yes. Yes, I was back. I felt like I was being cruel, but I just didn't want to get reacquainted. I didn't want someone all strung out on whatever, knowing where I had a house. A house that would sit empty most of the year. Sure he would act like I was his best friend until he needed some cash. Then he'd be there, stealing from me. Just looking at him made me seriously consider putting everything in storage when I wasn't actually staying in the cabin. And then, following that line of reasoning, I got a little angrier. I thought about all the effort, time, and money I put into assembling a livable home. I pictured him up there, eyeing my belongings with a truck in the driveway. I didn't want to come back and find all of my possessions in pawn shops. I began regretting coming into town at all. One of the reasons I bought the cabin was to get away from people. People like John Smalls. I was upset at myself. At John. At everything.

He was looking at me for an answer to his question. The man had overheard enough between Gwendy and me that I didn't feel like I could outright lie. Honestly has its cost.

"Sort of."

Again, it was the best I could come up with. Short and it avoided answering him directly. I tried to change the subject. "So what have you been up to all these years, Johnny?"

"Meth. Oxy." He smiled, his teeth crooked, chipped, and stained. "Coke when I could afford it or when it was given to me. Hell, damn near anything if I can get a hold of it. Well. Wait a minute, I guess not really. Not now. No more. See that was what I *USED* to be up to. Past is done and gone. Clean now. Almost 90 days."

He fumbled through three of his four coat pockets before finding what he was searching for. Johnny proudly held up a green plastic tag on a key ring. His face beamed. I tightened my lips and gave him an affirming little nod. Then all of a sudden something occurred to him and his expression changed. He quickly hid away his chip. For only a couple of seconds his face became stern. Serious.

"I know, I know what'ch yer thinking. I'm not supposed to be here having a beer, that I'm not going along with the program. But hey, you can't smoke beer, you can't snort it, and it ain't no pill neither. That was where all my problems come from. All better now. That ain't what I'm about no more. Did a little time once or twice. B and E. Possession. Ehh, well, really possession with intent, but it was bull shit 'cause it was all mine. Not much time, but the last one… That was a wakeup call. Fuck yeah it woke me up. Way the fuck up. I hate prison. You know sometimes I think that it's odd that it were something I had to realize. Hatein' prison. Right? Like I couldn't think that thought. That, 'prison ain't no good' without me being there. Like I couldn't know how much I'd hate being thrown into a cage without having been thrown into one a couple times. Stupid, right? Anyway, prison, it is counterproductive to my goals. I got goals now. Ain't going back is the biggest. Had a hard time a couple years ago. You wouldn't have heard, being gone and all. Dad killed himself, you remember dad? He always liked you. Dad killed himself and mom, well, mom was just gone one day. I just turned eighteen and she up and went. Was old enough then so I guess she thought it was alright. Didn't even take nothing, just left me. Night I came home, she just weren't there. Time to live her own life somewhere else I guess. She never did like it here, always said so. Without dad keepin' her there, well… She was still young enough to start over, so I guess she did. Miss her still. You know, tried to find her a couple of times? I'm not much of a detective though. Never got too far. Can't afford to hire a professional. And, well… If she wanted to find me, well then she knows where I live. Know what I'm sayin'? Same old damn trailer.

Anyway, mom gone and dad dead messed me up some. Wrong crowd and the wrong answers they tell me. But hey, that was then, I'm on my way up now. I got my goals and now you. Especially with you back Kent. Things are a changin' round here for me. I know it. It'll be like the old days!"

I unconsciously took another step back, what Johnny was asking of me was way too much to put on anyone. Especially someone who was essentially a stranger. My movement caught his eye and caused him to mentally change gears. Johnny took an uncharacteristically long pause and looked guilty.

"Aww man, fuck. Shit. I just remembered. Damn. I'm sorry. I really really am. So sorry about your house. Shit. Man. The fucking house. Know what I'm saying? Your house is gone. Damn. I know who torched your place though. God damned cock sucker, that's who. Fucking burned it down for a party, for a fucking party. When I showed up it was already halfway gone, nothing I could do about it. Not like I could have put it out. I couldn't. Ain't no way. I ain't no fireman. I could have tried. I'm sorry. Big fire, though. Big one. Was pretty damn cool too. Good music, heavy and loud, someone brought a DJ amp and some speakers. Lots of chicks there too, well maybe a couple. Huge flames, fucking bad ass time. Party went 'till dawn. Should have seen it. Shit. Sorry. Shit. Damn it, if you want, we can go kick his ass. God damn prick, he's still around. Burning down my friend Kent's house. Can you believe the nerve of that asshole? Damn, I hate that jerk. You wanna go? Ohh. He does have some kids now. Might be awkward. Ahh. Fuck him, let's get 'em anyways. Brats might learn a lesson or two from their dad getting a whoopin'."

Despite knowing better, I smiled. I started remembering what I liked about little Johnny Smalls. He was passionate, that much hadn't changed. He was also A-D-D as anyone could be. That too hadn't changed. He always did just keep charging forward. Where he ended up, you never knew, but he kept going.

"No. No, it's alright. Just relax John. My mom had sold the house by then. It wasn't mine any longer. If you were out drinking and looking for girls, we were years gone from that place by then. I'm not going to lie. I was a little sad when I saw it, but it's no big deal. OK? I just hope it was empty when it was burned down."

"Yeah, I'm sure it was. Damn banks foreclosing on everything 'round here. I'm fighting 'em right now myself. Bastards. Trying to take my place, from me. *MY PLACE.* Can you believe that shit? Miss a payment or two then all them letters and calls get serious like. Angry. Hateful even. Know what I'm saying? Can't talk to anyone at the bank when you are paying on time, miss a few and they wanna speak with you every single day. Shit. All I have left and they wanna go an take it from me. Fucking bastards. I'm working on it though, it's hard. Ain't no place to get a J-O-B around here. Ain't..."

"Kent," Gwen said, cutting in. She put a fresh beer in front of Johnny as a distraction. "I thought you told me you were running late for that thing you had to do. Best you hurry, if you wanna get there on time."

My angel. My cute bartending angel. I silently mouthed the words "thank you" to her while Johnny was distracted. I made a mental note to double my tip the next time I was in. She earned it by giving me a way out of the conversation.

Despite knowing better, in that short time Johnny had grown on me. It was fun to listen to him go off the way he did. However fun though, it was outweighed by not wanting to be stuck in the bar any more. I needed an escape and she gave me one. If I didn't take it, I knew it might have been my last good excuse for a long time. I grabbed onto my exit with both hands and ran.

"You're right Gwendy. I almost forgot. Thanks for the reminder." I looked at my watch and then at Johnny, shaking my head. "I really do have to get going."

"No worries man. Busy busy busy, you look the type. Busy that is. Know what I'm saying? Calendar all penciled in and shit, right? Dianne hold all my calls, am I right? Hah. Go do your thing. Good to see you again. I'll be around." He replied as I walked out the door. Just before it closed I turned around and gave Gwen a quick wave. In one gulp Johnny had already half-finished the pint of beer.

As I walked past the front window, from inside the bar, I heard Johnny yell loud and clear, "Good to see you again Kent. I'll catch up with you later man!"

By the time I got back to my car, I was in a daze. I had trouble processing what the heck had happened to me. Left home for lunch, spent nearly the whole day avoiding the sun sitting in a dark bar, met and socialized with an incredibly attractive young woman, drank too many beers, and then I ran into a crazy man I hadn't seen in twenty plus years. It was one heck of a day. I just sat in my car and quietly chuckled to myself.

Once I snapped out of the appreciation of my surreal afternoon, I put the car into drive.

Checking my mirrors to pull out of the parking spot, I noticed the telephone pole right next to my window. The sight was like a gentle nudge, waking me up from a comfortable dream, and making me realize I was still in the real world. A more sober world.

The pole was covered with sheets of paper. I had never before, or since, seen so many missing pet bills posted. The entire outside of the pole was covered with photocopied pictures of cats, dogs and even a horse. "Logan" and "Colt" had rewards. "Louis" and "Timber" didn't. Missing was a cat named "Cat" written in red crayon. Messages begging for help, all essentially the same. "If found, please call..." It was sobering. If it didn't actually sober me up, then the beer buzz certainly lost some of the euphoria it once had. The thought of all those missing animals was so depressing it bordered on sickening. I wondered why so many pets had run away, or worse how someone could be so twisted as to take them all. To cruelly disrupt so many families. I pictured at least one person crying for each of those posters. I started the car and headed off. I wasn't smiling any longer.

I made a slight detour when I remembered the reason I went to town in the first place. I stopped at a small local grocery store which wasn't too far out of my way. The store and its parking lot were all alone on a tree lined road. The tiny strip mall looked as though it had been built in the early fifties with a sort of midcentury modern style that was in need of repair. Light blue, chrome, and flickering fluorescent lights. Only two of the four smaller stores flanking the grocery were still in business. It gave me the sense of a hard fought but ultimately losing struggle against time. However, despite my initial expectations, the store was actually adequately stocked and had everything I needed.

I stayed at The Inn long enough that most of the day had slipped away. By the time I finished shopping the sun had completely set. Once past the lights of the strip mall everything around me turned pitch dark. Throughout the afternoon, the weather had once again become overcast, moody, and colorless. Without the sun defining the world, the sky blended into the ground. A wall of nothing. It seemed as if I were traveling alone through space.

I was a few miles from home driving down a fairly straight stretch of a single lane, bumpy, country road. All I could see, flanked on both sides, were corn rows forming seven foot high walls. The stalks were dead, dry, and ready to be harvested. Ahead, the fields crashed into a huge hill-like stand of trees. The road continued into the woods, burrowing through, and becoming an even darker tunnel.
I was almost to the trees when I felt chill run down my spine. Cold and paralyzing. Dread. Unexpected and out of place.

An instant later I saw... something.

Something standing in the middle of the road.

I slammed on the breaks. Not because I was close enough to hit whatever it was, but rather I knew didn't want to be anywhere near it. The car loudly slid to a complete stop. Anti-lock brakes violently shook everything and my grocery bags flew forward off the rear seats.

I was scared.

I could barely suppress the desperate urge to open the door, get out, and run which washed over me. Through me. Trying to control the overwhelming need to find safety reminded me of hiding under my blankets as a kid, afraid of the possibility just outside the covers. Afraid of the dark. Afraid of the things in the dark.

Once stopped, the dark fields wrapping around me were lit only by brake lights and a small amount of fall off from my headlamps. I felt swallowed by the dark.

Confined and claustrophobic.

Trapped.

All of that was in the back of my mind though.

I barely noticed my surroundings. Both my eyes were fixed straight forward and strained. Just within the range of my high beams, I saw "it." A shape that didn't fit into any pattern my brain wanted to apply. Halfway across the old neglected road was something that made no sense.

It was caught paused in mid-stride.

The thing looked like an old weathered scarecrow, tall and thin. Oddly broad of shoulder. Sank deep in its long drawn out face dark eye sockets stared directly towards me. Through me. Its arms and legs were too narrow. Stretched. Pointed fingers also far too long. It's neck humped and distorted. It's torso, misshaped beyond possibility. Everything was at an angle that didn't look natural. Perverted.

What I was looking at couldn't be what I was seeing.

And then, it was gone.

I saw it there for only a second after my car slammed to a stop. No more than two seconds for sure. While I was still trying to focus my eyes, it had jumped out of sight and back into the forest with a single bound. Afterwards there was nothing but empty road.

Just as I was about to relax my grip on the steering wheel I heard a scream. Or what I call a scream, or maybe a howl. It wasn't a person. It wasn't a screech owl, a cat's call, a fox, a dying rabbit, or any other blood curdling cry I've heard before. It was loud and penetrated my body. The howl made me tense up while shrinking into my seat.

And then, it too was gone as soon as I became aware of it.

I sat in my car as the seconds ticked away. At first I couldn't take my eyes off of the spot where it last stood. The longer I was there the more I felt vulnerable. I started glancing around and checking the mirrors. The corn crackled in the breeze. To my left and right the field felt like it pushed in. It felt like the stalks could be hiding anything. I wouldn't know until something was at my car. My heart pounded in my chest. I listened for anything other than the idling engine and my racing heartbeat. I waited.

Nothing. Slowly reason replaced fear. Once I calmed down, I knew my initial impressions had to have been wrong. "Eyes playing tricks on me, that was all it was," I told myself. I forced a halfhearted grin onto my face. I felt a little better.

I rationalized that sound I heard could have been my fan belt squealing. Or it could have been a dozen other mechanical issues. After all, the car had been jolted pretty seriously when I stopped hard. I told myself that what I saw and heard must have been unrelated. What I saw standing fifty yards in front of me was just a big old buck. The head it had sort of fit the profile. Its body looked thin because it had been standing facing towards me. Mentally I forced the image of a deer into the shape I had just seen. I changed both until it was not only possible, but the only possibility. I laughed out loud. I further pushed down my fear with a chuckle. It was just a stupid darn deer and my stupid eyes had played tricks on me. Alone on a dark country road, I had let a city boy's fear get a hold of me. I chastised myself for letting my imagination get out of hand. I thought that maybe the beers dulled my mind, I didn't know. A minute after it was gone I couldn't imagine the twisted scarecrow shape as anything *BUT* a deer. Before I put the car in gear and started back down the road I turned on the radio. I turned it up loud.

Even though I knew it was a deer, just before I got past the spot on the road where I last saw it, I hit the accelerator.

Ghost stories

"Scared by a deer? A stupid fucking deer? Really? Great story Kent.
Got any others?" Andy interrupted as he stood up and stretched.
"Wow. Right now I'm surprised that you even could muster the
courage to come on this hunt. You know, and I don't want to alarm
you Kent, but if you look around you'll notice that it's dark out here
right now."

He waved his arms around signaling that everything is engulfed in
darkness.

"We can't see more than fifteen feet away from the fire. Anything
could be out there. There are deer, and even *BIGGER*, *SCARIER*,
things out there *RIGHT* the shit now."

The professor smirked.

When Andy was finished, he plopped back down on his seat and
laughed to himself while shaking his head.

"I said I thought it was a deer. It was gone before I got a really good
look at it." Kent explained. "Whatever it was or whatever it wasn't

doesn't really matter. I guess my point is that what I saw scared me, and I don't care if you think it's funny. It scared me really badly, that's what I was trying to say."

"The mind does play tricks, doesn't it?" interjected the professor. "As I'm sure you both know the eyes just receive light. They only detect and process different wavelengths and transmit electrical signals. It is the brain that puts all that information together to form the mental picture we *THINK* we see. It is our mind's duty to make sense of the signals. All of us here know that the human brain is not infallible, it's easily confused. Easily… Manipulated. What you saw was a deer, just as you yourself said Mr. Williams. I'm sure of that. Using your own logic, what else could it have been? Hmm?"

Everyone was quiet for a few moments. Andy then cleared his throat.

"Creepy enough story I guess. Thanks Kent. You getting all girly scared reminds me of something else though. Something that really creeped me the hell out. Did you guys hear about them German kids in England? I just saw the story on some website. Holy shit, now *THAT* is a scary campfire story. You know? A real ghost story. One worth telling. We'll get back to you and your lame remodeling story later, but did either of you see *THAT* shit? Do you know what I'm talking about? Either of you? It was posted everywhere."

After looking around the fire and seeing nothing but heads slightly shaking no, Andy continued.

"Damn, I wish I could pull it up for you. Well, check this shit out. In the video I watched ... they said it was only a glitch in the surveillance feed or whatever. Technical jargon bullshit. Whatever, I bet someone lost their job for leaking that footage. It was fucking ghosts. See, these two German kids were following three or four feet behind their parents. You know, walking out of a subway station, some famous one, Kings Circus or some shit. It was in London, did I say that? It's in London. Anyway, the kids just disappeared and the parents obviously freaked out. Called the police. Asked everyone for help. Broad daylight and their kids were right behind them. Witnesses everywhere. Vanished. Poof. Not a trace of them."

Kent was looking off into the distant dark with his own thoughts, but the professor seemed to be listening, so Andy continued.

"Well, once the cops got there... Sorry. Once the Bobbies got there, someone decided to review the video surveillance. Freaking London has cameras everywhere. They don't give a shit about privacy rights. It doesn't do fuck all to deter crime. Fools trading away freedom for a false sense of security. Anyway. So, the police, they do a big search but never find the kids, but the tape. Damn. The tape showed what happened to them. Holy shit, I just got goosebumps. The tape showed them walking behind their parents, and then they were gone. Just gone. But check this out, before they vanished, for like no more than a split second you saw what happened to them. The video had like two or three frames or whatever that showed those kids getting half pulled into sidewalk with all these little hands reaching out of the ground. Yeah, little hands *ALL* the fuck over their legs. Grabbing at them. Dragging them into the earth. The German kid's faces are like in mid-scream. Horrified. Fucking creepy right? Right? Man you got the see the video. I really wish we had some service out there so you could see it. Anyway, it gets creepier. So, see someone did some research. Some ghost researchers. What they found was that in the beginning of WWII, before the Brits moved all their kids from the cities out to the country, a German bomb killed a bunch of 'em right there in that exact spot. School trip or something. What these experts are saying is that maybe those British kids were looking for some payback. Anyway, I read that shit online and saw the screen captures and the video. It scared me a little, just thinking about all those little ghost hands reaching out and grabbing at you, pulling you down there, with them. Maybe to hell, I dunno."

Feeling his tale was far scarier than Kent's, Andy looked around expecting some type of a reaction.

When Kent didn't say anything, the professor spoke up.

"I'm sorry Andy, I can't believe that. Because I can't believe it, it isn't frightening to me. I'm sure we can agree that man has created enough real horrors in the world without needing to invent ghosts and goblins. Not to belittle any beliefs you might have, but we are all adults here. Are we not? The children in your tale were probably kidnapped, or ran away, or any number of other more likely explanations. Even more probable, I believe, you may have fallen for a hoax. Video trickery, perhaps? We live in a tangible world. The supernatural simply does not exist anymore than good or evil exists. All of these misguided obsolescent ideas and concepts stem solely from the human imagination. I would suggest not losing any sleep over it."

Kent looked up towards the professor, but didn't say anything.

"I wasn't saying that the hands were real or nothing," Andy said feeling slightly chastised. "I'm just telling you what I saw online and how creepy it was. That's all. Ghost stories around the fire. Hell, Kent was just telling one. That's all I was doing."

The three of them were silent for well over a minute. The trees had quieted a bit and the only other sounds were the fire shifting and cracking. The temperature had dropped fifteen degrees since Kent began telling his story.

Andy cleared his throat.

"Anywho, now that I tried giving everyone the willies, I think we need to leave the relative safety and light of the campfire to head out into the pitch dark and the scary forest. Who's with me? Seriously? Fire's dying, and it's getting cold, are we going stay up? If so, we need to go gather some more wood." Andy suggested. Looking at West he added "We didn't intend to have this fire burn as large or as long as it has, so at this rate we didn't grab enough for the rest of the night."

"Agreed" Kent said adding a slow nod while standing up. "Let's go."

"Um, I'll help" chimed in West. "Let me get my shoes back on."

"No. No, that's alright. Kent's story just *FEELS* like it's taking forever. You must still be freezing. Stay there and keep warm. Rest up for tomorrow's hike." Suggested Andy. "Kent and I have this covered. This is an old hunting site. Someone, dunno who, cut up some wood into drag-able pieces a couple years or so ago. We'll grab a few of those logs, it's not all that far away."

Kent paused thoughtfully. He looked up at the professor like he wanted to say something but after a moment half shrugged and headed into the dark. Andy followed. After a few minutes of ducking under branches and walking around others both men arrived at the fallen trees they were looking for. It was a loose pile of hardwood logs and branches three or four feet tall and about fifteen feet in diameter, not stacked but rather simply dragged on top of each other to dry. The ones resting off the ground were perfect for a fire. The men circled around the wood, searching for few pieces which could easily be pulled out.

"So, um, what do you think about the professor there? Huh? Crazy dumb luck that that guy found us before he froze to death. You know we basically saved his life. Anyway it might be the cold, but I have to say, he seems a little off to me. Then again, thinking back through the cheap beer haze I call my college years, maybe he's not all that weird.

Professors, am I right? Anyway, do you want to take him in the morning or do you want me to do it? Unless you think he can make it by himself, but I'm not sure that's a good idea. I don't mind going, you know, I just would rather hunt. But I guess you would too?" Andy asked in between pulls on a log he was trying to yank free. Some of the branches were frozen into the ground, which he really had to put his back into before they broke free.

Kent was slow to reply, working on a log as well. "Let's wait until morning. Just decide then."

"Yeah. You're right, we can decide later. Maybe we do some rock, scissors, paper type shit. All I do know is that I want to get back to the ridge I was hunting today. I saw all kinds of moose tracks not to mention that cow. Did I tell you that? Oh shit, I didn't. I was up on the eastern ridge looking down into the muck below and saw her. She was a big female pushing through a lot of serious brush, some big bull is going to be looking for her before too long. I'm going to see him and then. Well you know. BAM!"

"Yeah I know. You'll probably miss. Anyway, let's worry about West and who gets to go hunting tomorrow. You ready to head back?" Kent said after man handling his own log free from the pile.

Both men dragged back a section of tree that was about ten feet in length and eight to ten inches in diameter. Dense wood that was heavy even dried. In the quiet of the night, the noise they were making was overwhelming. Progress was slow, but they didn't have that far to go. Most of the smaller branches snapped off within the first twenty or so feet of being dragged. Approaching the circle of fire light, the returning men saw the professor with his back towards them standing a few feet away from the fire. He was looking off into the distance and slightly swaying, almost as if listening to an unheard song. Kent noticed his fingers were absently tracing some initials long ago carved into the trunk of a tree.

"Hey. Whatcha looking at?" Andy called out.

West didn't reply at first. He lowered his head and slowly turned around. He kept his hand on the tree as long as he could throughout the rotation. He had a smile on his face. "Oh, nothing. Just thinking and, um… warming my… um… other side."

"Yep, he's a weirdo," Andy thought to himself. However, he continued out loud. "Ohh, well, get closer to the fire keep that blanket wrapped around you. It's your best friend right now. Though, I guess you're past any real danger of hyperthermia. Would have shown itself by now. You seem ok. Warming up all right?"

"Yes and thank you again for all you have done for me this evening."

Andy and Kent took their long logs and crossed them in the middle of the fire. Five foot sections of tree stuck out of the stone circle from all four directions. The professor looked at down at the fire, still standing.

Andy took West's body language to mean he had questioned the log placement.

"We don't carry saws big enough to cut this type of lumber and I'm not about to wear myself out using my little trail hatchet to chop this into picturesque perfect sized campfire logs. This isn't a movie set. Normally we keep our fires pretty small so we don't need all that much fuel. Plus we don't like to smoke up all our gear. However, since we are trying to keep you warm tonight, we need a little more wood than normal. This method is pretty easy and efficient enough. Once both of these ten foot logs burn in half, we end up with four logs a little less than five feet in length. Then we repeat the process. If we don't build the fire too much larger, what we have here should last the night. If not, you saw which direction we walked, there are plenty more of these where we came from."

"Thank you. I'll do that." He replied. "Now, are you two off to bed? Hmmm. No? I see. Then if possible, can we continue on with your story Kent? Settle back into our seats? Relax. Rest. I'm sure that you hadn't yet reached the end of your tale, you have yet to even mention the rifle in the case. I'm still quite curious."

"Yeah Kent, are you going to get to anything interesting? You know, besides giving me all this shit to hold over you? I'm sure Theresa, your *WIFE,* would love to hear about how you describe this bartender. Seriously though, mark my words Professor, this is just going to be a long story about how he shot a bear or a rabid squirrel or some other dumb shit."

"Maybe." Kent left it at that.

Andy shrugged and then gestured towards the log seats. "Alright then, if we're stuck hearing it, let's get on with it."

The three men sat around the fire. The air had further stilled and the night was almost completely silent. So quiet Kent could hear Andy lightly breathing from almost five feet away. Only the fire crackling away made any real sounds.

Kent began again.

All packed up, ready to leave

Well. Nothing else worth mentioning happened the rest of that week.
The Tuesday before Thanksgiving, I stopped by the Inn again, but
Gwen had already left by the time I got there. I only stayed long
enough for a beer which I drank in complete disappointment. That
was my last little excursion into town.

During those final couple of days I finished a few remaining projects
and began wrapping up my time in West Virginia. I winterized the
cabin the best I could, locked up what was possible, drained the pipes,
emptied the refrigerator, and turned everything off. As I mentioned,
the house was only about a four hour drive from D.C., but after taking
so much time off I knew I wouldn't be able to make it back until
spring. The last days of my extended vacation were used to visit my
mom for Thanksgiving. After the holiday I was back home, back to
work, and back to the real world.

Anyway, I loaded up the car but still had time to spare before I wanted
to leave. With nothing left to finish I decided to take one more, short,
hike around the property. The air had a chill to it and the sky was
overcast, but it wasn't raining or windy. I figured it was my last chance

to take in a bit more nature. Sitting on the porch stair, I had just laced up my boots when I heard a vehicle coming down my gravel driveway.

My first thought was that it had to be a UPS or FedEx truck. Delivery companies were the only visitors I'd had up to that point. No one makes the long and winding journey up the gravel driveway by accident. When I say the house is completely out of the way, I mean it. It's not even all that likely someone could stumble upon it. The road to the house splits three times, each with no markings. All other branches dead end into the forest or empty into a field. All except the road which leads to my house. Both UPS and FedEx had to call me to find the place. I toyed with the idea of putting up signs, but I decided the inconvenience was well worth the isolation.

The odds were that the visitor was just another delivery, although I didn't recall having any outstanding packages. I stood up and walked towards the driveway. I didn't have to guess who was approaching for very long. Having made the last turn out of the woods, I saw an old, beat up, rust brown, primer grey, and purple Ford F-150 pickup truck rocketing towards me with a huge dust cloud following close behind.

I had no idea who it could have been.

The driver of the truck must have seen me, because he thrust his arm out of the open window and began waving like mad. I couldn't see who it was because of the windshield glare, but naturally, I waved happily back.

The truck didn't slow and headed straight towards me. Being prudent I felt it necessary to take a couple steps off to the side, out of the vehicle's direct path. The Ford was just a few feet away from me becoming a causality when all four wheels locked up, scattering gravel everywhere. I shied away from the pelting and cringed at the sound of pebbles bouncing off my car. The pickup slid slightly sideways as it tried to stop. Before I even heard the sound of the parking-brake ratcheting up, which killed the last of the truck's momentum, the driver's side door was open. The purple wreck came to rest directly in front of me and out popped Johnny.

Johnny from the bar.

Johnny from my past.

He looked at me like I was handing him one of those giant oversized winning lottery checks. His face was divided by a huge toothy yellow smile. His arms were outstretched like he wanted to give me a hug. He had a jovial bounce to his step.

"Kent, Kent, Kent, *KENT*" he proclaimed. "Good to see you again man, good to see ya pal. Good. To. See. You. Hope you don't mind me paying you a quick little visit, since we're basically neighbors and all now a days. Know what I'm sayin'? Thought I might stop by and say 'hi' maybe finish out that conversation we was having the other day." Johnny stopped mid-step with an "I forgot something" look on his face. He spun around, and with two leaping strides was back at the truck. From inside the driver's side window he pulled out a six pack of beer cans, of which only four were left. I was sure the other two were empty and on the side of the road somewhere between where he bought them and my house.

"Brought some beers for us. Still pretty damn cold. Anyway, I was talking to Craig down at the gas station and he was telling me that he talked to Samantha and Brody over at the bank and they asked him if he knew you but he didn't but I did and they told me that you moved up here, 'cause Buck worked on your place with his uncle, so I was like, ahww shit that ain't all that far, I think I'll stop by for a visit. And here I am, damn yer driveway is pretty damn tricky though, almost gave up…Wait, what's wrong."

Maybe he noticed I still hadn't said a word. Maybe he saw the look of hopelessness on my face. Maybe he knew his visit was the last thing I wanted.

I had a sinking feeling that I was going to have to be a complete jerk to him to get him to leave. Rude enough to possibly end up making an enemy. Either that or I was going to be stuck talking for hours. Whichever I chose, I knew he was going to ruin the last morning of my vacation.

"Oh, nothing" I timidly said. "I was just getting ready to head out. Going to my mom's for Turkey Day. Long drive and all." I winced when I realized that with that statement he knew I was leaving for an extended time. I should have just asked him to, "Please burglarize my home." I searched his face for a reaction, but from what I could tell, he didn't seem to have noticed.

Johnny was looking over to where I had been tying my shoes. My day pack was sitting out as well as my hiking stick and a full bottle of water. He lowered his head and sighed.

"Look, man." He started before taking an extended pause. His face showed signs of inner turmoil or maybe he was just struggling with picking his next words. The silence gave me a chance to realize that it was the first time I recalled him taking the time reflect on anything. When he spoke again he started slowly and with some weight. "Look Kent, I know you don't want me around. I don't blame ya, sometimes I don't want to be around me neither. The truth is I really do want to catch up with ya. Everything was right back when you and I was here. I know we was just kids, but everything started going to shit for me not too long after you left. To see you again kind of gave me some hope er somethin'. That's all right to have, ain't it? Have some hope? And. Well. There's another reason I'm here. Man, just to get it out in the open, I need a little bit of assistance from you Kent."

I shook my head just a little. A tiny shake, but he saw it. The expression on his face was one of pure defeat. Almost in a whisper he continued.

"Naw, it ain't like that. I don't want no fucking charity or nothin'. I'm not begging, well, I am begging. Not begging for money like a bum. Begging you to hear me out. I just want some help. Just need you to hear what I'm sayin' is all."

I couldn't help myself. The unchanged grimace on my face said no, but in the end, I silently nodded to him. He pulled a beer free from its ring, handed it to me, and then opened one for himself. He took a large chug, wiped his chin with the back of his sleeve, and then stared down at his feet. I looked at the beer in my hand and then over at Johnny who was standing like a chastised child. I felt sorry for him and according to my conscience there was only one thing I could do. After a moment, I opened my beer and said "Alright Johnny I'll hear you out."

The weather wasn't great but it was still nice enough to be outside. I was going to listen to what he had to say, but I still didn't want him in my home. If he wanted to know what I had in there, well, he would just have to break in like any other criminal.

Johnny finished his beer in one long draw, crushed the can, and placed it gently on the ground next to his feet.

"Well," he started. "Well, the other day I told you about the bank. 'Member? How they're going to take my trailer and the lot it's on? Besides my truck I don't have much of anything else on this here green earth. Before you start saying anything, I'm not asking for you to give me no loan. All I'm asking is if you might take a look at some things. Some things I got, and make me an offer for 'em if you want them. That's all. I got 'em here. Back in the truck, if you're interested."

"I don't know Johnny. What kind of things?" I asked hesitantly. "I'm not buying stolen property. I'm not a fence. I don't need any trouble. I have my life together and don't want any legal problems."

"Kent. I told you earlier, it ain't like that. I ain't like that. I don't use no more and never really was a thief. I'm on the straight and narrow these days. This is stuff left to me." He paused. "And, if I'm thinking rightly about it, selling these would make me even more of a law abiding citizen. They're dad's old guns and I'm not supposed to have any due to my past record. Besides the truck, house, and some Creedence tapes, those guns are basically all that I got left from him. They're mine, not stolen. Know what I'm sayin'?"

I wasn't really into guns back then. I only occasionally shot the couple I owned. They were just tools to me. Tools I had enough of. I wasn't a collector like I am now and I wasn't interested in buying any more. On top of that, I normally don't like buying things from people down on their luck. Makes me feel like I took advantage of misfortune. I know people like Johnny are looking for solutions, but it still bothers me to do so.

I was stuck. Logically, I knew what to do, which was to tell him to take a hike. The less logical side of me wasn't as sure. He looked so desperate, and if they were his guns, and he was a felon... Well, he really could get into a lot more trouble just by owning them. If a parole officer saw those at his house, he could have ended up back in prison.

Before I knew it, I had made up my mind. Again, I just nodded to him. I motioned for him follow me back to his truck. He grabbed his empty can and got in step behind me. Once there, sure enough, sitting in the bed of the pickup was a rifle and two shotguns. They weren't covered, or in cases, or even wrapped up. The guns were just thrown in, naked to the world.

I looked at Johnny and shook my head. Convicted felon, open alcohol containers, and driving around with weapons he's not allowed to have. Weapons which were just lying in the back of his truck.

Johnny in response said to me with some embarrassment, "I know they ain't much."

I actually laughed.

"That's not why I was shaking my head at you Johnny. You were drinking and driving with weapons you can't legally own. Not smart. Not smart at all. I hope you had enough common sense to make sure they weren't loaded."

I took the closest shotgun out of the back of the truck, an old Remington 870. I looked at it for a second then worked the action. Sure enough, an unfired bright red plastic shell leapt out of the chamber.

"Damn it Johnny" I laughed a little more at how stupid he had been. "You really want to go back to jail, don't you?"

He just grinned at me, slowly realizing the possible consequences of his actions. Once it hit him, his face became stern.

"No. No sir. No, I don't. I do not want to go back to prison. Didn't think about all that. Man, that kinda just slipped my mind. Know what I'm saying? Sorry Kent."

He was right the first time though. The guns weren't much to look at. The 870 was the newest and least abused of the three. The other shotgun was an old Ithaca Model 37, which if I knew more about guns at the time, I could have identified by its single loading and ejection port. However, with all the surface rust and wear I couldn't even make out enough of the stamping to make a guess. I just knew it was in pretty awful shape.

The third. The rifle. Well, it's the reason I'm telling you this story. I didn't even reach in and pick it up to look at it. It was odd. It was odd and old, and it was filthy. Packing grease, dust, and dirt. It didn't look like anything more than neglected junk to me, so I didn't pay it any attention.

Johnny asked me for $400 for all of them.

The Remington, cleaned up, may have been worth $200 I thought. I found out later I was about right. I had little hope the other two were worth anything, especially in their condition. I didn't need or really even want any of them. At the time, before the Heller decision, I couldn't even legally keep them at home in Washington. Until getting the house in West Virginia, my other two firearms had been sitting in storage at my mom's. The Ruger 10/22 I had since I was a kid and the Springfield 1911 I bought for protection when I lived in Philly had been just collecting dust. I didn't want any more than those two, and even if I did want a shotgun, I certainly wouldn't have wanted what was in the back of that truck.

The rifle, I had zero interest in.

The little hamster in my head started spinning in his wheel. Working on an excuse as to why I couldn't help Johnny. Until I turned to see the most depressed face you could imagine on the out of luck man standing next to me. His pleading expression told me all I needed to know, I was his last hope and only friend. As a kid playing at Johnny's house I remembered his father owned several other and much nicer weapons than the three in front of me. I knew the sorry stockpile in the truck bed must have really represented the last, and the worst, of what he had left from his dad.

Without thinking I told him I would give him $500 for the lot, which was really about all the money I had remaining after the move. Johnny first looked confused and then ecstatic. He told me I had a "good eye" and that I was an "honest man," he was "proud to know." He waited as I went inside the car and dug out my checkbook. There was a slight look of disappointment when I didn't come back with cash, but he didn't say anything. When I asked him how bad he was in debt he just stated that it was his problem.

Johnny drank the remaining two beers while I sipped at mine. He proceeded to ramble on a variety of topics, and I'll admit it, I enjoyed myself. Once his last beer can was empty, crushed, and tossed in the back of his truck, Johnny excused himself citing "banker's hours" as his reason to go. I hoped he really was depositing the check, and not just rushing to get it cashed at some liquor store. Although there were more than enough reasons not to do so, I believed him. To me he seemed like he may have just been good man who had too much thrown at him all at once.

The whole exchange with Johnny only took about twenty minutes. After the dust settled and he was gone, I was no longer in the mood for hiking. I wrapped the three weapons up in an old blanket and put the whole bundle in the bottom of my trunk. At first I thought about leaving them locked up in the house, but changed my mind. I didn't want to take them home with me due to some very stupid laws, but while I was at my mom's I figured I could have them looked at by a professional. In the condition they were in I wouldn't use them, and not using them made them useless to me. I thought that if they could be cleaned and verified safe, then at least I would have gotten something out of the deal. If the guns weren't safe, I'd want to know that as well, at which point I would just get rid of them. Another reason I wanted to take them to a professional was to have them appraised so I would know just how much my little act of charity had really cost me. I repacked what I was taking with me on top of the guns and headed to my mom's for Thanksgiving.

The holiday was nice in all the ways it should have been, too much family, food, and football. I forgot all about the guns until I was getting ready to head home Saturday morning. I called a coworker and friend of mine, Pete, who I knew liked to go shooting occasionally. I asked him if he could recommend a gun shop someplace in Maryland near Washington. After asking me a few questions he gave me a name and address of a place he trusted and I stopped there on my back to the District.

Without much difficulty I got to the recommended shop which was descriptively called "The Gun Locker." It was located in an isolated concrete building with one door and one heavily barred window in the front. The solid steel door was covered in firearm related promotional stickers and was locked. I rang the buzzer and looked up to smile at the CCTV camera above me. A few seconds later I heard a loud mechanical click and made my way inside. It was a small store, with a glass display counter running the length of the room. Inside the case were nearly a hundred pistols and revolvers. On the wall behind it were dozens of rifles and shotguns of various makes and styles. I could see a workshop through an open door along the back wall. A large fellow with greying red hair greeted me while I plopped the bulky blanket down on the counter. His name was Scott.

The first thing he said when I unrolled the blanket was "what a pile of crud." Although he may have used slightly more colorful language.

I was disappointed in his assessment, but figured as much. We talked for a bit and I decided to leave the guns with him. He would clean them, see if they were safe to fire, and give me an idea of their value. I decided I liked the man when he at least attempted to hold in a chuckle after I told him what I paid. Scott didn't have much hope I'd get it back in value, though he did say the rifle wasn't overly familiar to him. He suggested, if I were lucky, it might have some collectible value. I told him there was no hurry for the work, gave him my number, and headed home.

I didn't hear from Scott again until early January.

The end of a 1,116 year reign

"And…?" Andy demanded impatiently. He was becoming annoyed. It was always hard for him to remain focused for too long. A bad trait he was only able to suppress while hunting.

"And what?" Kent complained. The constant interruptions were beginning to irritate and distract him. Although Kent was mostly accustomed to all of Andy's pointed assaults and mannerisms, for some reason they were starting to grate on Kent that night.

"And?" Andy loudly asked. "And you have *GOT* to pick up the pace of this story. Come on buddy. Seriously. I'm growing old here. Watch this."

Smiling, Andy dramatically cleared his throat, paused for effect, and began again.

"I went to West Virginia and bought a gun from an old friend of mine. The reason I carry it with me is… See, I could have retold the whole damn story so far in under 10 seconds. Now I feel bad about making those tampon jokes earlier. I mean, it's not fair to pick on you for being a chick if you are, in fact, a chick."

Andy looked over at the professor to see if he was joining in with his fun. He wasn't. Instead the professor was watching Kent with a straight face. Undeterred, the hunter turned back to Kent, grinning at his own cleverness.

"Jeeze. Lighten up. Can you at least give us a hint? Why do you carry that damn thing around?"

"Look. I told you, I'm telling this story the way I want to and only the way I want to. I can stop right now if you don't want to hear it. That's fine too," Kent challenged as he stood up, turned away from the men, and took several steps from his seat. He could barely be seen by light of the small fire when he came to a stop by the canoes.

"Alright. Alright. Don't go off pouting. But this better actually have something to do with guns. Or gear. Or at least something exciting. I'm not going to be happy if this is some type of romantic story about how you banged that hot bartender while lying next to your rifle. I don't have anything against guys embracing their feminine side and SHARING, but come on. There's no crying in, um, whatever the hell it is we are doing right now."

"We could just turn in for the night? No? If we are not turning in, I would still like to hear the conclusion, if that affects your decision to continue," the professor encouraged quietly. "I think it is quite engaging. Please, Kent, continue."

"Oh, yes Kent, please *please* continue," Andy mocked in a high pitched damsel in distress voice.

Kent had come to a stop in front of his rifle cases which were leaning on his canoe. He had been standing in front of them while the other two men spoke. After the chatter stopped, he reached out and placed a hand on the larger of the two containers.

"Come on Kent." Andy begged. "It was the best of times, it was the worst of times, and all that horse shit. Just tell us your tale of three guns," he laughed at his own pun. "Heh, that was almost pretty good. Literary and shit."

Kent picked up the bright safety orange tubular plastic case and walked back to his seat. Once he was again situated by the fire he placed the tube on his lap and then slowly looked up, first at Andy and then at the professor. Without needing to see what he was doing, he unlatched the snap hinge at one end of the tube and with care slid the rifle out of its protective container.

Andy and Professor West studied each inch of the object as it came into view. The first feature they noticed was that it was long, nearly four and a half feet long. Almost all of that length was the heavy but thin steel barrel and wooden fore stock. Next, the men noticed that the proportions seemed all wrong for what they expected, and that it obviously wasn't a modern firearm. The wooden stock was well polished with dense clear grain, but angled up in an unfamiliar way.

While beautiful, it was not without quite a few scratches and chips. However, those blemishes were worn and polished smooth with both care and age. The glossy wood and bright metal reflected the fire's orange and red glow. The gun looked warm. It almost radiated as if the firelight was coming from within the weapon itself. Despite the less than perfect finish Kent held the rifle reverently. He kept the weapon steady on his lap while he carelessly allowed the case to drop to the ground by his side.

"So what the hell is it, a hockey stick?" Asked Andy noting its odd shape.

"This is what I was getting ready to tell you about before I was interrupted. This was what the phone call I received from a Scott was about. The gunsmith's delay in getting back to me was because it took him a while to track down the rifle type, to verify it, and then find out whatever else he could for me. The two shotguns were cleaned up and inspected. They were nothing special and he deemed 'em safe enough to shoot. Common, mass produced, and with a lot of wear. As we both expected, they weren't particularly valuable. I still have them. This, however," Kent's hand caressed the stock. "This, while not quite unique, is very rare and very special."

"Do you want fucking a drum roll, Kent? Is that what you are waiting for? Damn, there is so much drama around the fire tonight."

Kent kept his eyes on the fire in front of him, gazing off into the space between West and Andy. Deep in thought he easily ignored the latter's smart ass comments. Both his hands were resting on the rifle, touching it with the care and respect one would use while handling fine art.

He pulled back on the hammer until it stopped with a click, shifted his thumb, and then rolled back the block exposing the weapon's empty cylinder. The mechanism made a solid, well oiled, metal on metal, sliding sound. It was a sound that was somehow greatly satisfying to Andy.

"This rifle here is closely related to the famous Remington M1867, which was notable because it's the first production rifle designed to use metal cartridges. It's also considered to be the rifle that saved the Remington Company from bankruptcy after the Civil War. Huge numbers of them were used by the Swedish and Norwegian Armies. While the M1867 was created here in the US, interestingly enough, our military never used it. Despite that, it was still the most widely fielded military arm of the late 19th century with some variant of the '67 being adopted by nearly every other military in the world. As such, the M1867 is a far more common rifle than what I've got sitting here. This weapon was licensed for manufacture from the Remington Company. It's one of those variants. However, this marking here, this is what makes it special."

Leaving the rifle in place on his lap, Kent rotated it slightly so the top was visible to both men. He gently tapped his finger just below the spot he wanted to draw attention to. Only Andy leaned in across the fire to try and get a closer look. Directly behind the rear sight there was a faded marking carved into the brightly polished metal. Andy was able to see some type of a shape before smoke from the fire irritated his eyes and forced him to sit back. Just before he pulled away, he got the impression that the engraving looked something like an octopus.

Andy returned his gaze to Kent and shrugged his shoulders. "And that is…What?"

"It's a stamp of the Crossed Keys of Saint Peter. Two keys crossed and tied with draping cords and topped with a triple layered crown. The papal coat of arms representing the keys to the kingdom of heaven. The symbolic keys Jesus promised Peter when he became the first pope. It's a symbol still used today by the Holy See and Vatican. This weapon here? Engraved with the Crossed Keys of the Vatican, this is a M1868 Papal States Remington. Otherwise known as the Pontificio. It's special because it was the only rifle ever designed specifically for use by the Roman Catholic Church. A weapon created for and used by the Papal States military in battle. If only for a few short years. Relatively few of these were ever manufactured, and most of them were lost or destroyed. There just aren't very many of them left. The rifle is very rare and especially so in this country."

Kent sighed with a hint of sorrow before continuing.

"International politics, the rebirth of Italian nationalism, civil infighting, as well as several consecutive military losses all contributed to the end of over a thousand years of Papal temporal power. In 1870 the Holy See was defeated by the Kingdom of Italy, and with that ended the official service life of this rifle... Among other things."

"So? What do you mean? Why should I care about that? You're being a bit oblique there buddy. Ya lost me and I hate to say this, 'cause I know I'm going to regret it. It's old, so what? You know me, history is kind of a bore. No offense to your field of study professor. I'm sure a lot of folks find it riveting but when it comes to the past, if it ain't sports history... well it's all just not that important and honestly all a little foggy to me." Andy jokingly asked. "Why do you care?"

Kent dipped his head in a slight nod. He paused in thought before continuing.

"I'm sure the Professor will correct me if I'm wrong, but as I mentioned, during the late 19th century the church reached its end as a temporal power. That is, as a power that controlled land in the same ways that traditional nation states do. The international situation at the time in Europe was in flux. After the Italian unification, King Victor Emmanuel the Second offered to *PROTECT* the Pope by sending his Army into Rome which would have been like Germany offering to send troops into Paris to protect it. Pius the IX called him a 'viper wanting in faith' and knew it to be a ruse. The Papacy hoped for French or German aid. Aid it needed to survive independently. Aid that never materialized. In early September of 1870 a portion of the Italian army marched into the papal frontier and advanced towards Rome. The invading Italian general chose a slow deliberate pace across the countryside in the hope that a peaceful, or at least non-violent, entry into the eternal city might still have had a chance to take place. While there was a popular sentiment for Italian self-rule that existed in the region, very few wanted an actual war with the church. Talks continued to fail and the Italian army continued its push further over the gently rolling, olive tree covered, Italian hills towards Rome. All the while the Papal forces used rifles like this one, maybe even this one, to lightly engage Italian units. They were delaying actions designed to give the church's remaining garrisons time to fall back from their outermost strongholds and eventually make their way behind Rome's walls. Those skirmishes were used to provide enough time to transport the church's the invaluable artillery. It was their only real strategic chance."

With another pause and deep breath Kent went on.

"The papal forces at the time were composed of the Swiss Guards and the Zouaves. The Swiss guards are the same guards you'd recognize today. They were as well-known now as they were then, but they only made up a small portion of Rome's forces. The rest were Papal Zouaves. Light infantry. The soldiers were young men and boys, unmarried, and Roman Catholic, who volunteered to defend their Pope, their city, and their faith. Volunteers that came from France, Austria, Germany, the Netherlands, Spain, and many other European countries. Even a handful made their way across the Atlantic from the United States and fought within the Church's ranks."

"The Pope's forces numbered just over thirteen thousand strong. Though, even less were actually behind Rome's walls defending the city when the day came to do so. Against them, those faithful few stood up against over eighty thousand Italians that marched towards Rome. The Papal forces were outnumbered almost seven to one."

Neither the professor nor Andy moved or said a thing. Besides Kent's voice only the continuing crackle of the fire and the slight breeze rustling the branches above could be heard.

"Without outside help, as Napoleon had provided before or as Bismarck once offered, Pope Pius IX must have surely known they were in for a fight they couldn't win."

"On the 19th of September, 1870, the Italian army reached the Aurelian Walls. Ancient walls made of concrete, brick, and mortar. Built sixteen hundred years earlier, the fortifications enclosed all 3500 acres of the Seven Hills of Rome. Walls that still stand protecting what was once the heart of the Roman Empire and the Vatican today. The invading army placed the city under a state of siege. Modern cannons were trained on structures that were built by Roman Emperors to protect against stone projectiles and arrows."

"Probably looking out over those walls Pius decided, that to prevent greater destruction than necessary, the surrender of the city would have to occur... but only after his troops had put up enough resistance to make it known that the takeover was not freely accepted. With a fight, history couldn't as easily be rewritten. The next day, after over three hours of constant shelling near Port Pia, a breach was torn through the towering Aurelian Walls."

"The highly trained and seasoned Piedmontese infantry corps of the Bersaglieri stormed into Rome like the Visigoths who ended the Western Roman Empire before them."

Andy was transfixed and listened intently to Kent describe the final hours of the Church. His mind easily imagined the siege, the cannons, the explosions, and smoke. The panicked yells, the destruction, the loss of life. He could imagine a pitched and heated battle and all that it entailed. For the first time all evening Andy was actively hanging on Kent's every word. The professor continued to remain unmoving and silent with his focus on Kent. His opinions he kept as his own.

"Young men and boys, volunteers all, in their red trimmed grey uniforms fired relentlessly at the Italian invaders with their M1868 Papal States Remingtons. The defender's determination was strong and with their bodies and bullets they stopped the invader's assault. They held the Italian army at the breach. Following a dogma similar to that of the U.S. military they were not content with just holding. "Instead, the Zouaves were in the midst of rallying and preparing for a counteroffensive to take advantage of the momentum they had gained."

"Then the order to surrender came down."

"Those men, after fighting back against superior numbers of well-trained troops were told to not only to lay down, but to destroy their arms. They were told to destroy their swords, their cannon, and their M1868s. Rifles like the one I'm holding, rifles built to defend the church. In the aftermath of the battle, several Zouaves were executed or murdered by the Italian forces following the surrender. One such, a proud Belgian officer who refused to give up his sword, was shot in the face. Even counting the criminal brutality of the Italian soldiers, the Papal forces gave more than they took, Fifty nine Italian soldiers were killed while only nineteen Papal Zouaves died that day."

"Rome, with the rest of the surrounding region of Lazio, was subsequently annexed into the unified Kingdom of Italy. The loss was also the beginning of a time of change for Italy and Europe. While only tangentially related, church's defeat coincided with the first seeds of Italian fascism that had been sown at the time, which ultimately lead to Mussolini's rise to power and Italy's ties to Nazi Germany."

"The surrender resulted in a treaty that left the governing body of the Catholic Church all but disarmed. Only a fraction of the Swiss Guard were allowed to continue to exist and even then they could only bear small defensive arms. Not that it mattered, even before the reduction in their numbers, they were never large enough to be considered a real force. The Zouaves were disbanded entirely. Nothing was allowed to remain that could have been a threat to the Italian Kingdom."

After another pause, Kent continued.

"After the Church's surrender and subsequent order to destroy its rifles, the rarity of these weapons was further magnified when nearly all of the remaining stock was shipped to North Africa in support Italy's failed attempted expansion into Somalia. The desert isn't the best environment for, well, anything and Italy's indigenous allies were not known for their meticulous maintenance of equipment. I have no idea how Johnny's father ended up with a Pontificio, very few are still around today. I treasure this weapon because, at the very least, it is an amazing piece of history."

"Kent. Wow. I wasn't even sure you knew how to read a book, much less learn some historical shit like that." Andy said breaking the silence. "Seriously though. That's a cool story, doesn't explain a damn thing, but cool."

Both the professor and Andy allowed Kent to pause before he continued on.

"Anyway. Back to where I left off. Over the phone, Scott suggested I take the rifle to a specialist because he couldn't place a value on it. Asking around he found a handful that were sold on auction, but all of those took place several years before. It was his opinion, however, that the rifle was worth a good deal more than the $500 I paid. I have to say I was a little shocked at what he was telling me, but when that wore off, I asked him the first thing that popped into my mind. Did he think I could shoot it?"

Switching immediately back to Kent's tale was too much for Andy's patience to handle. He tried again to move the story along.

"So what you are trying to tell us is that you are lugging around a God damn 50lb collector's item, for what fucking reason?" Andy asked in a flippant agitated manner. "Put it in a fucking glass case and dust it off once a year! People don't drag shit like that out into this type of shit. What the hell are you doing with that thing Kent?"

"It only weighs about 10 pounds," Kent started to say, but again was cut off by Andy.

"Whatever, did I miss an important part of your tale? Is this going to be even dumber than I thought it was going to be?"

The professor jumped in before Kent could reply.

"Yes. I mean no, not that your story will be dumb, but yes please explain. Yes indeed, explain why would you risk damage to an interesting but yet obsolete museum relic out here in the wilds of New

England?" The professor wanted to know. "Over a hundred years old it can't possibly still function as a weapon."

Kent reached into his jacket and from an inside pocket he pulled out a very large piece of brass and lead. Unique to the Vatican, it was a 12.7x45 millimeter cartridge. Kent held it up so the firelight would illuminate it for the others. In turn he showed it to both the professor and then to Andy. The bullet was nearly a half inch wide and the cartridge wider still. From end to end it was two and a quarter inches long. It was easily seen from across the fire. The brass shell looked brilliantly golden when the light from the flames played over it.

"If…" Kent left hanging, while his glare lingered on Andy, before he started again. "If you will allow me to finish telling my story, I think that I'll be able to answer all your questions."

West just kept his eyes on Kent and the cartridge, while Andy sighed before he chuckled to himself.

"Whatever. Go on, you lunatic you. Let's finish up this soap opera of yours." Andy shook his head and took a swig from his flask, but this time didn't offer to share.

Kent kept the rifle on his lap and gently rolled the cartridge between his fingers. The story continued.

Curtains and linens

"Shoot it?" The gunsmith asked me, completely flabbergasted by the question. "Wait? What? Really? You wanna shoot this thing? You outta your mind? Didn't you hear what I just told you?"

"Yeah, well I guess so. I mean, it's just an old stick if I can't shoot it. You know?"

"And so are most other antiques. They're just old sticks. Old rocks. Old pieces of clay. Old whatever. Doesn't mean people don't care about 'em. Doesn't mean you should use them neither. Hell, on my shelf right now I'm looking a C-ration from WWII. You don't see me eating it. It's just for display." Scott shot back as he labored to reorganize his thoughts.

During a later conversation he told me that he studied and researched the "Rome Question" and the history of the firearm more than he had anything else since he was in school. He told me it was one of the few times that the past actually interested him. I think Scott was a little disappointed that after all the background research he under took, he was ready for a lot more interesting questions than the one I asked him.

"Um, I guess so. I mean, you're not going to find ammo for it anywhere, and I do mean anywhere, but if you had some I don't see why you couldn't. Once I realized how old it was I stopped taking it apart and just lightly cleaned it. From what I saw it looks to be in good enough shape though. No stress fractures or anything that I could see. I guess, I mean, I'm pretty sure that it won't blow up on you." He thought about it for a few seconds more. "Make that mostly sure."

"Well then, that's some good news. Right? But so, no ammo for it? Is there a way to look into addressing that? I'm sure someone has something somewhere."

"No, actually, I highly doubt it. Maybe an antique dealer might have some. Definitely not picking any up off the shelf around here. This is the only rifle made that uses that particular round, it was custom for the Vatican. Might be able to find a box or two in some collector's stash. In Italy. Even over there, I don't expect you'd have much luck without the right connections. Connections I don't have and don't even know where to begin finding. You might not have noticed, but what I'm running here is just an ordinary neighborhood gun shop. I'll sell you a new barrel for your AR or help you pick out a shotgun, but that's about all I generally do. I'm not an international antiques dealer." Scott had been slowing down his words until he completely stopped and thought for a second or two. "Although, I guess we could have some rounds custom made, custom *HAND* made, but that my friend will not come cheap."

"How not cheap?"

"I'll have to look into it, but new rounds would be better than century old ones anyway," Scott said thinking to himself out loud as much as to me. "You know, just to be safe, we might need to slug out the barrel to double check that, and maybe even do a chamber cast. The markings all seem right for what it's supposed to be, but after a hundred years you never can tell what people could have done to the thing. I'll do you right and ask around for ya. Don't worry Kent, I won't charge you too much for all of the leg work I'm doing."

I could hear him smiling through the phone.

"All this history stuff got me interested though, been fun too. Hell, I even went to the library. Imagine me, greasy hands and smelling like Hoppe's #9, asking for help at the front desk. But you know there is just something about this rifle. I don't know how to describe it. It's more than just holding history. It's... I really don't know, don't have the words. It's just kind of cool. You know? Anyway, I got a few collectors, machinists, and hand loaders I can ask. People who know what they are doing. I'll give 'em a ring then get back to you."

We spoke a little more about his research and about the rifle. It was nice to see that he knew what he was talking about, and that he was an honest man. He could have easily told me that it was dangerous junk and kept it for himself.

It was a couple of weeks later when Scott gave me another call. He found someone who would make the ammunition I wanted. Despite being over century old, the technical and mechanical specifications were all still readily available. Once those details were looked up, it was just a matter of some machining. Specifically, it seems they were able to neck down a US .50-70 government case. Unfortunately for my wallet, those of course, were also hard to find and expensive. After giving the "go-a-head" I had twenty new cartridges for the rifle being made. I would have bought less, but it was the fewest the reloader was willing to set up for. I heard Scott clicking away on the calculator as he made out the invoice for the ammo and all his work. It wasn't a small sum. I mailed Scott a check for everything I owed him. Included in the price was also a profound sense of "what the heck did I just agree to spend how much on?"

However, even after the initial sticker shock, the idea of using - *ACTUALLY USING* - a real piece of the past made me a little giddy with excitement.

Winter arrived and every time it snowed I'd notice how many more inches of it Bucksburg got compared to Washington. Each time it snowed I'd day dream of getting stranded up there in my cabin. It would have been a nightmare for some, but for me, if I were well stocked it would have been a fantastic vacation. Unfortunately, I never made it there that winter.

It was early spring before I freed up enough time for a long weekend at the cabin. One Thursday afternoon I left work early and started the trip by finally returning to The Gun Locker. At the shop, I picked up the rifle, the two shotguns, and my custom rounds. For the money I spent on the ammunition I half expected the shells to be in some sort of a special case, something like you would see in the movies. Leather bound and lined in felt, or maybe brushed aluminum and clear plastic. Instead they were just stuck in an old used empty .300 Winchester magnum cardboard box. The corners were dented and a piece of the side was torn. Packing tape held it all together. Scrawled across the top of the box in a blue marker was my name. It was kind of anticlimactic. The three weapons I put in Scott's care were cleaned, oiled, and repaired to the best condition they could be. I was impressed at his work. On a whim I also bought a couple of boxes of shotgun shells, and some more ammo for my forty-five and twenty-two.

"You really oughta take that thing to an auction house, or maybe someplace like the NRA museum down off of 66 in Virginia." Scott told me. "I don't sell this kind of stuff. I'm doing my best here, but...

You know. I can't give you an exact value, just don't know enough about the market for something like that, but I do know that there is someone else out there that could tell ya. Hell, it might be worth a couple thousand bucks to the right buyer. I think it's a real collector's piece and in pretty good shape for something that's as old as it is."

I hated the way Scott was being a little insecure about his limited knowledge even though he had done a good job researching.

"Scott, you've done great work. I really appreciate it. And, to tell you the truth, I'm still not exactly sure what I'm ultimately going to do with it." I told him. "However, I bought the ammo, so I might as well try to send some lead down range. After that, I've got time to make up my mind. Older is better right?"

My joke flopped.

"If you say so," he said with a shrug. "In ONE PIECE and older IS better. But hey, it's your face. If it blows up on you, well if that happens, we never met."

I looked at him to make sure that last bit was a joke. After a few seconds he let out a roar of a deep belly laugh.

It took him a bit to rein it in to a slight chuckle, but when he did he continued.

"You're alright Kent, I like you. Anywho, I said it before, it looks safe enough to me. Eye and ear protection is never a bad idea though. In this case, you'd be a fool not to have some on. Shit, I'd even wear some heavy leather gloves for this one. Having said all that, you should be fine."

As I was packing up he suggested buying a real case for the rifle and not keeping it in my old blanket, but at that moment he didn't have anything long enough for the M1868. I paid the man for the additional ammo and thanked him for everything he had done. From there I headed out and got on the highway.

After leaving the shop it should have been a little over a four hour drive, however, that was without Capital beltway traffic. Heading to the Gun Locker before going to West Virginia was completely out of the way, but the politicians who knew what was best for me said I couldn't pick up the guns beforehand because I couldn't have them at home or in my car. There wasn't anything to do about that so I spent my extended time on the highway reflecting.

My emotions regarding the rifle were mixed. Part of me was ecstatic at the luck of it all. Being fortunate enough to stumble upon a rare historical treasure was a new experience, to say the least. Besides the monetary value, the idea of this rifle possibly being used a hundred years earlier to fight a war in Rome really spoke to me. It was exciting and really engaged my imagination. I surprised myself when I realized I completely understood the appeal of Antiques Roadshow.

Yet, another part of me felt guilty. From the little that I knew of him, Johnny really needed cash in a bad way. By selling me the rifle so cheaply he may have unknowingly thrown away his last real chance of getting out from under the bank's thumb. On some level I knew that I bought the rifle fair and square. Just as fair as the bank loaned Johnny money that he wasn't paying back. I knew I didn't owe him anything, but logic wasn't my issue. I *FELT* like I took advantage of his situation.

Just getting to West Virginia ate up the last of the afternoon. I was still an hour out when the evening darkened enough for headlights. All traces of the setting sun were gone by the time I turned off the highway, and by Bucksburg a fiercely cloudy sky made the night even darker still.

Somewhere along the way I made up my mind. After I shot it, I was going to give Johnny the rifle back. He needed it more than I did. He'd sell it, I'd get back the two hundred or so bucks I paid him for just that one gun, and then we'd be even. The rest of the money he could use to catch up on his mortgage.

The ammo on the other hand, I bought and it was mine. I was going to shoot it. If Johnny wanted to shoot the rifle as well, he could get his own darn ammunition. I figured in the end I'd feel good about myself and I'd still have the experience of firing it.

Especially if it didn't blow up in my face.

After the last few turns up the rough and meandering gravel and dirt driveway I finally saw my house. Waiting for me. Dark and empty. Arriving that night felt different than before. It didn't give me the same welcoming feeling I remembered. In fact it kind of gave me the creeps. For the first time I was bothered by knowing how isolated the house was.

Once parked in front, I stepped out of the car, and enjoyed a much needed stretch. In the distance a storm was approaching, which I felt before I even turned around to see. Through the trees, across the valley, and above the surrounding mountains, lightning carved its way through the jet black sky. The jagged explosions were still far enough away that I could only hear some of the thunder, but when I did, it was a deep lingering rumble that shook the earth. The sky was an amazing yet menacing scene. It was the same type of weather that as a kid I would imagine was a magical battle between gods or wizards. I leaned on the hood of my car and watched the dark black on black sky swirl, roll, and grow angry. Each violent strike outlined the horizon and temporarily burned the shapes of rounded peaks into my vision.

Eventually the wind began to stir and gust, kicking up leaves and causing the still bare trees to noisily scrape against each other. When a stray raindrop landed on my face it pulled me away from my thoughts. I had only planned to stay through the long weekend and relax a little, so I didn't bring much with me. Mainly I just wanted to reopen the house and get it ready for the season. The next time I visited I'd have nothing to do but enjoy myself. I grabbed some of my supplies and with arms overloaded I made my way towards the front porch. Almost immediately I could tell that something wasn't right.

I saw something move inside the house.

I stopped in my tracks.

There was no light coming from inside, yet I kept seeing flashes of something in one of the windows. It wasn't the lightning. It wasn't from anything reflected that I could tell. However, it *WAS SOMETHING*, without a doubt. After a few tense moments of staring at the same spot I realized I just couldn't make it out. It could have been anything or nothing, but despite my anxiety I needed to get closer.

Hesitantly I crept forward until I reached the steps that lead up to the porch. The deck was about ten feet higher than the first step, which meant I had to look up to see the window. It had been smashed open. Not a small round hole, like one created by a rock or ball. Instead it was a window which was very nearly devoid of all its glass. Only a few small sharp shards remained on the top and sides of the frame.

The movement that had scared me was just a white curtain. A curtain that danced between the inside and outside of the house with the wind. The fright in the shadows was only my imagination and something I ordered from Bed Bath and Beyond.

Unfortunately, the relief I felt from the simple and humdrum explanation only lasted for about a second. Past the broken window the inside of the house was still a pitch dark room filled with the unknown. My imagination didn't need any more evidence than that. The apprehension I felt earlier had transitioned into a sinking feeling. However, there wasn't anything I could do about it. I knew I had to go in. It wasn't like I could go home or call for help over a broken window…

…But I also realized that was exactly the same type of logic in movies that got people killed.

"It's only a broken window." I said out loud, trying to convince myself I was overreacting, that I was being silly, and that the chances were very good that the window was broken months before. Surely no one could still be in the house.

After I put the bags down I went back to the car and turned the headlights on thinking maybe it would help. It didn't make much of a difference, but at least the porch was lit if only a little.

Everything past the window was black nothingness.

I went to the trunk, unrolled the blanket with the guns, and took the Remington 870. Of the two shotguns, it was in better shape than the Ithaca. The thought didn't even cross my mind to grab the Pontificio. I loaded the 870 with four of the shells I had just purchased, racked the action, and loaded one more. They were only #8 shot target loads, but would have to do. I didn't buy any slugs or buckshot. After digging around for a moment I also found a flashlight that surprisingly worked. It was a lot bigger and brighter than the keychain light I was initially going to use to find my way through the house.

It's funny how a few minutes can have such a profound effect on perception. While driving up I was feeling safe and happy to be heading back to the mountains. Then, just ten short minutes later, I was nervous and arming myself to possibly take a life in order to protect my own.

When I winterized house I turned the power off at the main breaker. It seemed like a good idea at the time. Unfortunately, like most houses, the panel box was in the far corner of the basement. But for several, tiny, ground level, windows, there was no direct way for me to quickly get into the cellar.

I did consider going through a window instead of creeping through the dark house... and I would have done so too if the windows weren't locked... and I didn't mind wiggling on my stomach to get through them… and if I wanted to drop five feet head first onto the basement floor. Despite how bad that sounded to me, I almost wanted to try that way. Until I imagined coming face to face with a bear or a vagrant while stuck dangling half in and half out of the house. After that image, it didn't seem like such a great idea. Resigned, I cautiously went up the porch stairs.

After a couple creaky shuffling steps across the porch, I got to the door. I had my keys and light in one hand, shotgun in the other. Unsteadily I reached out for the door when everything changed.

BOOOM…. And a return to near total darkness.

The front of the house essentially disappeared while at the exact same instant a crash of thunder rolled through the valley. Loud enough to rattle the remaining glass in the broken window.

My heart skipped a beat as I jumped backwards. I could have died from shock or from nearly falling down the stairs. Somehow my heart managed to keep beating and I was able to maintain my balance with the heel of my foot hanging off the edge of the top step. I was glad I had kept my finger off of the trigger. If I hadn't, the surprise may very well have resulted in a shotgun blast into the front of the house.

The car's headlights had timed out.

The thunder, nothing more than a coincidence. My eyes adjusted. The only remaining source of light was the dim but bulky safety light I was holding. With the key already in hand, I made short work of the locks.

I gave the knob a turn and a slight push. The wind behind me drove the steel door open and inward until it slammed hard against the stopper with a crash almost as loud as the last thunderclap.

"I've got a gun!" I yelled into the darkness.

I figured anyone in the house would have seen me drive up the driveway. Seen me fumble about. Seen me walk back and forth between the car and the porch and finally they would have heard me open the front door with a slam. I didn't think I was going to surprise anyone, but wanted them to know I was armed. I tilted my head and leaned forward.

For more than a few moments I listened attentively but couldn't hear anything loud enough to be heard over the rising noise of the storm which had since closed in. The light rain beat out a steady wall of sound on the porch roof above me and on my car's metal roof behind. Louder still was the wind singing through the trees which battered their branches against one another.

With nothing else to do I took my first step past the threshold and peeked a little further inside. The small circle of illumination from the cheap flashlight darted over every surface visible from the doorway. Shining that timid little light around only made me realize how limited the area I could see really was. The darkness left most the room hidden and I could feel it encroaching in all around me.

Nothing about the situation made me comfortable.

The ground floor was laid out in a mostly open design, basically one large room with a couple areas partitioned off. The kitchen, dining room, and living room were all at least partially visible from where I stood at the door.

I noticed my TV was still there, but my sofa was pushed off to the side, turned over, and laying on its back. The loveseat looked fine and was where I left it. There were dried leaves blown all over my carpet and damp ones near the broken window. Of the kitchen cabinets I could see, some were open. Most were not. The bookcase, where I kept a few movies, novels, and odds and ends, was still standing but had its top most shelves knocked out. Items once on those shelves were scattered across the room. The bathroom door was partially open and I could see some of that room as well. Nothing in there seemed out of place.

I reached over with my non-shotgun hand and flipped the light switch up and down a couple of times. The power was still off, but I assumed as much when the motion detecting lights outside never turned on. Still, I felt it was worth the try.

I was fairly certain the room was clear but I was still anxious enough that I didn't really want to continue investigating. I tried to focus not on the creepy unknowns but on whatever positives I could come up with. Unfortunately, there weren't all that many.

Actually, I recall only two.

First and foremost I had yet to find anyone looking back at me with rape and murder in their eyes. An empty house without rape and murder is always a good sign. The second, if someone were staying in the house, I was sure they would have turned the power back on. At least that's what I would have done if I were trespassing and squatting.

In spite of my reluctance, I was able to get my feet moving. One cautious step at a time, I walked further away from what I unfoundedly felt was the relative safety of the outside. I trained my light everywhere I looked, and everywhere I looked I pointed the shotgun. With deliberate caution I pushed through and explored the remaining pools of shadows on the ground floor. Nothing else stood out as being overly good or bad beyond what I had already seen. I was sure the first floor was empty. My eyes hesitantly looked up towards the stairs.

"Hey. I'm coming up now." I proclaimed with faked confidence. I purposely lowered my voice half an octave. "I still have a gun. I won't shoot you, if you just come on out. I'll just let you be on your way. I promise. No harm no foul."

After a few seconds of listening to nothing but branches scrape the side of the house I added, "Really. I mean it. Come on down and no one needs to get shot."

Still no response.

I tried one more thing. I dramatically racked the action on the weapon. I was rewarded with that loudly distinctive Hollywood shotgun sound, which I hoped would scare someone out of hiding. You know the sound, the one that lets someone know you were serious.

However, by cycling the gun, all I actually accomplished was to fling a previously chambered loaded shot shell across the room. Feeling as dumb as I did nervous I rushed over to it, picked it up, and fed the shell back into the Remington.

With nothing else to do I guardedly made my way up the stairs.

While the second story was a little smaller than the downstairs, due to its layout I was able to see a lot less of it all at once. There was just one small hallway lined with doors. As I made my way forward, every shadow my flashlight created seemed menacing to me. I was convinced that shapes shifted at odd angles and I found myself repeating my motions to make sure those phantoms I expected to jump out at me were only caused by my light.

I went through each of the rooms and each of the rooms were mostly the same. A few items here and there were knocked over or broken, but nothing stood out as being missing. My bed might have looked as if it had been slept in or at least touched. Seeing the sheets messed up briefly reminded me of a reverse Goldilocks, I hoped I wouldn't find a black bear someplace that was just right for it. After checking the last of the rooms, I counted myself lucky. I didn't find anyone or anything.

I made my way back downstairs, turned the corner, and faced the open basement door. I also faced a childhood fear I had of cellars. I was scared of the dark, the monsters below, and the things that hid behind the stairs. Things watching from the shadows. Things waiting.

I dug deep for adult reasoning and convinced myself there was nothing to be afraid of. Even if there were, I had a loaded shotgun in my hands. My pep talk worked, mostly, but before I could change my mind I rushed down the stairs. Solid logic may have helped me get started, but it was the childlike fear of a hand grabbing my ankle from behind that was more than enough to prevent me from lingering. I made it down within a few rapid heartbeats.

Instead of the careful searches I performed upstairs, in the basement I made a beeline for the circuit breakers as fast as I could. The safety of electric light, real or perceived, was within reach and I went for it. The hairs on the back of my neck stood up. I was sure that something was quickly but silently rushing up behind me. It was a straight path to the metal breaker box and it was easy enough to open. I fumbled with the gun and light but managed to quickly flip the large main switch at the top of the box. Light flooded the room causing me to squint as I spun around.

I was alone. I was relieved. I laughed out loud.

The house came alive with inconspicuous whirring sounds, warm incandescent light, and blinking LEDs. I heard the water heater fill as the well began to pump. I heard the furnace light and fans begin to push stale air through the ducts. The house came alive with all the automation and conveniences electricity provides.

I put the untested shotgun down on the workbench and went to the gun safe I installed. I took out my forty-five, loaded it, chambered a round, and went upstairs. With the confidence of holding a known weapon and having the lights on I proceeded to search the house all over again. The second time through I added looking under the beds, behind shower curtains, and deeper into the closets. I even stuck my head in the fireplace and looked up the chimney. I turned on every working light in the house but still kept the flashlight on and with me.

The search took about ten minutes. When finished, even though I was pretty sure no one was going to pop out from under the kitchen sink, I still felt safer armed. I flicked up the safety on the forty-five and slid it into my waistband behind my back.

With my seemingly unfounded paranoia subsiding, I took the time to make a closer inspection of the damage. I tried to piece together who had been in my house. The more I looked, the more confused I became. It could have been a person, like my first impressions, but it also may have been only animals.

I noticed there were scratch marks on the hardwood floors. Not deep, but they seemed similar to what a large dog could make. I didn't see anything that looked like animal tracks, but that didn't mean there weren't any. Once I flipped the sofa right side up and slid it back across the room to where it belonged, I saw that the back of the chair was ripped. Long jagged shreds ran across half of the sofa. A large animal could have easily done that as well.

I continued to feel a little less violated after I realized there were none of the telltale signs of a home break in.

Thieves would have stolen most of what was in the house. With me away and no neighbors to hide from, they could have taken their time and emptied everything out. Teenagers would have left liquor bottles, beer cans, and used condoms. Maybe even have spray painted some band names or profound prose on my walls. None of that was evident. Any homeless living there would have left trash, eaten a few of the items of food I had in the kitchen, and left waste in the waterless toilets. That too was missing. Lastly, I reminded myself that if any of the aforementioned groups were in the house for even a few minutes they would have thought to turn the breaker box back on.

However, despite the majority of the evidence pointing to animals there was one detail that made me think I could be wrong. That someone actually had been in the house. It was a small discovery, but it made me feel very uneasy.

The back door was unlocked.

Any number of things could have broken the front window over the winter. A door, however, doesn't come to be unlocked on its own. Without an opposable thumb, most mountain critters weren't going to be very successful at working the deadbolt and the door knob locks. I was sure I remembered locking the back door before I left. Or, at least, I was pretty sure I did. Unfortunately, the more I looked around for additional clues, the less sense things made.

The broken window didn't have glass on the bottom sill, but there were still pieces of jagged glass on the sides near the top. Like something had climbed in. The window certainly was large enough for that. That's what an animal would do, climb in while knocking out the glass in the bottom of the sill. However, the window was right next to the front door, which *WAS* still locked even though a man could have easily reached in with an arm and worked the locks without risking a cut climbing through the window. That's what a person would do. Unlock the door, and not crawl in.

Frustrated, I swore I remembered standing in the kitchen and locking that door. I remembered I jiggled the handle. I was in there finishing up just before heading out for my hike. My mind shifted from the hike that never happened to Johnny Smalls. He was going through a rough time. Had he lost his house to the bank? Had he become homeless? Maybe he made his way to my house with the intention of robbing me but then... Maybe changed his mind? And then, he... What? Trashed my sofa and tossed the place? It was a stretch and it didn't make much sense, but he was the only person I could think of that might have broken in. Johnny was the only person who visited me up there.

But uncomfortable reasoning interfered with my short lived rage. I admitted to myself that Johnny was my prime suspect because I really didn't know anyone else in town. It wasn't fair to accuse him simply because I needed easy answers. The building itself wasn't a secret to anyone. Someone had lived there before I bought it, people had worked on it, and I had all manner of packages delivered there. Johnny wasn't the only shady character in West Virginia. He just happened to be the only shady character that I knew.

Johnny was mostly off the hook and just about everything else, with the lone exception of the back door, pointed to an ordinary old wildlife invasion. Free of glass, the front window was an open invitation for Mother Nature to come in and visit. What kind of squirrel would wanna live in a snow and ice covered nest out in a tree when it could have spent the winter on a dry and stylishly plush IKEA loveseat? I started to believe that maybe I just misremembered locking that door.

It was getting late and I figured the answer didn't really matter all that much. I still had to unload the car, and wasn't sure I wanted to do all the responsible adult things that came with being a responsible adult. Tasks such as cleaning up, fixing the window, and calling the police and insurance company.

I especially wasn't sure about notifying my insurance agent. Looking around, I figured the damage wasn't all that excessive. Six months before, when I filled out the homeowner's insurance forms, I assured them I would be in the house a lot more than I actually had been. There were some questions that I didn't want to answer which were sure to be asked.

As for the police… Well. A wise man, even one with nothing to hide, hesitates before inviting the state into his home. I decided to put the issue off until the morning.

I used a couple of pieces of plywood scraps, deck chairs, and a sun umbrella to cover the hole. I did a crappy job but it was able to keep most of the wind and rain out.

By the time I started unpacking the car, the storm had thrown itself into to a full frontal assault. Sheets of water blew horizontally through the open door and thunder shook the walls. I was soaked before I finished. I put the other shotgun, the M1886, and the ammo down in the basement next to the Remington. I kept the 1911 with me and headed upstairs. It was past 11:00 and it had been a long busy day for me.

The last thing I did was strip the bedding off and toss it down the stairs as reminder to do laundry in the morning. I eyed up my mattress and gave it a thorough inspection. It looked clean and didn't smell any different than a bed should. Just in case someone did sleep on it I flipped the mattress over and remade the bed with fresh sheets.

After the long day, I finally climbed under the covers and went to sleep.

Yet another unwanted interruption

"Kent!" Andy said exasperatedly. "Really? Come on man. Now you're telling us about your Goddamn laundry? Really? What's next? Did you brush your teeth that night too? Did you take a shit?"

"I'm not telling you about my laundry, I'm telling you what I found and what I didn't find," Kent calmly explained after he took a deep breath. "The whole break in thing was a bit of a mystery and I want you to understand what was going on up there. What I was going through."

The professor remained quiet as Andy shrugged his shoulders at him.

"What do make of all this so far Herb?" he asked. "I mean, for a second there I thought we might have had a story on our hands. He had the rifle, the point of this whole damn thing, his house was broken into... Put the two together and... and then he starts telling us about his sheets. Hey Kent, what was their thread count? Did ya spring for Egyptian cotton?"

"Well, I'm willing to keep listening, that is if you both don't want to turn in?" he replied after pausing to look back and forth between the other two men. "I'm sure he has a point."

Andy felt a little outnumbered, with nothing else to say he grabbed a small stick lying next to him and threw it into the fire with a little more force than was necessary.

"May I continue?" Kent sarcastically inquired.

Andy just shook his head and gave up.

Kent continued.

The police and a beer buzz

So… As I was about say, I was exhausted enough and should have passed right out… But I couldn't sleep.

In hindsight I should have just repaired the window a little better that night. The house already had been giving me an uneasy feeling but by knowing the building was essentially still open every little sound woke me.

There were plenty sounds during the storm.

I kept seeing the trees outside my window light up as the automatic motion sensors were triggered. The wind was blowing branches and leaves past the front of the house. The shadows in my room would shift or grow with the gusts. My imagination transformed everything I saw into something unnatural.

The last time I was there, just several months before, I had slept like a baby in that bed. It was so quiet and peaceful. So calm. Lying there that night, all I could imagine were *THINGS* crawling through the broken window, *THINGS* walking around downstairs, *THINGS* walking *UP* the stairs. Ancient, dead, hateful, and formless *THINGS* twisting shadows around themselves like fabric cloaks.

The open window was an invitation for only God knew what to come in. The wind and rain beat against the siding all night, providing me with an unending supply of noises to overreact to. Every time I woke, I glanced over at my otherwise useless phone to check the time. Each time only an hour or less had passed.

Even after the storm tapered off, the night seemed to go on forever. Eventually there was enough light outside for me to decide that it was officially morning. I'd given up on any hope that I'd feel rested that day, so I got up.

After having pretty much the whole night to think it over, the first thing I decided to do was call the police. Just so it was on file. I was sure it was nothing, but I decided I'd hate to find out later that something criminal had taken place there. I didn't want to have to explain why I didn't inform the authorities.

Seventy five minutes after I called, I heard a loud rap at the front door. I guessed someone hadn't seen the doorbell. Standing on the porch was middle aged woman in uniform. Not overweight, but not in shape.

She had greying brown hair that was cut short and held in place by her hat. The officer's stance was formal and her makeup free face was stern. She politely, but not pleasantly, told me her name and that she was responding to my call. I showed Officer Nancy Thompson in.

"I see you cleaned up." She said mildly annoyed. "You shouldn't have cleaned up. Don't ever clean up a potential crime scene. In doing so you make an investigation significantly more difficult and less likely to be solved."

"Um, sorry. I, ahh... Well. I didn't clean. Not really. I mean it looked mostly like this when I got in last night. Just flipped the sofa back over and brought some stuff in. The boards on the window were just to keep any more rain out. Really rained last night, didn't it?" I said pointing at the sofa and then around the house and finally to the window. "I'm no expert, but to me it didn't really look like a break in. So I didn't, you know, immediately preserve all the evidence. Still, I thought that maybe it could have been, so just in case thought I should get this on record or something and, um… you know, for my insurance and what not."

While I was speaking she walked over to the TV and looked at it. Then she looked over at me.

"Well, if that were the case, you should have called right away then." She told me that as if I should have known better, but I had a feeling it was more of her just wishing my call was on someone else's shift. "Is anything missing that you know of?"

"Ahh. No. Not that I noticed."

"Did you happen to see what broke the window? Rock, branch, dead bird? Anything?"

"Well. No."

"And… Mr. Williams, do you have anything of interest you want me to look at? Anything you want to show me? Anything at all?" She sneered through a strained smile.

I showed her the sofa with the fabric and padding scratched out. "Well, this wasn't like this last time I saw it."

She got down on one knee and looked at the rips in the sofa, looked back up at me, shook her head, and then back to the sofa. She ran her fingers over the torn fabric and then sighed.

"Animals." She stood up.

"Well, it was knocked over and pushed out of the center of the room when I got here last night. It's pretty heavy."

"Big animals. Anything else?"

That time I shook my head. Maybe I shouldn't have started with the sofa. Her face told me she was finished there. I wanted to mention my bed and the back door, but at the last minute I decided against it. It apparently didn't take her all that long to make up her mind, about the house and about me. Her attitude wasn't going to be changed by anything I could tell her, so I didn't try. I just put on the most positive face I could muster and smiled. I hoped she'd quickly be on her way.

"Animals." She curtly said. "I read the report of your call, you weren't here all winter. When you leave a house empty, out here, in the country, animals will get into it. You'll be finding fur or scat in the strangest places for months to come after something like this. This isn't the city. Nature is hard on houses up here, you need constant maintenance. You'll learn that your nice little country weekend retreat might get damaged. You're lucky though, this is nothing, it could have been a lot worse."

I thought to myself, "Yeah, I know. My parent's old house was burned to the ground." However, that was yet one more thing I wasn't going to tell her.

"You might wanna consider a caretaker. Someone who could check up on the place for you. I'm sure you could hire someone to do that for you."

"That's not a bad idea," I replied, still trying to appear chipper. "Although, from now on, I'll be staying here a lot more frequently."

"Uhh huh, your choice. Say, you don't have any pets do you?" She said looking around. I shook my head, but she must have not seen it. "Just a warning, but some household pets have been going missing or killed lately. Could be a pack of coyotes or wild dogs around. The winter and hunters usually thin out problem predators enough not to be much trouble, but this year… well this year they seem to be causing a small problem. If it's coyotes their range seems to have expanded a little closer towards town than I've ever seen. So if you're not familiar with the area, my advice for you is to keep your pets indoors."

"Sounds like good advice indeed, Officer. I have some fish back at home, but otherwise I don't have any real pets. Should I be concerned though? Meaning myself? I like to hike a lot."

"Of course you do. Listen, coyotes really aren't too prevalent around here and won't bother a full sized adult. Use whatever common sense you may have though, you need to be aware of your surroundings. There are occasionally black bears that do cause a small bit trouble. However, you'll be lucky to even catch a glimpse of a bear out there much less be attacked by one, they tend to stay away from people." She paused, as if thinking, shook her head, and then reached to her side for a pad and a pen. "I think we are finished here."

It wasn't a question.

She filled out a large form, which in essence only said that she paid me a visit. Her smug and superior attitude annoyed me, but I didn't let it show. I just kept an appreciative look on my face. One of the things I learned as a teen in Philly was to limit your exposure to cops. They have an important job to do, leave them alone enough to do it. If you do have to interact with them, don't argue and always show them deference. The police are always right, when they are not right, they are still right and you may just get arrested or worse.

I showed the officer out and wished her a good day. She had done what she could for me and she did it with enough professionalism that I really couldn't complain. I didn't like her attitude, but for as much as it bothered me, it really was only a minor unkindness. While I stood on the porch and watched her drive off I decided I wasn't going to call the insurance company. More than anything else, I just didn't feel like being on the phone getting the run around after my not exactly pleasant encounter with the police. I had driven up there to get away from dealing with unpleasant people and I didn't want any more than I already had.

The storm from the night before had passed, but the early morning was still a gloomy overcast grey. It was the type of weather that makes you feel isolated. Alone. It wasn't a good day to be outside so instead I focused my attention inside. I started cleaning up the mess with a little more attention to detail than I had done the night before.

While the sofa back was ruined by what looked like claws, I didn't immediately see any other real evidence of animals. Everything that wasn't in tatters looked clean. Furthermore, I didn't see the fur, feathers, or droppings I expected to find. Over the course of the winter, I thought at least a couple birds and chipmunks would have noticed the inside was a bit more comfortable than the mountain outside. I didn't even find any evidence of mice in the kitchen.

I filled up a kitchen trash bag with the leaves that had found their way inside through the broken window. After that everything else was fairly easy to clean. I put the few broken plates, cups, and a lamp in the trash. Everything that survived the winter went back to where it belonged. Putting the bookshelves back in order was the last of the bigger tasks.

While sorting the objects that were knocked off the shelves, I noticed something peculiar in the corner of the room. At first I thought it was a muddy pebble. I paid attention to it only because I wanted to remember to pick it up before I ran over it with the vacuum cleaner.

The bookshelf itself was a pain to put back together, but I eventually repaired it and restocked the shelves. Books, small knick knacks, VHS tapes, and an antique brass crucifix that my mom had given me were all put back and organized according to my own custom system of clutter. My method completely ignored any guidance from both Dewey and his decimals as well as anything feng shui might have prescribed. Just like a jigsaw puzzle, I was finished when nothing was left on the floor. I stood back and admired my handiwork.

Before I forgot, I went to the corner and picked up the small stone I noticed earlier. I was a few steps away from the trash can when I felt unexpectedly sharp edges on the "stone." It took me a second to figure out what was wrong. The rock wasn't a rock at all, but rather a dried blood covered tooth. Thinking back, I don't know why I didn't immediately drop it or toss it. Instead I rolled it around in my palm. Examined it from all angles. There was a disconnect between what I saw and what made sense. It was like when you forget you ordered a Sprite and take a sip expecting water. It was just so wrong. To me, the tooth looked like a human molar, hollow cracked roots and all, but again that just didn't make any sense.

Sure, it was a little off putting to find a tooth. All alone. In the corner. The officer said I'd find fur. If I did, at least it would have made the tooth a little less unsettling. I didn't discover any blood to go along with it. It wasn't like it was sitting in a pile of scat. The tooth was just resting there on the carpet.

After a few more seconds of examination I finished walking over to the trash and dropped it in. Obviously it was only a deer tooth. Like the cop said raccoons or foxes or something must have been in the house. I convinced myself I was lucky something didn't drag more of a carcass inside.

I started doing some laundry, mostly just the bedding I tossed down the stairs the night before. I carefully looked over everything I washed and did discover a very small amount of fur on blanket that was once on the back of the sofa. It was coarse and tan and I couldn't immediately place it. A deer maybe or some type of dog? I had dated dog and cat owners in the past, and I found a lot less fur than I would have expected if an animal had actually slept on it. Although it was nice to have some additional support for the animal break in theory, I still wasn't fully convinced.

By the time I finished the laundry the weather cleared a little. At first I considered going out into the woods for a quick hike. I wanted to clear my head and relax. Instead, I decided I was too tired to go through another sleepless night. To really sleep I needed to feel safe. For that I needed to secure the house and that meant the window needed to be fixed.

I pulled the double hung vinyl window from the frame and knocked out the remaining sharp pieces of glass before throwing it in my car. Looking down at it, for some reason, I just knew I'd have trouble getting it repaired.

"At least it's a still weekday, stores should be open." I mumbled to myself.

"Weekday," that word triggered something I had forgotten in the broken window, police, no sleep nonsense. Gwen, at The Inn, worked weekdays.

Although a smile crept across my face, I didn't want to get my hopes up. It had been four months since I was last there and I doubted she'd even remember me. Of course that was if she even still worked there or if she still worked on Fridays. In the end I figured it was worth the trip as I was going to have to eat somewhere.

Fixing the window came before heading to the Inn, so my first stop was to the little hardware store in town. Unfortunately, when I got there I found they couldn't help me. Double paned, insulated, windows were not something they could fix. They could cut me a piece of glass and sell me some glazing to repair a single pane window. The clerk made it very clear they could provide *THAT* service. My window? No. However, they did point me to a glass shop where I could be helped. Of course, that place was forty minutes away.

The glass shop was easy enough to find and the staff pleasant and helpful. I dropped off the frame and was told it would be finished in an hour or so. I noted the shop closed at 4:30 and that it was almost noon. I figured if I stood around and looked bored they might have rushed a little, but I still didn't want to wait. I wanted to go to the Inn. So I did.

When I walked into the restaurant, everything was just as I remembered. Much to my relief, that included Gwen working behind the bar. She gave me a sideways glance, and then a nonchalant double take. Subtle enough that I wasn't even sure if that's what it was. I raised my hand in a casual wave to her as I found a seat back near the end of the bar. I tried to keep the idiot smile off my face and play it cool.

"Hi Gwen," I said as she made her way towards me.

"Hi Stranger," she replied back. There wasn't anything familiar in her tone or her expression.

"Oh well," I thought. I knew it would have been quite a stretch to think that I'd have stood out so much that she'd remember me. After all, I had only met her that one time and I was sure hundreds of different people had come through the bar since. The ridiculous smile I sat down with vanished immediately. I was a little crestfallen and in turn I was embarrassed at myself for being so. Immediately I looked down at the lunch menu she slid me.

"We don't have Hop Devil on tap right now Kent, so what else can I get for ya instead?"

My heart skipped a beat. She *DID* remember me and not only my name but even what I was drinking. I know some bar tenders are just really good at remembering details so wanted to play it cool, but I felt like a kid hitting a homerun in little league. A huge grin split my face from ear to ear before I regained control. "Um, anything hoppy. Could you pick, if you don't mind?"

She flashed me a small quick smile before she turned to reach down into the cooler to grab me a glass. Way down into the cooler. And wow. She knew how to do that. Legs straight and torso bent only at her hips. If I hadn't been such a cynic, I'd have sworn that little show was to flirt with me.

With a filled pint she returned.

"Let me know how you like this one." She said as she slid the amber ale towards me. It was a perfect pour, white head expanding just over the top of the glass but not dripping down the sides. "So, where you been hiding at? I was beginnin' to think that ya might have found another hole in the wall to get a drink at."

"Oh. No, nothing like that." I told her. "Last time I was in town, I did stop in. Although I must have just missed you. There was an older guy working that day. This is my first trip back since then.

Unfortunately, I just didn't have a chance to get up here over the winter."

Gwen's appearance was a little different than I had remembered. Her red hair was cut shorter than before. She also wore a little more makeup, not that she needed it. Her tight fitting v-neck tee-shirt was tucked into her tight fitting jeans. This time her athletic figure, which hadn't changed, wasn't hard to discern through what she was wearing. I hadn't been dating anyone for a while, and maybe that hiatus was affecting my judgment, but looking at Gwen's face right then and there I decided she was the most beautiful person I'd ever seen.

"Older guy? Hmmm. Probably Mac, I'm guessing. Although he might have told you his name was Chad or McDougal. For some reason he's been trying to ditch his nickname, which ain't going to happen 'round here. Believe me, I've given up trying. But, yeah he's pretty much the only old guy who works here. So it had to be him. Anyway, I'm glad you made it back," she said as she strayed off to help the others seated at the bar.

The place was mostly empty and looked about same as my last visit. It was just me at the far end, one stool over from where I sat before, and two older gentlemen sitting together at the other end. They were the type of guys who looked like they lived their lives on those stools. She left me alone with my menu for the next few minutes. I have to admit I felt an ill founded pang of jealousy when I heard Gwen's song-like laugh in response to one of their jokes. I found myself looking at her significantly more than at my menu. I kept thinking "What was happening to me?"

Eventually she made her way back. "Are you enjoying it?"

"Excuse me?" I said with what I hoped was an undetectable level of panic. What was she asking? Did she see me staring at her again?

She nodded down at my beer and I realized a second later she meant my drink.

"Oh, oh, the beer. Yes the beer's good. Tasty. Hoppy. Thank you. Great choice." I was sure I was beginning to sound like an idiot.

"Good, I'm glad. We don't sell a lot of it around here. It's a local brew. Well, local to Morgantown. So what'ca been doing all this time up on that mountain all by your lonesome self?"

My heart skipped another beat. Wait, what? Did she? Did she ask if I were single? I wasn't sure, but I never really was, no matter how obvious. Just in case I was interpreting the statement wrong, I did my best to direct my reply past the implication. Forever the pessimist.

"Oh, repair work actually. Someone or something, I don't know which, got into my place over the winter. Broke a window and tore up some of my stuff. So far it doesn't look like anything was taken, which was nice, and besides my new sofa there wasn't anything else too big or expensive destroyed. Overall nothing too horrible. Unfortunately it did put a slight damper on my long weekend up here. But for the break in, I might have been able to make it down here a little sooner. Instead, I got up early and spent the morning cleaning, trying to get my window fixed, and being talked down to by an unpleasant cop."

With an attractive woman smiling at my every word I was feeling more confident and comfortable as I rambled on. The story just flowed out of my mouth. Hoping I was being smooth I threw in that little line about getting to the Inn earlier as a hint that maybe I was looking forward to seeing her again. I couldn't tell if she picked up on it or not, but I didn't push it.

"Aww, I'm sorry to hear about that Kent. Trashed your place, huh? That really does suck. But, hey. Like ya said, it could have been a lot worse. At least your house is still standing. Anyway, late or no, seems like you've got a perfect reason to kick back and enjoy a nice cold beer with me! You deserving it an all." She looked at me, her smile turning a bit mischievous. "Just out of curiosity, who was the cop?"

I cut short my sip of beer to reply. Caught up in the moment I just said the first thing that popped into my head.

"Oh, I don't really remember her name. Stern faced woman, who I gotta say, was a little unjustly harsh with me. A mean older lady, don't really know how else to describe her. About fifty I'd guess. Brown but greying hair. Nondescript really." Caught up Gwen's gorgeous eyes I thoughtlessly added one more detail to differentiate the police officer from the bartender I was gazing at. "No one would consider her a beautiful woman, that's for sure."

The more my reply lengthened, the more Gwen smiled. What I read as interest, I soon discovered was familiar recognition. When I got to the "beautiful lady" part she burst out laughing. I stopped talking, oblivious of whatever joke I told. I just knew that I was making her smile and took another swig of beer confident in my social skills.

"Hey Mr. Thompson," Gwen yelled down to the opposite side of bar. "This fellow down here just said your wife is mean and ugly!"

But for the quickness at which my hand clamped firmly over my mouth, beer would have been sprayed all over Gwendy and the bar. One of the old men at the end swiveled his stool towards me and sent me a peculiar tense look I couldn't immediately decipher. His compatriot leaned forward over the bar with a stony faced stare.

What the heck was I thinking, talking about people? In a small town, no less? Everyone knows everyone in places like Bucksburg. What did I think would happen? To pile it on, I had insulted a freaking police officer. Alienation is for the rich, and it wasn't something I could afford if I wanted to stay in peace. Even worse, what the heck was Gwen doing to me? Did she notice I was checking her out, was that punishment?

I immediately got to my feet. After choking down my beer I opened my mouth, but nothing useful came out, just a string of helpless random syllables. It was about then when both men I was addressing started softly chuckling.

"*EX* wife, and while it's true she never were much of a looker, at least at one time she might of had a couple favorable qualities a man could appreciate. I did marry her after all, and that was solely my choice." He said with a smile. "So I'm guessin' it must have been you this mornin'? Ya know, she might have been in a better mood, if you didn't make her late to the meeting we had setup. We was goin' to talk about our daughter's educational options after she graduates this semester. Which meant we were talkin' money, and money ain't much of a pleasant subject between us. I'd guess the prospect of having to speak with me probably put her in an unagreeable state of mind before even dealin' with you and your little issue."

I was barely paying attention to what he was saying. My mind was struggling to find an acceptable excuse.

"I'm so very sorry, that was unacceptably rude of me. I was in a bad mood, and tired, and I wasn't thinking..."

He cut me off.

"No worries, you don't need to apologize to me. I'm not the one you dinged. Knowing that you're who she met, well, she said quite a few things about you this mornin' as well. If I were a judge, which I ain't, I'd have to say you're both 'bout even City Boy who likes to take long nature hikes. But then again as I said, I ain't no judge and it ain't my place." He chuckled to himself and then went back to his beer, apparently reaching his "socializing with strangers" limit for the afternoon.

"Not cool. Not cool at all!" I forcefully whispered leaning in towards the bartender. I was really pretty darn angry about being thrown under the bus like that. Yes, I knew I was the outsider, but the treatment still felt like a betrayal to me. The worst of it was that I thought, for a moment or two, we had been making a connection.

I was just about done with The Inn and glad I hadn't yet put in a food order. Gwen looked at me with a huge smile on her face. I wasn't sure what she was thinking or what I would do, but I wanted to patch something up with the locals if I could. After a second I asked Gwen "If you would, buy them both a beer on my tab? Please."

I said "please" through gritted teeth.

I looked down at my three quarters full beer and wondered how fast I could drink it without looking like I was drinking it fast. I wanted to get out of there and back to the safe comfort of being alone, but I wanted to make my exit with at least a small amount of dignity. I decided that she wasn't going to drive me out of the bar, if that were her goal. Even at the time I recognized the flaw in my logic.

Gwen shook her head slightly with a little bit of disappointment.

"Relax, I'll get the beers for 'em, but just letting you know I'm sure you just made Dan's day. Nancy and Dan have been divorced for the last 18 years or so. From what I gather, I don't think they even liked each other even while they *WERE* married. In fact, their dislike for each other is near legend around here. Lighten up, Kent. It was all in good fun, everyone got a laugh out of it. I didn't do you wrong."

She finished with a smile on her face, but her demeanor shifted slightly towards seriousness.

"Though just a little advice, if I were you, I wouldn't make it a habit of spreading people's names around like that. You know, some folks 'round here actually do love their ugly wives!"

She finished with a huge grin and went to deliver Dan and his friend a pair of Bud long necks.

I worked on my beer as I worked on my predicament.

I didn't know what to make of the scene or of Gwen. Was the joke on me? I wasn't sure. She seemed friendly enough after the incident. I watched her as she spent some time with the locals. They looked down the bar towards me, then went back to talking, and then looked back a second time a minute or so later. It was obvious that I was still the topic of conversation. Although I couldn't be sure without overhearing what was said, it did seem to me like Gwen was doing her best to make sure everything was alright.

"No bridges burned, Kent." She quietly said as she returned. "Free beers go a long way in this place, and you didn't have all that far to go. So the question is, you going to stick around long enough to get some lunch or did the mean lady scare you off?"

We both looked down at my nearly empty pint glass. Logically, I knew I was in over my head with that girl, but I didn't want to leave any longer. Her smile really was that inviting. Checking down the bar I saw that the two old guys were back to their beers and their conversation. With Gwen leaning in, way in, the urgency of my departure didn't seem as pressing. One more glance at her face and it was decided.

"Yeah. Sounds good." With all the awkward beer sipping and waiting I had my head down in the lunch menu for a while, so I had already had something in mind that sounded good. "I'll get the turkey club on untoasted rye. With fries instead of chips, please."

That "please" came out entirely different than the one just a few moments before.

"Coming right up, Kent." She walked over and put the order into the terminal. "By the way, your next beer is on me."

Gwen made herself busy which left me to my thoughts, the first of which was, what was I doing there?

Except on a very few, very rare occasions, I never sat alone at a bar. When I did it was never by design and never for more than a few minutes. Never for more than one drink. Two times in a row, however, I found myself staring at a doppelganger behind the looking glass who apparently did day drink alone in a dark bar. I spent the next ten minutes or so looking at my reflection in the mirror past the liquor bottles. My mind wandered. I thought of my future. Of what I wanted out of life. Of things... well... just things. When I reached again for my glass it was full. Somehow Gwen poured me a new beer without me even noticing. I looked around to thank her and saw her coming back from the kitchen with my sandwich.

"Here ya go." She dropped off my plate and looked up at me with these huge, sad, puppy dog eyes. "Are you still mad me?"

Those eyes of hers just made all my defenses collapse. I wanted to wrap my arms around her and never let go. It was a dirty weapon. Even though I was still a little agitated I couldn't bring myself to expressing it.

"No, no. Not at all. Just a joke, right?"

"Yes Kent, just a joke" which she said with a little extra force behind "just a joke".

166

"So, um, enough about my problems, what have you been up to all winter?" I couldn't help myself but to relax a bit more.

On the drive there I thought of the last conversation we had. I realized it seemed like she asked a lot of questions and I did a lot of the talking. For the hours I spent chatting with Gwen, I didn't really know all that much about her, and that was highly unusual for me. My modus operandi was to ask open ended questions and let everyone I meet tell me all about themselves before I shared too much. When it came to Gwen, it seemed like I rushed into telling her everything I could about myself. I didn't know much more about her other than her name, where she worked, and interestingly enough, that she didn't like sweet potatoes.

"Oh, a little of this. A little of that. You know, nothing exciting." She replied to me. "Been taking a lot of extra shifts lately, so that makes me even a little more boring than usual. But that Kent, that there's a story for another day. Maybe next time you're in I'll tell you more about it."

She had done it again, albeit, this time directly. She deflected my inquiry without revealing anything about herself. However, I tried not to take it too personally, and at least it wasn't sleight of hand. Being a private person myself, it made sense. Keeping a closed mouth when you're standing across from a bunch of barflies is, if nothing else, a matter of personal safety. The good news was that she did leave me that small opening to get to know her better. Maybe she was flirting with me, if only a little bit. "Next time" indeed.

"Alright, that sounds like a plan, Stan." I said. "Unfortunately, next time might not be for a while. I'm only staying up here for the weekend this time around, and I'm not even sure when I'll be back. Come Monday, I'll be back to work in the District."

"Normally I'd just have to say that it's your loss, Kent. However, well, remember what I just said about picking up some extra shifts? This particular weekend I picked up Saturday too. So if you find yourself hungry, or thirsty, or for whatever other reason you might have, stop by before four and I'll be here slinging beers to the early weekend crowd tomorrow."

She flashed me another one of her amazing smiles and turned to help another pair of men who had just taken stools near the center of the bar.

The afternoon pleasantly flew by in a blur and each time Gwen returned we spoke a little more, a few minutes here and a few minutes there. Eventually the bar filled as the town's work week came to an end. Our talks got shorter and shorter. By 3:30 many of the stools were taken. Thirsty patrons were standing behind me ordering their drinks over my shoulders. The chatter in the bar became loud and excited which replaced the hushed somber tones of earlier. Gwen became far too busy to really converse with me, and the last couple times she came by it was only to refill my beer and share with me a smile. I looked around the room, then at my watch. It was sad, but I had reached the end of my stay.

"Gwen." I called out as she walked past with six beer bottles in her hands. She glanced over her shoulder back at me. I made a little "check mark" sign in the air with my finger. She nodded but gave me an exaggerated pouting face before going back to work. A minute or two later she came back with a black vinyl bill holder with my printed tab inside.

"Sorry to see you leave, Kent."

"Yeah. I have to get out of here before the glass shop closes. I need that window installed. I could barely sleep last night. Besides, spending the afternoon with you I just doubled the amount I've drank in the last month. I'm a lightweight, and you don't take it easy on a guy."

"Oh boo who, you're holding your own. You've gotta trust me, Kent. I'm a professional. Anyway, I've gotta run too. See ya around?" Gwen asked, her eyes expressing a little more honesty than her persona usually allowed.

In an attempt at sounding cool I shot back at her "Never can tell."

She threw her head back and laughed as she walked away, "All right Jack Burton. Say 'Hi' to Wang for me."

I didn't even realize I had been imitating Kurt Russell from Big Trouble in Little China, but she spotted it instantly. Gwen just kept surprising me. She watched cheesy cult classic movies too. I pulled out my wallet and looked down at my bill. She had comped me nearly all my beers. Despite my standard self-defeatist attitude, I had begun to think that maybe she did like me.

It wasn't until I was walking out and didn't get accosted by an aggressive homeless looking man that I remembered I wanted to ask Gwen about Johnny. I wanted to know if he still came in and when or where I might be able to find him. I still wanted to offer him his rifle back. Of course I was only disappointed in myself for a moment before a toothy grin formed on my face.

"I guess this means I *DO* need to come back tomorrow" I said to myself out loud.

The words came out odd, not really slurred, but not quite naturally. Being interested in a bartender can lead to an awful lot of drinking. I hoped I could keep up.

The drive to the glass company and back home was uneventful. I wasn't used to day drinking, so I drove the speed limit and made overly conscientious choices. Driving wasn't the smartest or safest thing to do, and told myself I wouldn't do it again. Luckily I was basically the only person on those back roads.

Once I was safely at home, I easily put the repaired window back into the frame. In under a minute it was snapped into place and my little chore was finished. If my various detours were included, "fixing" that one window took almost an entire day of work. Thinking back to Gwendy it wasn't a bad day by any stretch of the imagination, but a full day it was.

While I was lurking in the dark depths of a dive bar, the sky had cleared up for the most part and the weather slightly improved. There were only a few lingering clouds high above. Gazing out through the spotlessly clean and repaired window, I watched the sky turn from a desaturated blue into an amazing orange and purple gradient. Where the sun had sunk below the tree covered ridge a fiery glow radiated upwards before fading into the darkening heavens. Dusk arrived and with it a few stars had begun to shine. A day before I had left the street lights and trash of the city behind and ended up spending nearly twenty four hours indoors while just outside were the beautiful wilds of the West Virginian countryside. I walked away from the window when my breath fogged up the glass. It had grown chilly outside, but not cold enough that my jacket couldn't render the night comfortable.

Needing some of the space and fresh air I drove over a hundred miles for, I went outside for one of my favorite ways to relax.

The fire pit in the backyard was full of leaves, and that was just fine with me. More fuel for the flames. The winter winds had littered the yard with enough fallen sticks from the oaks above that within a few moments I had collected what I needed to start a fire. To keep it going, I had plenty of split lumber from the cord I bought the fall before. The stacked logs were all hardwoods that would burn long and hot once lit.

Despite being a little damp from the earlier rain, the tinder immediately caught fire. I sat down close enough to the flames that I had to be mindful of my shoes. The warmth on my face was just what I needed. It felt amazing. At least as warm and amazing as it felt spending the afternoon with Gwen. I threw some logs into the flames and settled deeper into my seat.

There is some type of ancient but everyday magic in a campfire. While sitting in front of one there's a kind of primal calm that washes over you. Hypnotic flickering flames take you to a deep place of reflection and thought. It wasn't very long until I was fixated on dancing red and yellow flames, glowing coals throbbing white and blue, the calming scent of wood smoke, and the crackle and pop of the logs.

I kept the fire as large as I needed to keep up with the increasing chill of the evening. Otherwise I just sat back nursing a bottle of water while all the light from the sky faded away but for the few flickering pinpoints above. My entire world became nothing more than what I could see by the light of the fire. It was exactly the type of peace I was looking for.

Of course, it wouldn't last.

Nothing good does, but I guess that just makes us appreciate those moments more when find them.

At first the approaching disturbance unnoticeably blended into the sounds of the fire. Pops that were not wholly unlike steam violently escaping from a piece of wood. Until those pops got louder. Until the sounds started echoing off the surrounding bare forest and house. Sounds I eventually noticed no longer had been coming from in front of me. Glancing around, I saw the trees off to side start to light up. A car was coming up my driveway, loose gravel popping from beneath its tires. I cringed just knowing it wasn't going to be good news. I didn't want to be interrupted and I couldn't think of anyone I wanted to see that night that was likely to pay me a visit.

I got up and followed the stone path around to the front of the house. After an hour in the dark, next to a small fire, my eyes had adjusted to the gentle warm glow of the soft flames. Turning the corner I was blinded by the harsh glare of advancing blue-white headlights. I couldn't make out anything beyond the basic shape of a vehicle, which was the height of a car.

The headlights came to a stop a little further away than I would have expected. Almost immediately I heard a door open and the piercing lights jostled a little as someone exited the vehicle. My eyes slowly grew accustomed to the brightness and begin to make out more shapes. Was that a roof rack, I thought?

No. When I pieced it together I knew it was a light bar on top of the car. The police had come to pay me another visit.

The first thing I thought of was "what did Gwen do to me?" Then, more accurately, I revised it to "what did I do to myself with my big mouth?" I went into panic mode. I figured the cop from this morning must have found out I called her ugly. It was the only reason I could imagine for the police to come back. Officer Thompson was angry and wanted to enact some country justice on the city boy. Maybe arrest me on some trumped up charge? Maybe just beat me down? I was all alone and there wasn't anything I could do about it. I stopped dead in my tracks once I came to the conclusion. My hand raised, frozen in place, shielding my eyes. A flashlight was added to the blinding mix few seconds after I heard the door open. It was pointed right at my face in a power play to further limit my vision.

"Mr. Williams? Kent Williams?" A man's voice called out. Not a woman's, I hoped it could be a good sign. Maybe. The beam from his light lowered to my waist. Another good sign. Maybe I wasn't in trouble.

"Yeah, that's me. I'm Kent."

The officer started towards me, closing the thirty or forty feet between us. As he approached I was able to make out more and more details, the first of which was that he was significantly shorter than I am. Maybe only five foot five. Five foot six inches at the most. For such a small man he had a booming deep authoritative voice. I too started taking a few cautious steps to meet him halfway, never straying from the beams of his headlights. My hands I kept in front of me and visible at all times.

As I may have said before, very few police officers are actually bad. The crooked cops playing the villain in the movies are few and far between once off of the silver screen. Even knowing that, they still exist and it's still wise to be leery of men who can wrongly lock you up or end your life with little or no consequences for themselves. Even honest cops make mistakes. However, my initial anxiety had begun to shift slightly towards curiosity. Why would an officer decide to drive all the way up to see me? Did he find out something about the house?

"Um, hi. Can I help you officer?"

"Yes sir, maybe answer just a couple questions if you don't mind? Or actually, really just one right now. Have you seen a little girl around here? Likely she'd be the only one, but the one I'm looking for is thirteen, short black hair, about as tall as I am, and goes by the name of Tammy. Tammy Crammer."

No need for me to think or pause. I shook my head.

"No, I haven't seen anyone, but to tell you the truth I've been out all day. I was running errands and then had something to eat in town. Only got back here, oh, about an hour or so ago. I guess I'm saying she could have been here. How long has she been missing?"

"Not all that long, maybe just a couple hours. This isn't really a search. Just keeping an eye out is all. Got a call from a nervous friend of mine. Thought she might just be out walking around, maybe. Family lives on the other side of the hill." He pointed up the mountain and over the horizon. "'Guess 'bout two er three miles or so as the crow flies. I heard about your break in, I thought maybe it could have been kids. Maybe her and some of her friends wanted a place to get away to. Maybe this is the place they found. Maybe she'd make her way back here not knowing you returned this weekend. Maybe."

"Well, like I said, I haven't seen anyone here today but that doesn't mean she wasn't here. If it were a bunch of kids who broke in, at least they were decent enough to not steal anything from me." I paused. "You know, I haven't been upstairs or in the basement since I got home. There could be a scared girl hiding there, not wanting to get caught, or something. You wanna come in and look with me?"

"No sir, I don't think that will be necessary. I don't think that's very likely. However, I would appreciate it if maybe you'd have a look while maybe I could do a quick loop around the house through your woods. Do you mind? Do you mind if I take a walk around your property, sir?"

"No, no, not one bit. Go ahead. I'll yell out to you if I find anything in here." I said pointing at my house. "If I do, I'll just talk to her. I won't try and stop her from leaving or anything."

He just gave me a tight smile and a nod before he headed off into the blackness with his flashlight leading the way.

With that I went inside, completely relieved I wasn't in trouble. A relief that only lasted long enough to transition into some type of thick smothering guilt. Guilt that I found relief in a little girl missing. I tried to remember, what was it like being thirteen? I guessed that was fifth or sixth grade. When I was in middle school I recalled thinking that I was old enough to be out on my own. Most kids that age actually probably are. Where I lived, however, it was a lot easier for me to get the space I needed from my mom. In Philadelphia I could walk half a block and be at a friend's house. Out in the country sometimes miles separated homes, much less homes between where friends might live. School districts covered half of a county in places like Bucksburg. Being able to get out from under your parent's scrutiny without a car might only mean taking a walk through the woods. At thirteen there were more than enough reasons to want to get away.

Once back in the house I called out, explaining that I wasn't mad and that she shouldn't be scared. I explained I wouldn't press charges if she just came out. I let her know that the police were worried. With no response I searched in all the likely hiding spots, a task I was getting fairly good at it. The whole process didn't take long, even doing a pretty thorough job. As far as I could tell there hadn't been anyone in the house after I left that morning. Satisfied I was alone, I made my way back outside with another pair of water bottles. I didn't see the officer so I sat back down next to the fire.

But for the occasional faint and distant cries of "Tammy" the night was quiet and peaceful. After a while even those sounds were so muffled by distance and trees that I could barely discern them from the breeze. Soon after that I couldn't hear anything at all.

About twenty minutes after I last heard the officer, I saw a flashlight rapidly scanning in a 360 degree arc through the trees. Moments later the officer came hurriedly out of the forest towards me and the campfire. His pants legs and shirt sleeves were damp and his boots muddy. I noticed an angry red scratch across his cheek. During his approach he kept his light pointed just in front of himself at the ground when he wasn't scanning behind. If I didn't know better, my first thought was that he looked disoriented.

"Any luck?" I asked. He wasn't looking at me, but back into the woods when he replied. His light shining on the area he just walked out of.

"No. No. I thought. I thought maybe I saw something a couple times. Something out there. Tried to follow at first, but then I... It was nothing. No, it was a deer. Damn thing was... There was nothing."

I wasn't sure but I thought he sounded a little rattled. When the officer turned to face me, I held out the second bottle of water to him.

"Sorry, water is all I have to offer you, but it's yours if you want it."

Shaking his head, he held up his hand. "Thank ya, but no thanks. I've still got about a gallon of coffee left in the cruiser."

He looked over his shoulder out into the darkness again. I could see that he was working through his thoughts. I heard him take a deep breath and then he slightly shook his head. He silently looked off into the distance for over a minute before he turned halfway back around.

We made eye contact again. It took him a second to regain his composure. A little calmer he said "So, you were saying you ran errands in town? Get your house straightened out? Get that smashed window fixed? Read the report this morning. Heard what happened. Tough luck."

"Um, yeah." I said. "It'll all be fine. Damage was really minimal. Nothing that can't be replaced."

I wasn't really interested in talking about my house, and was far more concerned about the missing child that might be lost in my woods.

"So what's next, Officer..." I asked him, hanging on the last word.

"Greene. Name's Greene. Well, if you notice anything additional let us know. Otherwise, I'm sorry to say, your incident is already closed. You might not ever find out what happened."

I shook my head at him. He noticed, but still didn't track what I was asking. He didn't seem to catch my meaning.

"No, pardon me. What I meant was what's next for your search?" He had an anxious expression on his face, and he hesitated answering. He waved his flashlight into the woods once more before fully turning back to me and replying.

"Ohh. Well, hopefully nuthin'. I'm sure she's fine. I'll check back in with her parents. Maybe she's already at home getting her ear chewed off by her ma. Maybe she's still out there, but relatively safe in some sixteen year old boy's car. Maybe she's doing something else altogether. Still..."

I didn't quite feel comfortable the way he just stopped and left the word "still" hanging. He wasn't looking at me but up the mountain and off into the distance.

"Still, um, what?" I said before hastily adding "Officer Greene."

He took his eyes of the wood line where they had drifted again and tilted his head sideways and skyward. He paused thinking for a few seconds. I saw some of the tension in his stance relax a little.

"Aww, nuthin. Just a thought's all." He paused again as if he wasn't sure how to proceed. The silence had started to become awkward.

"You can tell me." I told him. It seemed the right thing to say, though I really didn't even know what I meant by it. Maybe it wasn't something he could tell me, I didn't know.

"No, it…" He started before stopping himself.

He shifted his head from the odd angle it was at and looked me in the eye. People always seem to open up to me, maybe it's my face, maybe it's my demeanor, I don't know. Whatever the case, he continued and ended up unloading on me. Though when he first started it was less talking *TO* me than it seemed like he was processing his own thoughts out loud.

"Well. From what I understand you don't spend a lot of time round here. This is some sort of, ah, vacation home you got? What I'm asking is you don't have any roots here?"

"Well no, but sort of, and I wouldn't call this place a..." I was cut off. I wanted to register a protest to his description of my house, to try and stop any more misperceptions, but he waved me off and kept talking.

"Don't matter none for what I'm a gonna be saying. Point is, maybe you ain't caught up on all the local goings ons, is all. Maybe you didn't hear that earlier this month our department got itself a missing person's report. Young mother that wasn't home when she was supposed to be. Hasn't been seen since. Husband's whole world has fallen apart. Now he's raising a baby girl on his own, that is, raising her when he ain't calling us begging for any new information we don't have or when he ain't hanging up those flyers he puts everywhere. Nothing terribly unusual in someone going missing, here or any place else. Sad as all hell, but not unheard of. Maybe it was foul play, maybe an accident, maybe she just found somewhere else to be. People just disappear sometimes, that's just the kind of sick world we all live in. You know? We'll continue to do our best looking into it, but we don't really have any leads. Anyway, while we have that one missing person's report, well..."

I waited, but he was lost in his own thoughts, this time staring into the flames of my camp fire. He didn't seem to want to reply until I nudged him on. Even then he didn't look directly at me.

182

I cleared my throat. "Well?"

"Well, it ain't nuthin. Not really. Not like we got a, well, like I said it's nothing. But the facts being what they are, facts, maybe just maybe more than one person went missing around here recently. Maybe."

This time I did wait. We just stood there for about ten seconds or more. Eventually he shifted his gaze skyward again in thought. He seemed to be putting it all together for himself instead of conversing with me. Vocalizing what he had been thinking or feeling, and maybe for the first time, expressing it.

"I guess I'm just frustrated about Tammy. About the whole darn town right now. I gotta feeling. A bad one." Officer Greene took a deep breath and sighed. "This ain't a secret. I'm not saying nuthin' others haven't already whispered about. If you weren't little more than a tourist I'm sure you'd have probably heard it too. So don't go reading into what I *AM* saying. Maybe it's not big news, but being in a small town, people do love their gossip. You could hear this anywhere if you wanted to ask. So, the thing is, maybe some folks who moved on, didn't. See what I'm saying? Not everyone has someone to miss them, and maybe some of those didn't just pack their bags and get."

"Are you saying there's maybe a string of disappearances in...?"

"Damn it!" He exclaimed cutting me off, irritated. Although I read it as he may have been more irritated at himself than with me. Wherever aimed, the outburst was short lived. After a second he regained control and continued in a conversational tone. "Darn it. I knew I shouldn't have opened up my mouth to you. Haven't you been listening to the words I've been saying? I didn't say nuthin' but 'maybe'. Just a maybe. Maybe I don't like it. That's all. That's all I'm saying to you. I just don't like it. Goddamn it Tammy, where'd you go and run off to?"

Once again he looked up into the night sky and shook his head slightly.

I just nodded to him in agreement. He looked like he may have finished speaking, but I didn't want to say the wrong thing, I didn't want him to raise his voice at me again. His demeanor was vastly different than it was before he went into the woods and it subtly changed even more as we spoke. From calm and confident when he drove up, to agitated and confused, finally to annoyed. I felt like if I said the wrong thing he would just clam up, frustrated with the difficulty he had expressing himself, and then he'd leave. I was too interested in what he was telling me to let that happen if I could help it. People possibly going missing in the mountains that I just moved to was something I felt I needed to know.

When I was sure he wasn't going to continue, but before the silence grew too long I spoke up.

"I understand why you're out here. Makes perfect sense to me, you're worried about the missing girl. You're worried about Tammy. Sounds like you might even have at least some good reason to be concerned."

184

He looked at me for a second then let out a short snort of a laugh. It was out of place and unexpected, but he laughed a real laugh. For a while his whole attitude changed for the better.

"Yup, I guess I am here 'cause I'm worried. You're right Mr. Williams, if I'm to be honest with myself. When I headed out here I thought I was just keeping busy. Proactively doing my job and all that. Until you said it out loud. Thing is though, we're both wrong. The worrying has got to be too much as there ain't nothin' to be worried about. I don't know why I went off like that. It's silly really. She's fine, gotta be. I think it's just that Tammy is my daughter's best friend. Lynn and her have been damn near inseparable since kindergarten. She's stayed over at our place as much as she's been at her own. Those damn giggling girls stay up all hours of the night gossiping and listening to that horrible boy band music. You know, they're closer than sisters and, and well, I kind of almost see her as another daughter. Listen to me going on." He looked a little embarrassed, laughed one more time, and started walking around the side of the house towards his cruiser. "I'm sorry to have bothered you Mr. Kent. Best be on my way. I don't know what got into me tonight. Have a good one, sir."

He turned to walk back to his cruiser which was still running with its lights shining on the front of my house. I walked with him, though I stayed a few feet to the side and never got too close.

"Don't worry about it, it wasn't a bother. You didn't interrupt anything really, you saw what I was doing tonight." I tried to comfort him as it was pretty obvious the whole affair had him concerned. "Hey, anyway it's normal to worry, but like you said earlier she's probably fine."

"You're right. I'm sure she's fine, but darn, these kids sometimes. Teenagers? Know what I'm saying?" He asked, assuming incorrectly I was also a parent. I didn't want to interrupt, so I didn't bother telling him otherwise. A little of the gloom returned to his voice. "They make such piss poor decisions sometimes. You know? Were we ever that plumb stupid back in the day? Damn water heads, one an all. Even if I'm just speculating, and there really isn't anything more to those couple of missing losers, drunks, and druggies, everyone knows there is an aggressive pack of dogs or maybe even a bear out there killing livestock and pets. Hell, I even heard talk of a pumas returning to the area. Now these dumb ass kids are goin' 'round daring each other ta go out at night? To prove they ain't scared of that stupid Terror Man crap they're all talking about? Sometimes I just gotta shake my head and wonder if they got any sense these days. Must be all the TV rotting their minds or something."

While not actually yelling, the more he spoke the louder he became. The louder he became the thicker his Appalachian accent. Again it seemed he was more venting to himself than actually talking to me. Even if he were talking just to himself, I had to ask him a question.

"The, uh, what man?"

"Oh nothin', really truly. Nothin' at all." He laughed it off and waved at me dismissively before continuing. "Stories. Just kids telling the same ole scary tales we told to each other twenty years before, and most likely the same ones our parents told each other twenty years before that. I'm sure wherever you're from you heard the same types of dumbass stories too. Kids being kids scaring themselves and whatnot. That was definitely not worth mentioning."

He paused in thought. I expected him to expound on the local legend or keep expressing his disappointment with the youth. I was wrong. He changed gears and went back to speaking with a more formal police officer tone.

"On second thought, if you don't mind sir, I would like that bottle of water you offered me before. It seems that maybe I've already had a bit too much coffee this evening. The way I'm talking, I can't seem to focus."

"Um. Yeah, sure." I jogged back and got him the extra bottle that was sitting beside my lawn chair. "No problem and I'm sure it won't come to this, but if you need help looking around here for, um, Tammy let me know. Last fall I did a lot of hiking and I might be able to help if you think she is out there. Pretty familiar with at least the immediate area. Heck, hiking was part of my plan for tomorrow anyway so when I go I'll keep an eye out for anything that might be important."

"Thank you sir, I do appreciate it." The formal, in control, police officer was back. He turned to go. Stopped, took a step, and then stopped once again. He turned towards me. Again his voice softened and lost some of the law enforcement authority it just had. "Listen. I do appreciate your help and you seem like an alright guy Mr. Williams. I just want to let you know that Nancy Thompson may be a hard woman to get along with, I know that as well as any man, but she is a good woman and a good cop and you don't have no right talking about her the way you did."

My heart fell through to my stomach and I felt physically ill. I started shaking my head furiously.

"NO! It wasn't like that at all" I tried to interject and defend myself, but he held up his hand and loudly drew out the word "now" until I stopped talking. Once I ceased resisting he continued.

"Now, I know from experience she may have treated you a might bit unprofessionally, and you could have in turn been upset. Hell, sometimes I think some powerfully mean thoughts about her myself and I consider her a dear close friend. But, and I'm just being honest with ya, you're an outsider and we're a community. Talking about people or taking sides in arguments you don't know nuthin' about with a bunch of strangers in bars is *NOT* the way to make friends here. You understand me?"

"I'm so sorry, this really just getting out of hand it wasn't like that at all. I didn't remember her name and was asked to describe what she looked like and all I said was ..." Again, I was cut off.

"Don't care. Just passing on some free advice. Do what you will with it, it bein' free. Thanks again for the water. We'll let you know about Tammy if we need to."

All I could do was quietly thank him as I stood there embarrassed. I was so angry at Gwen, her little joke put me in the worse social position I could remember. I wasn't even sure that what I had said was even all that bad. The story must have had grown in its retelling, I only hoped it wasn't retold all that much. The way he spoke to me, only god only knew what Officer Greene thought I had said about his coworker and friend.

I walked back to the fire but was no longer in the mood to just sit there. Did the whole town hear about my little jab? All I wanted to do was amuse Gwen a little. I kicked the biggest log off the fire and sat down. Feeling sorry for myself I watched the flames slowly flicker away. When the last light sputtered away I poured the remaining water from my bottle on to the coals. The fire wasn't Boy Scout safe, and a strong wind could have reignited it, but I deemed it safe enough with the ground being as wet as it was. Between not getting much sleep the night before and drinking beer all day I was tired and just wanted to call it a night.

I went inside, locked up the house, and got into bed. I tucked myself in, closed my eyes, and tried to drift away into sleep. But... something felt subtly wrong. Even with the house locked and the window fixed. I felt uneasy. Unsafe.

Eventually exhaustion won and I fell asleep. A sleep that didn't last.

Sometime after midnight...

BOOM.

The entire house shook. Trinkets on shelves, pots and pans, and the windows rattled.

My eyes flew open, but I otherwise didn't move. I couldn't move. I was frozen in horror. Instead I focused on anything that could be heard over my rapidly pounding heart. While I was asleep a massive thudding sound had rung out from downstairs. A single boom that was loud enough to be felt. While adrenaline pumped through my veins, I laid under the covers in silence and in terror. The dream I was having moments before was of shapeless twisting nightmare creatures full of panic and dread. Creatures that swam in a sea of black blood under a full red full moon. Eldritch creatures reaching for me. The noise that awoke me seemed to have brought that dream to life. I felt almost dizzy with disorientation. Without moving my head, my eyes darted over to the window. I could make out the trees contrasting against the dark sky. There was no wind that I could discern. In the only act of defiance I could make, against the petrifying fear, I moved just enough to shift my head to look down the hallway through the open bedroom door. Nothing moved.

I waited. There was nothing but darkness, but my fear didn't abate. My foggy head continued to swim.

Cautiously I sat up just enough to look around and waited another minute with no other sounds or movement.

Even with my hands shaking and heart pounding I started to think that I imagined the noise. Maybe it was a part of the bad dream? But for the distress I was feeling, there wasn't anything out of the ordinary. In the silence it could have been something small that only sounded loud. It could have been a water bottle in the closet rolling off a shelf. It could have been a branch falling onto the roof. It could have even all been just in my dream. Thinking that, I still couldn't understand why I was so scared. I couldn't understand why I was too scared to even move.

I was about to try and focus on falling back asleep when the house shook with another explosively loud bang followed moments later by the sound of something breaking. Glass for certain, maybe some metal. Something had been smashed.

Fear and instinct drove me.

I jumped out of bed and threw myself into the corner in an uncontrolled lunge. My white knuckled hands still clutched my blanket. I knew that there was no ignoring those sounds. Those sounds were not part of a nightmare. Not a part of my imagination and I wasn't misinterpreting something minor. It was so loud, prominent, and unexplained that I was gasping for air in fear. More than fear, I was terrified. I felt sick I was so scared. It wasn't a squirrel on the roof or a mouse in the pantry; it was something big and forceful. I huddled there cowering in the dark waiting for, something. Then I remembered that my 1911 was still in the dresser drawer and within reach.

I turned on the light and opened the night stand. Once the weapon was in hand I fell back into the corner. I pulled the slide back slightly and when I wasn't rewarded with seeing brass in the chamber I yanked it all the way back and let go. A round loudly slammed forward. The weapon was hot.

It could have been the gun in my hand or having the light on or just time passing by. Whatever it was, I was able to start thinking a little clearer. While still nervous, my mind went to Officer Greene and Tammy, so I thumbed the safety. The time I needed to remove the gun from safe wasn't much more than a fraction of a second, but it could have been enough time to prevent me from firing at someone I would regret.

For the second time in two nights I found myself yelling out into the darkness "I'm armed!"

My voice was higher pitched, more strained, and more broken than the night before.

After my calls were answered with silence I elaborated a little. "Is anyone down there? Officer Greene? Tammy? If someone is down stairs, just let me know and we can talk. Don't make me call the police or shoot you. Alright? Hello?"

Nothing. I took a deep breath and timidity made my way out of the bedroom, down the hall, and towards the stairs. I turned on every light I passed. As I got to the top of the stairs, I crouched down and crept forward one painfully anxious step at a time until I could see into the living room through the wooden railing. I looked through the slats near the top of the stairs like I was some excited kid on Christmas morning trying to get a peek at the gifts under a tree. Except on Christmas no kid was ever as terrified out of their mind as I was.

Everything in the living room was dark but undisturbed. Everything was as it should have been. Everything except the front porch, I could see it. Light shone through the window. One of the motion activated flood lights had come on. Something outside had moved.

I called out again from top of the stairs. "Hello?"

At that stage I wasn't expecting an answer, but I listened for one. I started to feel a little less trapped by fear. I wasn't going to spend the whole night stuck between the two floors, so I made my way down. Once at the bottom I used the light switch and felt a lot better after the room was fully illuminated. I then made my way to the front door. Every few steps I looked behind me, just to be sure.

My fully extended, shaking left arm to tried the door knob. I gave it a twist and found it still locked. Relieved, I went to the window and looked out onto the porch and into front yard. With the light on I could see out to the driveway and a little past my car.

Again, nothing.

Then I noticed… the shadows weren't correct. There was something wrong. I thought the view from the window was a little darker than the night before. I hesitantly got my face as close to the glass as I dared. Close enough to smell the new glue and vinyl. As close as I was, only a few additional degrees of visibility were added. I still couldn't see directly below or right up against the outside wall.

As soon as I saw what I could, I hurriedly backed up. The thought of some Hollywood style jump scare like in the original Amityville Horror pig demon thing showing up on the other side of the glass was too much for me.

On my way to check the backdoor I went through the house turning on lights. That door too was still locked. A quick look around the room verified that the windows were all still closed. I was alone inside the house, or at least that was what I convinced myself of. I could have gone back up to my bedroom. I could have tried to go back to sleep knowing that the house was secured. However, I also knew that wasn't going to happen.

To really assure myself, I needed to look into why the porch light came on. I needed to figure out what those sounds were. Sounds that I had already, once again, began to doubt how loud I remembered them.

The automatic lights were on a five minute timer. They were still lit. It took me at least four minutes to rally my courage and make my way down stairs. Realizing I didn't know when the lights were triggered only added to my apprehension. I wanted to wait. Wait until the lights went out again, that way I'd know nothing had moved for at least five minutes. While I hoped nothing was there, it could also have meant something was just waiting still for five minutes. I reasoned I was better off with the lights on when I opened the door.

Standing as far away as I could I quickly jerked open the door and stepped back into the living room. The pistol in my right hand rose as I pointed it into the dark void. My right thumb rested on the safety of the Springfield, my index finger hovered near the trigger.

I waited.

Nothing burst through the open doorway.

Nothing moved outside.

One last time yelled out, that time with anger. My fear had begun to dramatically subside. "I've got a gun. Do *NOT* screw with me. Things can get really ugly really fast. Be smart. Come on out."

My breath clouded in the frigid air that rushed through the doorway.

With no reply, I stepped forward and poked my head out. My pistol pointed everywhere I looked. There was no one on the porch or in the yard for as far as the lights penetrated the darkness. For a second I smelled a faint musty animal odor in the air with what was oddly mixed with scorched oil. I took another whiff and it was gone, replaced with an indistinct odor of rotting meat, which too rapidly faded away leaving me again in doubt of my senses. I walked to the edge of the front steps and looked out into the yard. My eyes scanned as far as they could into the night, but I still couldn't identify anything out of the ordinary. I wished that my flashlight wasn't back in the car, but there was no way I was going down to go get it.

The night was nearly silent. I could faintly make out a few frost covered leaves rustling in the very slight breeze. Everything was exactly as I expected it to be. I struggled to recapture the odd odors I thought I may have smelled, and inhaled deeply through my nose. The cold air burned but all I could make out was the wet earthy forest and a little wood smoke from the smoldering campfire on the other side of the house. I started doubting myself again. Really, how loud was that noise? Did it really come from downstairs? Maybe I was just freaking myself out? I lowered the sidearm in my hand. Things really didn't seem as frightening as they did minutes before.

However, there was still something that wasn't right.

Upon turning I immediately saw the problem. At the far corner of the covered porch one of the two flood lights, which normally shone into the front yard, wasn't on. In fact, it was ripped off the wall. Short electrical wires hung dangerously out of a hole near the ceiling and the smashed light was on the deck. The porch was only about eighteen feet long. To investigate the broken light and the yard beyond would only take a few steps.

I didn't take a few steps. I took many small and slow steps. I inched over to the edge and looked into the yard and the forest beyond it. My eyes adjusted a little. Again, I didn't see anything I didn't expect to see, but my visibility was far from ideal. I looked down at the smashed floodlight at my feet. I looked back up to where it was mounted on the wall. Nothing obvious pointed to who or what had destroyed it. The breaking sound, at least, was accounted for and proven real.

There wasn't anything else to see from the deck. Dressed only my boxers and a tee-shirt, the cold was getting to me. Nothing could have convinced me to walk around the house in the dark so I turned to head back in. Then I saw the exterior side of the door. Head high in the steel door was a six inch wide circular depression.

I walked up and touched it, feeling the contrast between the dent and the rest of the door. The crater in the steel was almost three quarters of an inch deep. I used my own fist and gave the door a solid bang just below the dent. My punch didn't even flex the steel. It was pretty obvious where the pounding noise had come from. I shivered at the thought of how much force it would take to bend the door. I immediately spun around again and backed into the house. I felt vulnerable from behind. I locked the door. I gave the knob a good tug to make sure that it was secured. I double checked the back door and windows.

After seeing the dent, I wasn't quite ready to go back to sleep. Instead, I sat on the stairs and waited until the porch light automatically turned off again, then I waited another ten minutes to make sure it didn't turn back on.

It took a while for my heart rate to slow down to normal. I felt how long of a day it had been. I felt how much it wore on me. I was exhausted, but I couldn't stop thinking about what had happened.

Someone had hammered on my front door with enough anger and energy to put a large dent into a steel security door. Sure it wasn't a bank vault, but it wasn't like it was some cheap wooden interior door. No, it was a door designed and manufactured to stop people from gaining entry. The door did its job, but it took a beating in the process. Then I had to wonder about the light. Was someone drunk? After punching my door, did someone decide that even more violence was needed? Someone angry enough to pull the light off the wall before leaving? And if someone wanted in, why not just break the window again?

My best guess was that the dent in the door could have been made by a pissed off very strong man or maybe something like a large black bear. Those were the only two possibilities I could come up with. However, be it a man or bear, without seeing either, there wasn't much more to do.

I could have stayed up all night, but I realized that wasn't much of a short or long term solution. I needed sleep. The doors were locked, and so were the windows. If someone were going to get into the house, they were going to have to break something. A door, or more likely, a window. With the state of mind I was in, I was sure I'd hear anything like that. If I did, I'd be right there with my gun. As the fear faded away I told myself if it were a person, someone would pay for screwing with me. That much I was certain.

I left all the lights on, and went back to bed. I kept my gun on top of the night stand. I didn't unload it. I forced myself to try and get some rest, and eventually I did, though it turned out to be yet another long night of waking up every hour.

Always the good guy, Kent

Kent paused in silence looking across the slowly dying fire towards the professor. The professor in turn stared back at Kent and his rifle.

After about thirty seconds of silence Andy spoke up.

"Dude. It's really getting late. You gotta recognize that if the professor weren't here, we'd be up and out hunting in an hour or so. We might have to finish this another day, man, I can barely keep my eyes open."

The late October morning still didn't show any signs of the coming sunrise, but it was approaching.

"No, I don't think so. I'm almost finished. You can go to sleep if you like. I think the professor might stay up with me. He seems interested."

"If you wanna. Look, I'm really fucking tired and this story is really dragging ass. Plus, I already figured out how this is all going to end.

I'm guessing a black bear decided it liked your house and thought you were a big ole pussy. It storms in and you shoot it with your antique rifle. Hell, maybe that chick Gwen is even there. You end up saving the whole fucking day and end up getting laid. Everything wraps up with you being a *BIG DAMN HERO* and all that. Tell me that ain't right?"

Kent didn't respond, and with his silence, Andy resumed pleading his case while looking back and forth between the other two men seated across the fire.

"Look Kent, I'm sorry to steal your thunder, but you've been telegraphing your ending. You'd make a bad boxer and a worse gambler. Especially with the whole door banging part. A man would have broken the window and climbed through. And denting a steel door? Need to be a huge animal or a guy with a sledge hammer. You'd hear and recognize the difference between a hammer and a fist. Know what I'm saying? We all know the end to this story. You're just taking your good ole fucking time getting there. Come on West, back me up here, buddy."

The professor turned his head slightly to make eye contact with Andy. He had been so still for so long that his stiff movements seemed out of place. Andy, who was generally oblivious to subtly, instinctively reacted to the change and cut short anything else he was going to add.

"Yes." Professor West said.

The unnatural absurdity of it all got to Andy and he just laughed off the oddness he felt.

"Yes? What the hell, man? Come on. Yes to what? Yes, you acknowledge that I've been talking to you? Yes, the story is over? A little more info from you might be helpful. See there Kent, West here is so damn tired he can't even think straight. It's time to continue your long ass tale another day."

West went back to looking at Kent. "Yes. The night has about come to its end. You gentleman should rest. I've disrupted your plans enough for one evening. I'd hate to ruin your tomorrow as well. I believe that it is time to put your antique away and we can finish your, as Andy said, tale some other day. Perhaps over dinner, once we are all back safely in civilization?"

Andy gestured to West. "See? Everyone here is done for the night. Come on Kent, it seems to be agreed upon. I'm fucking beat."

Kent didn't immediately reply. His hands still rested gently upon the Papal State's Remington, although he no longer played with the cartridge he once held in his hand. His eyes, slightly unfocused, looked distantly through the fire. Just as Andy was about to pressure him again, Kent shifted his gaze and replied.

"No worries. Professor, you can sleep in my tent. The blue one behind you. I'll just stay up until morning and keep the fire going. I'm not all that tired anymore. Maybe that coffee was a bit too much for me. I usually don't drink any caffeine before bed. Now I'm borderline jittery. I'll watch over the camp until the sun comes up. Maybe I'll even have some breakfast ready for you guys. Sound like a fair plan? The story is almost over, but if neither of you will be awake to hear it, then it doesn't really matter. Does it? Listen, if you're both too tired to stay up, please guys, go and head off to bed."

Kent looked over to the professor to see if his offer was accepted, but instead of a verbal reply West just curled his lips into a slight grin and shook his head. Andy didn't notice West, but instead responded directly to Kent.

"Yeah, always the good guy, Kent. I guess maybe you're right. It be a pretty huge dick move for us to turn in and leave this guy out here in the cold. Thanks for offering to bite the bullet and let him stay in your tent. You're a better man than I, Gunga Din!"

Andy stood up and paused. After a few moments he sat back down on his log and shook his head.

"Aww, fuck it. Damn it, I guess I'll stay up with you. If you're pulling an all nighter, I will too. Hell, I'm a couple years younger than you are old man. If you can hack it, I can hack it. Plus, some part of me still wants to know why you lug that big ole gun around with you. I've been going over it in my head, and I'm beginning to think it can't just be sentimental, like if that gun saved your life or some shit, that would just be another reason to put it in a glass case. Maybe I did get the ending wrong, but if it's not that, well. I mean. I mean if you just wanted stopping power in an unusual ass round, you could've went with something like, ah, I don't know. Like a fifty caliber Beowulf or something. At least then you could possibly find cartridges and parts for it and it be built on a modern weapons platform. If you just wanted some really stupid stopping power you could have always got something ridiculous like a five-seventy-seven Tyrannosaur. But, no, instead you decided you want to drag around a freaking ancient musket or whatever the fuck it is. I gotta love you man, but you're crazy. Bat shit crazy. So there's gotta be a little more to this. Right? At the very least, I wanna hear more about this piece of ass you keep talking about. I wonder about how much of this your wife knows, especially the way you keep talking about this Gwen chick."

Kent briefly shut his eyes and shook his head.

"There is something more to my story. I'll tell you that much, but I'd really like the both of you to hear it. Hear it in the order it happened to me. The way it happened to me. If you're too tired Andy, well, there isn't much of a point to staying up just to keep me company. You know me, I like my quiet time. I'll be fine up by myself and I'll tell you both what happens and how it ends in the morning. What do you say Professor Herb? Once the sun comes up, I can start up again over a hot cup of Joe?"

"Well now." He said with a slender tight lipped smile on his face. "If you are telling this tale, at least partially for my benefit, I would hate to ruin it by going off to sleep. Even more so if it's also going to be a horror story, which you seem to irrationally insist upon making it. Well it just won't do to have you tell it in the light of day. Am I correct, Mr. Williams?"

"It may not receive the same reaction from you in the morning, no. But I'm not trying to make this a ghost story Professor. I'm just telling you the events the way I remember them. Now as for finishing it tonight, if I had my choice, I believe now would be the perfect time. At least while there is still time."

West cocked his head, and looked out through a small break in the trees overhead.

"Hmm, we might make it to the end of this story. That is of course if your tale is truly coming to its completion."

Andy looked back and forth between the other two men. Once again was slightly confused by their exchange.

"What the fuck are you two going on and on about? We still have a couple hours left before first light, and even longer until the sun makes it over the hills. Am I missing something here? You guys are acting a bit weird." Andy snickered out loud. "God damn it you fuckheads, nothing personal professor, you guys haven't been making too much sense. Snap out of it. This is just some ridiculous story Kent wants to tell so he can hear himself speak. Horror story? Still time for it? Kent, I know you enjoy talking about your emotions or whatever, but I still just wanna hear about something at least somewhat exciting. Am I, you know before too long, going to hear something exciting?"

"Well, I can guarantee you that at the time, I was excited. All I can do is tell you what happened to me. Maybe you'll find it exciting. Maybe you won't, I don't know. However, for what it's worth, before too long we'll be getting to the gunplay you've been waiting to hear about."

"Hot-diggity-damn. You hear that? Kent is going to talk about some gunplay! Hello? You may not have heard what I just said Herb. You should be as excited as I am. A couple hours deep into this story and Kent's going finally going to tell us something interesting." Andy kicked the logs on his side of the fire further in. The agitation and extra fuel caused the flames to grow and completely reveal everyone's faces for the first time in hours. Andy, who couldn't leave any possible slight left unused, leaned over to West in faux confidentiality. "You know, of course, somehow Kent's going to make his bit of shooting actually boring?"

"Boring or not, Andy. I guess it seems we're all in agreement. If that's the case, I'm going to continue." Kent also kicked some of the half burnt logs on his side further into the flames as well. Fiery orange sparks filled the air before disappearing into the night above.

I watched a bird kill itself

The peace I so desperately wanted to find in West Virginia, the magic I felt when I first returned, continued to elude me. My sleeplessness and exhaustion didn't help.

Just like the evening before, but far far worse, every sound woke me. Instead of just imagining something in the house with me, each creak filled me with fear. It wasn't the same panic I felt as with the bangs, but with every ordinary noise I expected something to bust down the door and storm into my room. Tear me limb from limb. The worst part of the evening occurred after I realized it wouldn't be all that difficult for someone to climb up onto the porch roof and in through one of the second story windows.

After that thought, the night seemed to last forever.

It wasn't until the sky started to lighten, when that grey blue band on the horizon started to form, that I was finally able to really fall into a restless sleep.

I know I finally was able to get some real sleep because I remember dreaming. I remembered dreaming because those dreams were horrible. I don't so much recall what happened in them, they were just emotions more than anything else. I only remembered how they left me feeling. Drained. Drained with a crushing sense of dread. Dread and sadness.

As part of a recurring theme, like everything else good, my rest that morning also didn't last. With another startling sound I was once more yanked out of sleeping nightmares and into another one while wide awake.

I sat straight up in bed.

The same banging had come back and again I was scared.

Only, that time it wasn't the same.

For starters, it was light out and I was startled not terrified. My room was well lit. The sun had risen, though with a quick glance out the window I knew it wouldn't be visible through the heavy cloud cover and mists.

I had to hear the pounding again before I was sure that those noises weren't what had woke me hours before. The new bangs, while loud and forceful, were just knocks. First a set of three then closely followed by a second set of four.

A few seconds after the banging at the door, I heard the doorbell ring.

I was still in a semi-dreamlike mindset and wasn't able to fully appreciate what was happening. I reached over and grabbed the Springfield again. I checked the chamber and it was still loaded. I took a deep breath, re-safed the gun, and got out of bed. After the doorbell, everything remained quiet for the fifteen seconds or so that it took me to make it to the stairs.

My sleep deprived senses had slowly come back online, and I realized that anyone knocking on my door wasn't very likely to be a threat. Like the night before I found myself ducking down a little so that my head was close to the floor so that I could see through the railing.

It was the police.

At my house.

Again.

Just like the morning before, it was Officer Nancy Thompson. I saw her face pressed up against the newly replaced front window. She saw me and we made eye contact. I waved to her with my empty hand and hurried down the stairs while she took a step away from the window.

Far from being completely soothing, my first emotion was still relief. The knocking at the door wasn't that of a murderer or a bear or even worse a murdering bear. All of which are good things to not see at the front door. My second reaction was less satisfying. I couldn't believe that I was once again speaking with the cops. I had gone a dozen years without so much as a parking ticket, and then three times in two days I was face to face with a law enforcement officer. With so much contact, the unfamiliar novelty had worn off and I'd become at least a little accustomed to the visits. The new normalcy I found, combined with a lack of sleep and the emotional exhaustion of being terrified all night, left me in a place where I wasn't nervous that she might have been there because I called her ugly. Mostly not nervous.

As I neared the door a quick glance at myself in the mirror showed me that I wasn't exactly ready to talk to the police woman.

First thing first, I put down my gun. If you want to live you don't meet the police at the door with a gun, or anything for that matter, in hand. For good measure I buried it under a stack of newspapers and mail. Second, I was wearing my boxers and a tee shirt. I wasn't going to leave her waiting any longer by putting on some pants. But I did what I could by rotating my boxers so that the fly was slightly off to the side. Once I confirmed that I probably wouldn't be charged with indecent exposure, I opened my dented steel front door.

"Mr. Williams, I'm sorry for," she paused and reshaped the rest of her sentence into a question, "awaking you, at 9:45 in the morning?"

Even though I could tell she was trying to be nice, it still came off as condescending and judgmental. To be fair to me, it was a Saturday morning. Her greeting wasn't a great way to start the conversation.

"Yes officer, I did just wake up. Yes officer, I'm sure that I reaffirmed what you already thought about me. Yes, Officer this was one more reason to dislike the lazy new guy from out of town." Of course I didn't say any of that. I kept my mouth shut and just nodded which allowed her continue.

"Officer Greene was going to come by this morning, but he changed his mind and thought that maybe I should." She had finished but then decided to add, "Since your house was on my way back to the station."

I didn't know what to make of that. Did Greene think that I should apologize to her? Maybe he thought she might want to apologize to me? Maybe he thought that the two of us should just get to know each other a little more. It also could have been that my house really was on Officer Thompson's way into work. I didn't know. Whatever was going on, I wanted to make it go as easily and as quickly as it could for the both of us.

I hesitantly took a chance, "Good news, I hope? Tammy make it home last night?"

"Yes. But more likely no. There is some possible good news but as far as we know she is not yet home. I was asked to let you know the status of Officer Greene's search for the little girl, and to see of you could still look for her during your, um… Recreation. If I recall from our meeting yesterday, you said you enjoy hiking. I also understand that you offered to look around for Tammy as you hiked this morning. Or afternoon."

I ignored her obvious opinion of my sleep schedule, but instead gave her a quizzical look. "Why the yes and no?"

She returned my look with a deep exasperated sigh and continued on.

"It seems the young Miss Crammer, while not actually home, may be accounted for. Very early this morning we received word she had been spotted. However, there is the possibility that the information obtained by the mother may have been fabricated."

"Um, OK. So what you're saying is that there is a thirteen year old girl still out there missing, but her mom thinks maybe she's somewhere that's relatively safe, but no one really knows for sure?" I asked.

"Basically correct. While Tammy's mother was reaching out to her daughter's friends last night, one of them indicated she had seen the missing girl and thought that she planned to do some shopping with some other friends of theirs, after shopping Tammy discussed staying the night with yet a third group of friends. However, Officer Greene, using his own CI feels that the provided information may be suspect. Tammy's friend may have believed that she was spending time with an older male that Tammy's mother didn't approve of, so there is a possibility of subterfuge. Both leads are being investigated"

I thought to myself how odd it was that Officer Thompson was being so police like and using so much jargon. She wasn't nearly so formal the day before. Business like, yes, but not as formal. CI? I doubted she would have known the details of the conversation I had with Officer Greene the night before, but for her to say Greene had talked to a confidential informant instead of simply saying he asked his daughter seemed a bit much to me.

"No worries. I'm sorry to hear that. I did plan on heading out so I'll give the woods between here and the top of the mountain a good walk through. There isn't much on the trees, um you know meaning leaves, so I should have a pretty good field of view. Any idea what she was wearing?"

"Thank you Mr. Williams, and no. Her mother wasn't sure how she was dressed. Apparently she is in the habit of changing multiple times throughout the day. Once again, we appreciate your assistance in this. Good day."

As she was about to turn and walk away I stopped her with another "Um."

The reason I initially tried to delay her was to apologize, but as soon as I started I realized I had no idea how to say it. I couldn't be straightforward. "Excuse me, I'm sorry I told your ex-husband I thought you were frumpy bore." That wasn't going to work, but neither was trying to sugar coat it. Instead I decided upon continuing to ignore the elephant in the room and to head in a completely different direction. Maybe if I were as nice I could be, the unpleasantness would fade away.

"If I find, um, Tammy in the woods, should I, um, do what? Like tell her to go home or maybe just give you a call?"

I sounded like some sort of an idiot.

"If you find anything you can call the police station and make a report with the receptionist. She will direct any information provided appropriately. Also, while hiking remember what I told you yesterday about the local wildlife. You're pretty far out here. This time of year the bears are beginning to stir and are hungry. Here on the east coast, black bears are usually only a problem for people who sneak up on them while they're with their cubs. So don't. If you see one or hear something big, generally yelling out something like 'HEY BEAR' is all you need to do to get them moving on."

"Thanks for the advice, and believe me, I'm going to heed it. I was scared out of my mind last night when I think a bear banged on my door a couple of times. Ripped down one of my lights. I could barely sleep the rest of night. Look what it did to my door."

I pointed at the large dent in the steel and took a step further into the house so that she could take a closer look without having to completely shut the door. It was located a couple inches above her head, so

Officer Thompson had to look up at it. She stared at the indentation, then at me, and then shook her head a little as she took a step back to get a better look at the whole door.

I waited for her to say something.

"Officer?"

"Yes? You think...? Hmm. You actually saw the bear that did this?"

"Well no. Whole thing only lasted a minute or so and woke me. So no, I didn't. Um. I just heard it as it beat on the door and then I heard the sound of it attacking my lights. Like you said, I'm thinking it had to be a bear. I mean I guess it could have been a strong guy or something. But, why? Bear makes more sense. It must have been scared off when I made my way down stairs. I didn't see anything outside. I'm just glad it didn't break the window again since that was what probably did it over the winter, you know?"

She looked back up to the large dent, and ran her fingers over the smooth surface. She looked back at me.

"Well. To be honest, this doesn't seem all that normal to me. Not really. I'm no expert, but the couple times I've followed up on bears getting into barns or chicken coops, they usually try and claw their way in or just lean real hard on something. Not pound doors down like this. I wouldn't have thought this bear damage... but I also wouldn't put too much thought into it. As I said, I'm no expert. Could have been a bear. Animals do some pretty random things out here. I'm sure it isn't anything to worry about. If it were a bear, it probably won't be an ongoing problem. Especially now that it knows someone is home, and like you told me yesterday, now that you'll be here more often your scent will be more prominent. I'm sure it will stay away for good."

Not a bear? I wasn't sure what to make of that. Of course it was a bear. Did she think it was a person? If she thought it was a vagrant or some sociopath she would've told me, right?

However, I didn't focus on it, I still felt really awkward around Nancy and was struggling to find an answer to what I could do about that.

She looked back over her shoulder to her patrol car parked in my driveway. She was about to speak up, with what I assumed was her exit. The need to apologize was fighting to get out of me and I knew at that moment it was my last chance. Still without a clue as to what I was doing, I jumped in with both feet.

"Listen Officer, um, I don't have any brewed yet, but I could offer you a cup of coffee in about five minutes if you'd like. It's the least I could do for you for having to come all this way out here twice in as many days."

She just stared at me. While her stern flat expression was unchanged, her dark eyes bored into me as she tried to read my intentions. The look was intimidating, and she knew it. She probably used it to great effect as police officer.

Then the expression on her face softened.

"Is it the least you could do for me after driving all the way out here, or is coffee the least you could do for me after commenting on my appearance with my ex-husband and his drunk loser friends?"

I was mortified, she *HAD* heard about it. I cursed myself for not just letting it go. We had been both dealing with it and being civil, and then I had to bring it out into the open. I wasn't prepared for her being so direct, but I was going to talk anyway. I was hoping something would leap off my tongue that would get me out of my mess.

Just as I was about to start my babbling, she stopped me by continuing.

"Don't even bother trying. It's alright. Really. While I didn't hear what you said first hand, I have a feeling that the little incident was at your expense nearly as much as it was at mine. I'm sure that vapid little girl wasting her life away as a bartender thought it was just wonderful fun putting you on the spot. Good laugh for everyone? Right? Anyway, it doesn't matter to me. None of that matters. Small people talk about people. I know what I look like and I'm fine with it. If Dan wants to spend his days getting drunk in a dingy bar and watching some little hussy's ass walk back and forth, well, it's completely up to him. I'm no longer his keeper and I'm happily free of him as my burden."

Her tone was more human than the formal police woman I started speaking with. There was real venom when she spoke of her ex-husband and almost disappointment when she spoke of Gwen. I didn't have the background to contradict anything she had said, so I didn't.

"Listen. Nothing that afternoon happened the way I planned it. It all came out wrong and by the time I realized the damage had been done. I'm really sorry."

"It's alright. Small town. I'm sure back in Washington D.C. you can talk about people behind their backs with complete anonymity." Until she flashed what appeared to be a strained smile I wasn't sure she was joking. Officer Thompson had turned out to be a lot friendlier and understanding than my first encounter with her had led me to believe. Knowing that only made me feel like more of an ass.

"Well, thank you again. I'm glad I was able to finally apologize to you. I've been feeling horrible about the whole thing since it happened. So what do you say about that cup of coffee?" I asked.

"No thank you, that's alright. I have to get back to the job. There is still a lot to be done this morning. Just keep an eye out for the missing girl, if you would."

"OK. That sounds like a plan. I'll make my way out shortly. I'm sure she's fine, but if she is up there I'll find her." I cocked my head over my shoulder indicating up the mountainside.

Since she arrived the older police woman had went through being indifferent, angry, humorous, and then lastly a touch sad. Her reply took with it the slight smile she had been wearing.

"I hope you're right. About an hour ago Greene called the county Sheriff's department asking for help. This looking like it will become a full scale search. He's really worried about Tammy."

She paused in reflection and then shook her head to dismiss whatever thought she kept to herself. Nancy purposely looked me back in the eye. "I have to go. Thank you. And thank you for your help and your time Mr. Williams."

The gravity of the situation left me with little to say.

"Yeah, no problem," was all I managed. I stood in the doorway until the she got in and started her car. I heard her drive away as I sunk into the couch. Besides being drained and tired, I also became depressed. Nearly everything that weekend felt wrong. Besides the actual moments spent with Gwen, nothing else was positive.

Worry. Fear. Dread. Hopelessness. Anxiety. Frustration.

On that partially destroyed sofa I felt them all. I borrowed from the bank everything I could, and for all that debt, I purchased the exact opposite of what I wanted. Gone was the warmth and safety I felt just a few short months before. Gone was the magic I thought I'd recaptured. Gone was everything I expected to find. Looking around I hated where I was and wanted to pack up and leave.

Despite all of that I did my best to try to deny myself the luxury of wallowing in self-pity for very long. A few minutes were enough. I fought against the malaise and focused instead on the little bit of good I saw. Foremost of which was Gwendy. She had all but expressly and personally invited me back to the bar. Well, maybe. With all the signs and my high hopes, I still didn't want to read too much into the conversation. There was still a solid chance I may have just been a good customer, but it was possible that something a little more was happening between us. For just the cost of a few beers it was worth the chance. At the very least, as Officer Thompson suggested in a roundabout way, I thought I could look forward to enjoying the view.

Before I headed back to the bar and to Gwen, I needed put in some time outside looking for Tammy. The clear skies from the night before were a thing of the past as the morning was a miserably foggy and overcast mess. Anything further than thirty or forty yards disappeared as the mists became impenetrable. The fog and the sky were a uniform shade of grey that merged together. It wasn't the type of day I would normally choose to be out in the woods, but I had no choice having told two different police officers I would take a look. Even if it wasn't for the police, I'd have still went out if I thought I could help someone find a lost child.

As I left the house the big dent in the metal door stood out begging for my attention. While the destruction irritated me, more importantly it made me realize that I'd feel a lot safer being armed walking through forest. I didn't want to startle a groggy bear without some means of personal defense. So I grabbed the 1911 again. Without a proper holster I stuck it into the back of my pants and headed out.

I chose one of several trails leading from my porch and headed off into the trees. I didn't have to walk far before I lost sight of the house. Colors and sounds were muted in the damp weather and soggy leaves. Desaturated. Dull. Surrounded by grey haze I felt alone in the world.

Within about five minutes of walking, the uncomfortable hunk of metal rubbing against my lower back had to go, so I moved the gun to my front pocket. There, it was too big to completely fit, and the handle awkwardly stuck out of the top and felt unbalanced. After five more minutes of hiking I decided I would just have to keep my forty-five in my hand. I made a mental note to that I needed to buy myself a real holster if I were going to carry on a regular basis. After the gun was sorted out I made good time towards the summit.

The forest was still a few long months away from developing the thick and lush green underbrush it would have in the summer. Being virtually barren of foliage, I was able to cut an easy trail as well as see a fair distance before the mists obscured my surroundings. I took any game trail or natural pathway that lead me in the general direction that I thought officer Greene pointed towards the night before. Mostly I just headed up the hill, but I also frequently meandered off in an attempt to cover a little more ground. With no set track I always detoured towards anything that stood out as unusual or interesting. For instance, in nature horizontal lines are rarities, so I always checked those out. Each anomaly I investigated was usually only a rock oddly jutting out of the ground or a weathered and ancient looking standing stone. I didn't find anything obviously man-made along my way other than the occasional old faded beer can or shotgun shell. Nothing that made me believe that Tammy had been there.

About once every five minutes or so I would stop moving, take a deep breath, and listen for any sounds out of the ordinary. Almost nothing that day stirred in the forest. The silent hill I climbed seemed dead. Empty. After listening for a bit, I would call out to Tammy and then wait patiently a little longer hoping for a reply. Each time nothing called back. Even my echoes were swallowed by the forest and fog.

Everything was still and everything was quiet.

It was about an hour and a half into my hike, when I began to get a strangely familiar uneasy feeling.

At first the dreary weather reminded me of the burnt out church I had seen on Main Street. The overcast rainy day, the crumbled building, the soot, the sadness that hung in the air. Then I remembered the funeral I attended there as a boy and with that came the familiar of loss of my father. I remembered the nightmares I just had the night before, and all of those which had woken in the years before that. My mind sped up and flashed between every frightening or depressing memory I had until they all morphed into one miserable sensation.

Having those feelings right then and there didn't make any sense.

I knew that.

I was looking at the same trees, the same soft damp ground, and the same fog that I had been looking at all morning. Everything was the same yet somehow everything felt different. Felt wrong. The more I focused on the sensation the more my fear seemed to grow. I started to feel anxious. It's almost too cliché to say, but it was like there was someone just out of view and watching me. That too felt familiar somehow, like déjà vu. My mind flashed back to whatever it was outside of my house the night before.

I tried to shake the feeling. I told myself that my change in mood was just something to do with being alone in those ghostly grey woods. It was depressing, being out there, hating to acknowledge it but still half expecting to find a dead child. I figured what I was doing paired with the claustrophobic overcast sky and all the colorless barren trees were all just too much for me. Any other time or place and I would have been fine. Months before while hiking that same hill I didn't feel anything like that.

I did what I could. I forced myself to think back to all the warm, safe, and fun times I had alone in the West Virginian countryside. I thought of hot sunny afternoons lying under shade trees. Of tubing down lazy rivers. Of deep blue skies and the fiery red sunsets that followed. I told myself that my mood was all in my head. Fear is the mind killer, the little death, and all of that.

It didn't work.

Instead of looking past my dreary surroundings, I swear I started seeing silent shapes and shadows moving through the fallen clouds. Faintly I heard multiple twigs snap in the distance, but not once was anything close enough for me to see. No two of my senses were able to verify one another. I came to the conclusion that either something was out there stalking me, or I was losing my mind. Imagining things.

For the first time in my life, standing alone in that forest, I made the rational decision to doubt what I saw and heard. It was my only logical choice. Fantasizing the existence of shapes was a more comforting option than having actual things moving around in the grey void. Having spent years of my life walking about Appalachia I understood that there was likely nothing in those woods for me to fear. Irrationally at the time, however, I wasn't so sure. I was getting scared and the longer I stayed, the worse it became. With no real options, all I could do was continue onward, so I did. One step at a time.

With each stride those dark feelings grew.

I didn't get very far before the continuing uneasiness inside me matured into real tangible fear, and with that came the same sick feeling I felt when I was ripped from sleep the night before. All my conflicting thoughts and emotions became ordered and clear. I emerged from a general fearful haze and I began to remember specific events with shocking clarity. My mind flashed back to the autumn before when I saw that thing, that tall scarecrow looking deer creature in the road by the cornfield. Once I touched on that memory, I remembered more and more of the event. Maybe that night wasn't the first time I felt that scared? I wasn't sure, but maybe my fear went back even further. Maybe it was something that I had always known. Some instinctual primitive dread those years away from the mountains had buried. I wasn't simply experiencing an elevated feeling of anxiety or nervousness. There was something specific eating away at my sane mind. More and more clicked into place until I *KNEW* that my dread was something that I felt before. Not just the previous night or months before on the road. I knew that same painful horror from other places and other times. The heart pounding and crushing terror had always been with me, buried deep beneath the surface.

The epiphany was like waking from nightmare but still seeing it still there. Sitting up in bed and seeing that your nightmare followed you back to your room and was staring at you. It was a chill that went to the core of my soul. Doom that had absorbed, twisted, or destroyed everything else I could think or feel. Doom that knotted my stomach, made me tremble, and made my legs weak. I felt a cold sweat start to form on my brow.

It was about then, while I was fighting the hopelessness and horror that was welling up inside me, that I noticed the birds.

At first there were only a couple, but even those few were far more than I had seen the whole drab morning in that dead forest. One or two of the animals flew past me, ducking and dodging between the trees.

Then, more followed.

Blue jays, sparrows, crows, hawks, finches, and birds I recognized but never bothered to learn the names of, flew by me. Birds of all sizes rushed past, some close enough to be within a few feet of me. All of them coming from behind. Every second their numbers seemed to double. I watched more and more fly past. The dozens rapidly turned into hundreds, all flying the same way. All flying up the mountain.

I've seen homogeneous flocks of blackbirds or starlings before. I've seen huge amorphous murmurations pick up and move, fly through the sky like living swirling clouds of black smoke. Seen thousands of their uniform dark shapes casually hop from tree to tree or across fields looking for food like a swarm of locusts.

What I saw on that mountain was nothing like that.

What I saw was every bird in the forest flying in one direction as fast as they could. The chattering sounds they made were so loud, that compared to the silence of the rest of the hike, it reminded me of a long and drawn out high pitched scream. Paired with the flashing streaks of the animals flying by me, the sounds of their wings beating was so disorienting that I needed to grab a nearby sapling to help steady myself. The scene was completely unnatural and unlike anything I'd ever experienced.

I watched a small grey bird, maybe a sparrow, fly at top speed and graze the side of a tall thick oak. Its tiny head hit the tree with such force that it made an audibly sickening crunch as its hollow bones shattered. A few tiny feathers exploded outwards from the impact and then drifted away like dandelion seeds in a breeze. The small bird's body briefly tumbled through the air before it landed on the damp leaves covering the forest floor. Afterwards it laid motionless.

I had watched a bird kill itself.

My frenzied mind knew there was something I needed to recognize through the horror that was taking over. Something I needed to understand. Something of real immediate importance. Something I needed to face it before I completely shut down. The profane scene with the dead sparrow in front of me had given my fear the last little something it needed to latch on and pull me over the edge. In just a few short seconds after the first birds flew by, it happened.

My mind simply broke. I connected the dots and came to an understanding.

The birds. They were being driven. Driven up the hill from the direction I had just come. The birds, they weren't just flying past me, they were flying away from something. Flying away from something coming up the mountain.

Something coming up the mountain following me. I immediately twisted around, and stared down the slope and into the fog.

As abruptly as it begun, the massive wave of birds had dwindled to only a few. I watched the last of the stragglers approach. The birds appeared out of the mists, raced towards me, and then past. A lone starling had lagged behind the rest and seemed to struggle to get up the hill. After that final bird was gone, the forest once again became silent. Silent, still, and dead. Nothing but the slight shifting of the fog changed or moved as far as I could see.

Without consciously doing so, I realized I had raised my weapon and had it pointed down the hill and out into the forest.

Using my fear as a tool, which by then had fully gripped me, allowed panic to burrow further into my broken psyche. My heart pounded in my chest. My hands shook even more.

I tried to tell myself that the terror wasn't rational, that a lack of sleep and a rough night of being besieged by a bear had clouded my judgement. I tried but my efforts were fruitless. I kept going back to the memory of that thing looking at me from the middle of the road. Hollow eyes staring from its uncanny unnatural shape. I knew I had lied to myself that night. I knew what I had seen wasn't a deer. Furthermore, I knew the same thing was out there with me at that moment. I couldn't take my eyes off the forest below, I was too afraid. I couldn't move. I didn't even want to breathe, like exhaling alone could give me away.

But breathe I did, and with each new breath a stink started to fill my nostrils. Had it been any stronger I would have gagged. Instantly recognizable as rotting flesh, it was the odor of a carcass left out to decay. The smell, again, was more complex and was laced with a lingering hint of burnt motor oil. Death and decay, fire and ruin. The rancid stench was just one more sense which attacked my crumbling mind. I knew I couldn't keep my sanity together much longer.

Then just at the edge of my vision, a large shadow caught my attention. It caught my attention because the shadow moved. Or, at least I thought it did. I couldn't be sure of what I saw, but there was something in the mists, a dark shape taller than me and I thought I had seen it shift a little. Not much, if at all. Maybe, I didn't know. I turned my head a little and tried to focus, but it faded into the background fog.

I concentrated intensely on that spot, willing my eyes to put a form to whatever I instinctively knew was out there. Like if I strained my eyes enough I could cut through the mists, but all I saw was the same empty flat grey that I saw everywhere else.

Then, out of the corner of my eye, far off to the right I saw that same or similar shape appear again. That time however, when I turned, the dark shadow didn't fade into the background. It just stood there, boldly, just far enough away that I couldn't make out any details.

Everything was still enough, long enough, that I began to doubt my eyes.

Then it moved.

I watched it clearly take a step closer.

Just moments before my instinct was to find safety in being still, by not attracting any attention to myself, by hiding in plain sight. Those moments were gone. As soon as I saw that large shape step towards me my mind screamed out one thing.

RUN!

I ran.

I ran as fast as I ever would run again.

Adrenaline pumped through my muscles. Panic won and had taken complete control over me. No conscious thought remained. I lost any directed will and bolted away with no plan or direction. Primitive and animalistic, I knew just I had to get out of there.

I don't have any recollection of the first part of my flight up the hill. I don't recall anything but blind terror.

What I do know was that the worst part was turning my back on the forest. Turning my back on the shape, turning my back on what was out there. Not knowing what was going on behind me was the terrifying fuel my legs needed to propel me on. I ran in an ungraceful flat out scramble.

I ran until my lungs burned and my sides hurt.

Then I ran some more.

I didn't follow the trail I was on, having lost it as I got away. I pushed through whatever was in front of me. My only desire was to put some distance between me and the shadow crashing through the forest behind me.

But no matter how scared you are a sprint like that can't be maintained indefinitely and even less so running uphill through a heavily wooded forest. Still, I moved as fast as I could crossing fallen trees and going over rocky ridges.

Even slowed, in my panic, I stumbled often. Branches slapped my face and hands, my knees ached and were bloodied from falling. Regardless I pushed on through the pain with everything I had.

I only dared to glance back a few brief times, which was about as frequently as I could while running at that pace. Each time I hoped wouldn't catch a glance of whatever it was behind me. My risks were rewarded because each look back revealed nothing, save the iniquitous swirling grey fog.

However, seeing nothing didn't provide me with any solace.

I knew it was still out there.

I heard it.

I could still smell the rotten dead stink in the air with each of my deep gasping breaths.

I could feel its dark presence.

Exhaustion eventually caught up with me, the cramp in my side felt like knives stabbing with every breath. I lost my footing with even more frequency. My legs felt like rubber, and I had trouble lifting them as high as I needed. More and more my foot would catch on something which caused me to stumble and fall. I can hike all day, but I've never been much of a runner. I knew that I didn't have much left within me.

I also knew that when I didn't have any more reserves, it would all be over.

I had run for almost fifteen minutes. There was a small clearing ahead. It was a flat, level, timber-less piece of land with minimal undergrowth. It wasn't very big, no more than twenty or thirty feet wide and roughly square in shape, but it was clear and open enough that I risked another glance backwards. I desperately needed the peace of mind that I wasn't about to be tackled or snatched at any moment.

When I turned, in that quick glance behind me, I saw something. I saw something rapidly gaining on me, closing the gap between us with incredible speed. Something tall. Something just barely visible in the distance, but clearly visible enough to know it was real. Something that had arms and stood on hind legs. Something that was seven or eight feet tall. Something unnatural. Something that appeared to be bounding towards me.

The sight horrified me enough to redouble my need to flee. A fear that could have drove my fatigued body forward with renewed speed. I should have done just that. Kept running. Instead I *HAD* to know what was out there. I could no longer leave my doubts to imagination. I needed a better look and to do so I kept my head turned behind me for no more than an extra second. I tried focus on what was coming out of the mists.

Then, in an instant, my view was ripped from creature and the distant wood line. It was forced up to the silhouettes of dark branches against the monochromatic sky.

Something had caught my leg upon entering the clearing and caused me to twist around and fall backwards.

The back of my head crashed hard against a flat stone lying on the ground, not enough for me to see stars but still it throbbed in pain. With that pain I found I could refocus my attention. If just a little. I looked down and saw that my pants leg was ripped and caught on an old cast iron section of fence that had fallen over and was hidden in the brush. My leg was scratched and bleeding. I was lying on my back, but still had the same overwhelming urgency to get away from the dark form in the forest. I kicked the stuck leg, once with no success and then twice more. Which each kick the fence cut further into my flesh.

My jeans ripped, and pain shot through my calf, but with my third try I broke free. I scrambled, crab walking backwards, as fast as I could.

I desperately searched for my pursuer. I scanned the tree line, only to find myself alone in the center of the clearing. A clearing I would have run through in seconds had I not fallen.

The dark shape was no longer where I had last seen it just seconds before.

I moved backwards another foot or two before stopping. I thought I saw a shape drifting away. Then… nothing.

And I waited…

And waited…

Thorns dug into my downturned palms and scratched deeply into my arms. I looked around and found that once again nothing in the woods seemed out of the ordinary. At the very least I no longer saw any shapes moving in the distance. I struggled to slow my heavy breathing and listened for any sounds. The forest had returned to being still and dead quiet. The only real evidence I had of the experience was a faint rotting stink which faded to nothingness as I sat in the leaves and thorns.

I looked down at the gun in my hand and wondered why I didn't fire it when I had the chance. I felt disgusted at my cowardice and confusion, that as scared as I was, I didn't even think to shoot.

After a few minutes I cautiously sat up and checked the back of my head for blood. Luckily, there wasn't any evidence of a cut, although a lump had already begun to form. My lungs still stung. There was a faint taste of blood in my mouth. My heart was still racing and felt like it was about to burst from my chest, but from where I was sitting, I no longer saw any reason for any of it. My excitement was still there, my anxiety was still there, I was still visibly shaking, but the crushing dread that I felt had faded away.

I didn't know what to think and at that moment nothing made any sense to me. I felt a little crazy.

I tested the air with a little laugh. Just a snicker. It felt good.

I thought I might have lost my mind. The laugh really seemed to fit the situation. "Like a madman" I told myself. That made me laugh even more. Seeing terrors and cackling about it, "what was wrong with me?" I thought. The joyless outburst became an acceptance of the confusion and fear. At that point I knew I was probably losing my grip on reality, which was once again a surprising relief compared to actually being chased and hunted through the forest.

I started to laugh again but it was immediately cut off as I heard something behind me. A fiercely loud rumbling sound ripped through the quiet forest.

"Bahwooaaaaaaa"

I focused my entire being on the noise. I spun around in the dirt and bushes, and raised my weapon. My thumb released the safety as I brought my off hand up to steady the shaking forty-five caliber pistol.

A second or two passed.

I re-safetied my weapon and lowered it.

I was able to identity the horrible sound I had just heard. The noise that came roaring out of nowhere was a large diesel truck, downshifting, and growling out an abusive burst as the engine revved high to slow down the vehicle. A few seconds later I was able to make out the sound of heavy tires rolling by and kicking up gravel. I was somewhere near a road.

With everything that was going on inside my head, something as mundane as a truck had brought me back to what I felt was reality. I was still out of breath and shaking from both fear and fatigue, but the world seemed just a little bit more ordinary. I looked all around again, and there just wasn't any sign of anything to be afraid of.

After standing with a little difficulty I took my first hesitant steps in the direction I was originally running, which conveniently was also towards the truck I heard. As I neared the tree line, at the edge of the clearing, I saw a couple more sections of wrought iron fence like the one that caught my leg. They were in disrepair and covered in vines but still standing. I also noticed chest high stonework pillars at the corners of the rectangle and two more that may have at one time held a gate. I passed all of that without paying it any mind and walked back into the forest.

Not long after re-entering the woods, the mist and trees parted enough for me to make out an asphalt road thirty or so feet away. In my flight I would have reached it in a few extra seconds if I hadn't fallen. I recognized that section of pavement as the state road that ran along the top of the mountain. The road which eventually leads down to my road and eventually my driveway. I had made it as far as I wanted that morning.

I was about three and a half miles from home.

Still uneasy and apprehensive about being surrounded by the forest, I jogged the last couple of yards until I was standing in the middle of the road. I couldn't have gone any further at that accelerated pace if I had to, so I rested. I was completely spent.

It was overwhelming how much of a relief it was to be standing on that road. A man made thoroughfare carved into the hillside that snaked through the forest. A product of civilization that represented man's triumph over nature and over the unknown wilds. Alone in the wilderness it seemed like anything was possible, but there on the road, strict rules applied in the domain of man. Unsubstantiated fear could be conquered there. The road was the last piece I needed to fully dispel the terrors that gripped me and to begin putting back my fractured psyche.

There are very few truly wild places left in North America. Places that have never been touched by the influence of man. Forests that have never faced the saw or ax. Especially on the east coast. Because there is so little of it, people forget that throughout most of our brief history the only safety to be found was by cowering in our small villages and towns. Precious little islands of protection in a big and dangerous world where men needed to come together to survive. The deep dark forests were given wide berth for a reason. Look no further than old children's fables and fairy tales. Little Red Riding Hood. Hansel and Gretel. Children sent out alone into the woods simply were not expected to return. That went for adults as well. Banishment often was just another form of death.

Despite all that I had just experienced, I yet again pushed it aside and welcomed a return of reality and common sense. It was like the memories of the darkness and fear had been drained away. At that moment I was having a hard time remembering exactly why I was so afraid. The whole event had become foggy in my mind. I realized how ridiculous I had been, running like a lunatic through the woods. It was heavily overcast, yes, but still daylight. I had plenty of visibility. Did I really see or hear anything out in those woods that was a threat to me? A shadow that I thought had legs? Was that it? On top of everything else, I was also armed with a full magazine. I could have defended myself against any animal I came across. I told myself that I simply had too much happen to me over the previous two days and I let it get the better of me.

Walking with a small limp in my fatigued steps I started down the road towards home.

I felt better once I put a little distance from where I came out of the forest behind me. The fear and panic, once lifted, continued to be replaced with a forgetful light headed daze.

Another ten or so minutes after that, I calmed enough to remember that I still should have been keeping an eye out for Tammy. I wasn't really afraid any longer but even so I decided I wasn't going back into the woods. My rationale was that I needed to get home and that the road was the quickest route. Still I wanted to be helpful, so every hundred yards I called out the missing girl's name.
In little less than an hour had walked almost all the way to my driveway. Thankfully, the way was all downhill. I was just about to the first turnoff when I decided to yell out once again for Tammy. My

strained voice had become rough and my vocal cords hurt each time I shouted. I was losing the volume I had earlier in the day, but what I had left was still enough to carry.

Surprisingly, instead of the all too familiar silence, I heard a 'hello' not too far off into the distance.

I answered with another shout, this time my own questioning "hello" and waited. Then yet one more, a slightly louder, 'hello' was returned.

The response was a lot clearer and was focused in my direction. Unfortunately, unless Tammy was a chain smoker, I knew the person responding to my shouts was a gravelly voiced man.

I stood my ground and began scanning the area for movement when it occurred to me that calling for a little girl with a gun in my hand might not be the best first impression. I put the Springfield back into the belt of my pants and made sure my jacket was pulled down far enough to cover it.

A few scant moments after securing my weapon a man appeared out of the mists, walking up the mountain road. He wore a blaze orange baseball cap and similarly colored vest over his Realtree camouflage jacket with muddy jeans and well-worn boots. He was a large man. Athletic or hard worked, likely both. Lean muscle, chiseled shaved jaw. While big he also looked young, eighteen years of age at the high end.

Carried in his arms was a Remington model 700 rifle with a synthetic green stock and a large scope.

I raised my hand in greeting. Before I had a chance to say anything to him, another man also came forward out of the mists on the opposite side of the street. He too wore blaze orange hunting safety clothing and also carried a firearm. Instead of a scoped rifle, he was armed with a shotgun clad in camouflaged hardware. Where the first man was obviously young, the second was the opposite. Grey and wrinkled, his face showed hard decades of experiences. He couldn't have been under sixty five. Yet despite his apparent age, his eyes were active and alive. Neither man showed any signs of being winded from the walk up the steep mountain hill.

When the two were completely out of the haze I walked forward. We continued to approach each other until about fifteen feet separated me from the closer of the two. The younger man, in front, stopped and a second later the older man did as well. The senior man was still about ten feet behind the first and stayed on the opposite side of the road.

I knew that it wasn't going to be a friendly neighborhood chat, there was tension coming from the other party.

"You looking for Tammy? You, um, Williams?" The younger of the two men asked in a deep voice that seemed too old to be coming from him.

I nodded. I was feeling nervous about the encounter and wished I still had the forty-five in my hand.

"Yes, to both. I told the police I would look around this morning. I'm Kent Williams. Recently moved here, just up the driveway."

I pointed without taking my eyes off the pair.

The younger man looked back at the older, who in turn nodded to him. They shared a few moments of unspoken, unmoving communication, the subject matter of which I could only guess, until the younger man turned back towards me.

"Mr. Greene said I might find you out in the woods. Whadn't expecting ya ta be walkin' down the road."

"I started out in the woods. Hiked a zig zag until I got to the top and found the road. Up there just before it splits off on to this one. Figured I'd look around this way on my way back." I had no intention of telling strangers that the city guy had scared himself silly walking through the forest. My reasons were my own and didn't matter. It was the truth and it seemed sufficient as an answer for the armed teen. He nodded back to me in either understanding or approval.

"Up by the old Schneider family plot? Yeah. Makes sense ya comin' back this-a-way," he said to me. "I'm Jack. That there is Henry, my Uncle. Tammy's my sister."

I tipped my head towards each in turn. "I'm sorry about your sister. I guess this means she hasn't turned up?"

"No. Not that we've heard, and you wouldn't have been a yellin' for her if you'd found her."

I frowned and non-verbally agreed, then all three of us just kind of stood there. The meeting had become awkward. Normally I would have filled the silence with some meaningless small talk, but I could tell those two weren't the type for pleasantries. At about the point when I thought I'd be forced to say something, the older man in the back, Henry, spoke to Jack. I could barely hear him.

"We should git moving. Ask him," he flatly stated.

I tilted my head quizzically at Jack.

"We're going to keep looking. Wanted to see if you'd have a problem if we ended up looking around on your property."

"God no! Not at all" I promptly replied. "Something like this you can go anywhere you like. If you think she is around here, I can look around some more too."

"My family thanks ya, Mr Williams. Right now we're headed back to the house, we've been out since just before dawn. We need some news and something to eat. We'll go out again after that." He looked back to confirm with Henry, and then continued. "Hopin' it ain't necessary, but if we do go back out, we'll go on from our place and walk down the mountain, towards yours, then past it and down to the river. Anyway, that's our plan for now."

"You think she's around here, lost maybe?" I shouldn't have added the 'lost' bit. I think Jack took it as bit of an insult.

"Naw," he said shaking his head at me. "She wouldn't be lost. She grew up here, knows this place as well as I do. Hell, she has her own tree stand not too far from your land. I don't know where she is, but if there is a chance she's out there... well then I'll be out there too."

"Understood. Listen if you need anything from me, don't hesitate to ask." Imagining them coming up to the door for help reminded me of the night before, I continued with a question. "Actually, speaking of asking. Do you know if anyone paid me a visit last night?"

"Excuse me, sir?" Jack asked.

"It's nothing really. I just wondered if someone you knew may have come up to my place last night. Maybe someone looking for Tammy? After Officer Greene came by, and after I turned in for the night someone banged on my door. Banged on it so darn hard it could have been a bear. Officer Thompson looked at the dent this morning and told me she thought otherwise but she wasn't sure. Ripped my outdoor light down too."

246

Unlike the slow glances both men gave each other before, this time they quickly made eye contact, though they still didn't verbalize anything. I initially took it as them thinking it might have been Tammy, so I wanted to quickly stop that so as to not get their hopes up.

"Listen guys, if you're wondering, I don't think it was Tammy. First of all, no one was there when I got to the door. I even called out her name. Secondly, I don't know of a little girl that could have beat on my door like that. It was loud, and I mean really loud. Shook the whole house. On top of that, the dent in my steel door was a little bit higher than my head. So, like I said, I thought it was a bear. Still do actually. I was just wondering, that's all. Doesn't really matter."

While I was explaining myself, I began to think they might have recognized something based on their expressions. As I continued they kept knowingly looking back and forth between each other. Once I finished, they both returned their gaze back to me.

It was the older man who spoke up next.

"Naw Mr. Williams, twasn't nobody we know disturbing yer rest. Sorry, but we can't help ya thar. As we said before, we're 'bout to be gettin' goin', but we do thank you for your help this morning, though I wish it might have been a bit more successful. No matter what, we'll be seeing you around. Neighbors and all."

"No problem, and I'll be looking the last mile or so up to my house as well." I said pointing back in the general direction I thought my house was.

Jack started walking again, but this time slowly at a diagonal to reach Henry on his side of the road. They both gave me one last head nod before just before we passed. We never, got within ten feet of each other.

A couple seconds after turning my back on them Henry called out to me. I stopped and turned to face the man who was almost obscured by the mists.

"Oh, Mr. Williams, bit of advice. Being from Washington D.C. an all, don't know if you're the type that owns 'em, but if I was you, I'd be carring a gun while walking around out here."

Any other time, any other place, I would've immediately followed up a statement like that with some questions. I would ask 'why' for starters. Standing there, at that time, I didn't need an answer from them. I didn't even need to ask. I just knew it to be the right advice. Instead of thanking him, or saying anything, I reached back and pulled out the 1911. I kept the pistol pointed at the ground but brandished it with a little side to side flourish before returning it to the back of my pants. Both Henry and Jack nodded. Henry muttered "good man" and with a slight wave turned to keep walking up the road.

As I watched them go I caught the slightest hint of movement up the hill on the high the side of the road. When I turned to more directly face it I realized I was seeing a fully camouflaged man walking out of the bushes to join the others. Unlike the Jack and Henry, he wore no safety orange and was nearly invisible. While we were talking he must have only been twelve or fifteen feet away from me. I either walked right past him or he crept up on me. No matter which, he purposely chose to stay out of sight. These men may have been searching for Tammy, but it seemed to me they were prepared for something else. The third man was carrying an AR-15 with a standard thirty round magazine loaded. He also had a half dozen more mags stuffed into the pockets of his tactical vest.

As with the other two men, we made eye contact and he tilted his head in greeting. Once acknowledged, he quickly flashed me a smile through his thick beard. I read that as he knew he was able to sneak up on me. Like he beat me in a contest I wasn't even playing. Immediately after, he too turned his back to me and continued up the hill. All three were gone, back into the mists, in under a minute.

Again, I felt a chill run through me. Nothing on the same level as before and it felt more internalized, but was still a sense of ill tidings. I wondered yet again, what I had gotten myself into? If I should have ever bought that house? The armed men seemed odd to me, but after the few initial tense moments, standing there talking to them was the first time in hours I felt truly safe.

The last mile to the house didn't take long, even with cutting some corners and going through the woods and brush looking Tammy. When I got back I was exhausted. The hike was one thing, but combined with my run, and lack of sleep I was physically beat. Real or not, the experience in the woods also left me equally emotionally drained. Instead of going straight inside, I sat on the deck. I found a seat that allowed me the farthest view down the hillside. The overcast gloom was still pretty heavy so I couldn't see far. Part of me still wanted to keep searching for the missing girl. Although I also understood I wasn't likely to be much more help until something was more formally organized. Without orchestrated guidance I would likely just be wasting my time. The one place I was asked to look, I was fairly certain she wasn't. My pattern had covered a lot of ground, or at least it did until the very end.

My mind flashed back to the panic attack. I found it difficult to remember what had me so scared and I felt ashamed at how I responded. I just couldn't recall exactly what caused me to snap. Instead I worried about what would have happened if I had panicked further out, when I was deeper into the woods and away from the road. If I had lost my nerve and ran somewhere that lead me away from everything. Well, that thought gave me goosebumps.

After a while I stood up and went inside. Tammy wasn't going to be found sitting there and I didn't want to be looking out into the mists any longer.

I laid my handgun back on the table from where I'd grabbed it earlier and put the pile of papers back on top as well. I was heading towards the sofa to rest when I saw the clock.

2:30 was a lot later than I thought it was and wanted it to be. I still had a small chance to salvage a little of the weekend. If I hurried I still had time to get to the Inn and see Gwen.

There was another reason that I wanted to go into town. I couldn't stand the thought of being alone any longer. Being alone and surrounded by the swirling mists.

To get ready I took the fastest shower I could. In and out. Afterwards I addressed the cuts on my leg which only needed a little gauze and tape. Both of which I had in the first aid kit. Out of the limited collection of apparel I had with me, I put on the best clothes I had. My outfit it wasn't anything fancy, but my pants weren't torn and my shirt didn't have paint on it. Twenty rushed minutes later I was on the road.

I had become an old hand at navigating the small country roads into town. Even while keeping an eye out for missing teenage girls, I was looking for parking on Main Street with a scant thirty minutes remaining of Gwen's shift. I told myself to relax, that there was no need to hurry and that I was just looking for something to eat. If Gwen were around, well, then that would be an added bonus. There was no reason to get my hopes up. After all, I thought, she was just being nice to me because I tipped well.

I lied to myself a lot back then.

None of that mental misdirection lowered my frustration when I couldn't find a parking spot within a couple blocks. Saturday afternoon was a busy day in the small town and the lines of cars and old beat up trucks parked along Main Street showed it. Block by block, nothing. I kept looking down at the clock as minute after minute of Gwen's shift slipped away. I eventually found a spot halfway down the street, and then headed up the sidewalk towards The Inn in as fast of a walk as I could manage without going into a jog. By then my limp was barely noticeable but still hurt a little. Lying again, I told myself that I was nearly running because it was getting chilly as the sun started to set and I only wanted to be out of the cold.

With the restaurant in sight, I watched a man hurriedly make his way out of the Inn walking quickly, also almost in a jog, towards me.

The collar on his light flannel jacket was flipped up. He had one hand clutching it closed while the other was thrust deep into a pocket. His face was down, dealing with the damp chill the best he could. Once we got a little closer, through his thick mess of hair, I recognized his face. It belonged to John Smalls. Just my luck. Even though talking to him was on my list of things I wanted to do that weekend, I wasn't happy to see him then and there. He was just one more delay, one more obstacle.

The urgency of Gwen's shift ending was one thing, but there was also something about just meeting John on the street. Standing in the cold and blurting out that he was about to be a lot less broke. It wasn't really the way I imagined giving him the good news. It lacked the sense of theatrics I was visualizing. My self-sacrifice deserved at least that selfishness didn't it? I considered walking past him without an acknowledgment, figuring I could have always caught up with him some other time. However, he looked up at me. A few steps after that his face lit up with recognition.

"Kent. Kent. Kent my man, you're back in town? Awesome. Awe. Some. Good to see you, good to see you." He exclaimed as he pushed his arm out for a handshake. I did the same. He gripped my hand firmly and shook vigorously. He also held on a bit longer than I was comfortable with.

I gave him a quick, hopefully non-obvious once over, trying to judge how bad off he was. I needed to know if he was going to hit me up for cash right then and there or maybe just later. My appraisal took a moment. Something about Johnny didn't fit into the mold I tried to place him. Something about him was different.

What was "wrong" I discovered was that he looked better. A lot better. His clothes were cleaner, his hair while not cut was washed, his face wasn't as pale, and his cheeks weren't as sunken. He was still a little rough, and his teeth were the same dental nightmare as I recalled, but something positive had happened to him.

"How you doing Johnny?" I asked. Testing the waters.

"Good man, good. No bullshit, that type of good. Since we last talked, since you so kindly helped me out, everything has been coming out all right for ole Johnny here. Really man, like I said no bullshit." Johnny nodded his head with a tight-lipped sincere smile on his face before he continued. "Fucking A, I'm glad to see you Kent. Gotta thank ya for that money. Gave me the time I needed. Shut that asshole at the bank's mouth right the hell up, that's for sure. Fucker. I owe you one buddy. A big one. At the very least I gotta buy ya a beer."

He glanced back over his shoulder, towards The Inn. When he turned to me again he had a look of trepidation on his face. I cut him off from what I assumed was offering to buy me a beer that he couldn't afford.

"Actually, I've been meaning to look you up myself." I told him. I wanted to control the conversation so I could hopefully speed it along. I didn't have time for a drink or a conversation with him and still be able to talk to Gwen. "I have something I'd like to talk to you about, but now isn't really ideal. I'm kind of in a hurry. You'll like it though. It's some pretty good news."

"Understood. Say no more. Under. Stood." He said with a look that started as relief and then changed into one of skepticism. "Have to tell ya, I'm a little curious Kent, people don't come around looking up Mr. Smalls with any news other than bad on their mind. But I trust ya, we go too far back for me not to, ya know? If its timing? Well. That's just a thing. Don't worry about it. Honestly, it ain't a great time fer me neither. You see, technically I'm on the clock right now. I'm working. I got a job. No. Shit. *J. O. B..* Job. I'm a working man. Hell, I think I might even be paying taxes!"

I glanced up at the Inn, and then back at Johnny while I cocked my head questioningly. If he were working, why was he coming out of a bar?

Johnny, turned his head to see what I was looking at and then back at me smiling.

"A man can have a lunch break can't he? An, I only had one. A light beer at that. The way I sees it, having one beer for lunch takes way less time than actually ordering food, waiting for them who cook it to cook it, waiting for someone else to bring it to you, waiting for all that other horse shit. Too many links in the chain. Too much process. Too much time. See what I'm saying? Me, I just run in, say 'Gwendy Gwen Gwen give me your finest light beery beer', I drink it down, throw my money on the bar and I leave. Five minutes, in an out. If everyone else took such short lunch breaks, well, there still be plenty factory jobs left in America for one thing I can tell ya."

"Hey Johnny, no worries. I'm not judging, I was just wondering."

While I did listen to what he had to say, all I really heard was that Gwendy just served him a beer. She was still there, I just needed to hurry.

"No, no, no. I knew you wasn't judging me. Not you Kent, I was just s'plaining, was all. I got nothing to hide, see? I work for Pat now. I'm officially the head, well, you know. I'm officially the only assistant at Patrick Galloway's Handyman Services. Me and him, we got us an understanding like. He knows what I'm doing here, and it's all good. I told him I'd grab a quick lunch after I picked up some materials at the hardware store. He told me fine, and just ta be back by 4:00."

"That's great Johnny. I'm glad to hear you found a job." I sincerely told him, as I looked down at my watch. It seemed both of us had 4:00 deadlines and if we kept talking, neither of us would make them. "Anyway, I do need to speak with you, but obviously now's not a great time. I don't want you to be late for job."

"Truth, right there. Truth. As much as I owe you, I owe Pat more, and don't wanna let 'em down or nothing. Both you and me know he took a chance with putting me to work with 'em. We're a good team though, he sees that now. At first he told me straight I was only hired till he got back on his feet. Old fool. Nope. Wait. WAIT! He ain't no fool. I take that back. I got nothing bad to say about that man, hear me? Well. Pat, see? He somehow he startled himself or some shit, jumped back 'er something and ended up falling down his basement stairs. Broke his leg in three spots and couldn't drive his truck with that big old cast he has on. We got to talking at the bar one night and I told him that I had a truck that I can drive. He told me to meet him at 7:00 in the morning the next day, and you know what? I was there at 6:30. We been working together since. He's almost off his crutches and I'm still working with him. I think him mixing pain pills with his Jack and Coke helped me get the job more than he'll admit though. That was then, but now that I'm there, we're both getting something out of it. You see I'm doing a lot of stuff he don't wanna, and he's also teaching me somethings I wanna learn. Plus, you know, he pays me for my work. He says that's capitalism. When two people trade and get what they ask for, everyone's happy. That's why everyone says thank you when you buy something. See?"

"Heh, that's a pretty decent summary, better than some I've heard. You should be a professor. The job sounds great, I'm really glad for you Johnny. I'll have to meet Pat one of these days. Actually, now that I think about it, I might have some work for you guys too." I paused with a genuine smile. "I have to say, you do seem to be doing a lot better for yourself. At least a little better off than when we last met."

"You ain't kidding me none, Kent" he said with all the seriousness he could muster. "I'm going to be alright. Having a bit of good luck has really helped me. Givin' me the chance I needed. It all started with you coming back ta town. Like I told ya it would. If you hadn't helped me, I'd have lost my place. Being homeless, just don't know how'd it have turned out. I don't know what I'd have done."

He just left it hang, the implications weren't hopeful.

"Anyway, I was wondering if I could stop by sometime soon. Like I said, I've got some good news for you."

"How 'bout after work. I mean my work, not your work. You ain't working right now, is ya?" He said smiling at me with a silent chuckle. I'm sure I could have met up with him later that night. I could have had a beer or two with dinner and driven over afterwards. But, I just didn't feel like it. I wasn't in the mood for anything else that day. Plus, I still hadn't shot the rifle yet. I really did want to fire it at least once.

"Tonight, um. How about tomorrow instead?" I asked.

"Long as it ain't too damn early. Don't know what I'm getting into tonight, if you know what I'm saying. And I think you do. Am I right?

Its payday since we're finishing the job. Pay. Day." He grinned at me broadly.

I knew what he meant. He was likely to be hungover or still drunk in the morning.

"Yeah, will do. It won't be too early. Maybe lunchtime? Look, you have to head out before you're late for work and I'm starving. So let's just, um, talk tomorrow."

"Starving, huh? Maybe you're hungry for something alright. I think maybe you just wanna get in there to see that fine looking bartender who's been asking 'bout you." He cackled. "Get your ass in there you dirty ole dog you. I'll see ya tomorrow."

I heard him still laughing to himself as he walked away. My world narrowed down to a single sentence. I could only focus on what he had just said to me. She had been asking about me? Gwendolyn, the hot bartender, had been asking about *ME?* The biggest stupidest smile formed on my face.

Did you kill a man?

Kent stopped speaking when he saw the professor awkwardly shift his legs by planting them widely. Stretching. The professor in turn stopped moving when Kent stopped talking. West, who looked like had begun to stand, had since froze in place.

Even Andy took notice of the interaction. This was about the first time he wasn't at least partially off in his own thoughts since Kent had stopped talking about guns and focused on what Andy saw as bullshit.

"Hey? What's up?" He questioned, looking around.

Kent didn't respond, but the professor slowly turned to look towards Andy.

"Well," he started and then stopped. Herb again made eye contact with Kent. After a brief pause he fully extended his legs and stood up straight. With no reaction from either of the hunters he again turned to face Andy. "I just wanted to stretch. Nothing more. Pardon the pun. Nothing, besides me, is up, Mr. Warren."

Andy didn't believe the professor and the critical expression he wore on his face showed it.

"What the hell is with you guys? You're both really acting fucking strange. Seriously Kent, for the last hour you've been taking this story way too, I don't know, intensely or some shit. Monsters in the woods? What really happened out there? Did you take some mushrooms or acid? Did you really see something? I'm beginning to think you really need to just get to the point. I'm beginning to think there is something more to this. I mean the way you were describing it, sure sounded like you almost shit your pants out there. Why? What the fuck, man? Are you telling us a campfire story or is this a real fucking story? I'm not sure I can fucking take much more. And what about this chick you keep talking about? Way to personal. Something is going on with this story of yours and I don't like feeling lost. Lost is how I'm fucking feeling right now."

This time no one replied and Andy was left to his own frustrated thoughts. Both Kent and the professor had their gazes locked together through the dwindling smoke and flames of the fire.

After a few seconds passed, Andy explosively shouted out a new thought that had just occurred to him.

"Holy shit Kent! Hold on. Did you fucking kill a man? Or that Tammy girl? Or, oh shit, that piece of ass you keep talking about? I mean, you've been with your wife for nearly as far back as this story goes. So you couldn't have dated her for long or anything. Is that what this is up leading to, did you fucking shoot someone? I don't believe you'd ever purposely commit murder Kent, but... Shit. Maybe you scared yourself so much you accidentally shot someone out in the woods? Is that what the fuck happened that weekend?"

Kent just shook his head, but the professor cut off any spoken reply he might have been preparing.

"Yes, Kent. What *IS* your ghost story leading up to? Did you use that religious symbol of yours to take a life? To take someone from this mortal plane. To send them to the great beyond? Send them to your hell, maybe?" He said with a sneer and a bitter hissing laugh.

The change in Herb West's speech and attitude was so abrupt and out of character that it startled Andy, who stood up. The confused absent minded professor they had grown accustomed to had seemingly suddenly become mean spirited man with a cutting tone.

"Am I missing something, you guys? I'm serious! Do you two know each other or something? Seriously, what the fuck?"

Andy started pacing back and forth a little behind the log he was previously sitting on.

Kent did the best he could to de-escalate the tension with a light chuckle.

"No Andy, come on man. Don't let any of this get to you. To answer your question, I think you would have known if I had accidently shot someone. I would have told you, that be a burden too large for me to bare alone. Next. Yes something serious happened, but I didn't murder anyone. As for the West, no I've never met the professor before tonight. We've never crossed paths anywhere or at any point in time. I am completely sure of that."

The professor added "I'm sorry Andy. I've never been very good in social situations. I can see how my comment could have been interpreted as unacceptably rude. My fatigue must be catching up with me. Again, I apologize."

Kent finally took his eyes off West and gave Andy a reassuring smile. He then looked back at the skinny academic and said, "If you'll have yourself a seat again, I can finish this up pretty quickly. If you let me get to the end, Herb, I can assure you you'll definitely find the conclusion of this story of interest."

"Oh, I have a feeling I can guess the outcome, but agreed, it is of interest to me. Finish your tale." The professor looked Kent in the eye, then down at the weapon still resting on his lap. West then slowly sat down. "Finish telling us this, tall tale, of your antique rifle."

The way he said "antique" it came out like a pejorative.

Kent glanced back over at his friend. "Andy, I'm almost done. I promise. The rest of this story takes place all in the same weekend I was just telling you about. From the Saturday night I was just describing, there's a day left to recount. When I'm done you'll know something about me that next to no one else knows. It's important to me and I trust you that much."

West sat on his log smiling in response to Kent's statements. He didn't bother putting his blanket back around his shoulders or leaning in towards the warmth of the dying flames.

Andy wasn't convinced that the odd behavior was because everyone was tired, but he went along with it. Kent was being sincere, he knew that much. He too sat back down and with his booted foot he kicked a burning log in front of him a little further into the fire and tried to be lighthearted. It wasn't his best effort.

"Now I'm pretty sure I really know where this is going, somehow by the end of this you're going to tell me that you used to be a woman, am I right?"

"You'll just have to wait Andy. You'll just have to wait."

"Yeah, yeah. I'll wait Miss Kent."

Kent adjusted the rifle on his lap and started retelling the story.

Damn, son

I opened the door and walked into the bar. It was about as crowded as it was when I left the day before. Far too crowded for my tastes. Gwen was working with someone else behind the bar. I recognized him as Mac, the only other bartender there I knew.

Mac was a tall older fellow, with thinning silver hair, red cheeks, silver mustache, and a beer gut. He wore and old stained denim apron and had a huge smile on his face as he laughed with a couple of patrons. Gwen couldn't have been any more different from him at that moment. Besides being young and gorgeous she was scowling at a group of women who kept pointing violently at their receipt. Obviously there was some type of disagreement going on.

After getting my bearings, I made my way further into the bar and headed towards the one lone empty stool I saw. As I pushed through the light crowd Gwen saw me. Her face changed completely. In an instant the sour look was gone and replaced with glancing shy smile. As obtuse as I could be, all doubt was removed from my mind. Gwendy was interested in me. I couldn't believe my luck.

She quickly finished dealing with her bothersome customers and walked down to the empty stool I was taking.

"You almost missed me here tonight, I have to say, that would have been a real shame Mr. Williams." She let me know as she leaned in across the bar top.

"It wasn't my plan. I did want to get here a little earlier. Just couldn't make it happen. My day was a lot busier and stranger than you could imagine Gwen."

"Really? Loafing around in your house, looking at the scenery? Did you fix yourself a cup of tea? Earl Grey, maybe? Read a mystery novel? Smoke a pipe in front of the fire? Whatever it was your day couldn't have been any busier than this mess!" She exaggeratedly held up her arms indicating the crowded room full of mostly men drinking away their paychecks.

"Is that what you think I do? Nevermind. Well, for starters, I had a woman wake me up this morning." I waited for some type of reaction but didn't receive any. "Let me rephrase that, a police woman woke me up this morning. Our good friend Officer Thompson."

"No? Shut up."

"Yes, and no I won't. It happened, and by the way, she's not your biggest fan either. So, thanks again for yesterday. I appreciate it."

Gwen shrugged off that comment by rolling her eyes, shaking her head, and giving me a "whatever" face.

"She used to love me when she needed a babysitter. So what... Did she go out there to tell you off? Holy crap. What a mean old crotchety bitch."

I cut her off before anything else was said about the officer. "No it was about something else and luckily for me, when it did come up, Thompson was not as angry as I thought she'd be. Anyway, she wasn't the only cop that came by since yesterday. An Officer Greene came by to have a chat with me last night."

"You're shitting me? Come on Kent. Two police visits since I've seen you? You some type of bad boy, huh? You in trouble with the law?" She said with a sly grin on her perfect lips.

"No, don't believe I am. But yeah, I had three visits in twenty four hours if you count the first one I requested."

"Well, bad or not, I always did have a thing for the popular boys. You seem awfully popular," she said to me in an obviously over the top type of flirt. "So come on, spill the beans. Really, you in some kind of trouble? Is someone after you? Maybe the mob? I kind of had you pegged for the straight and narrow type. Now I'm not so sure."

"Ease up that wild imagination. No I'm not in any type trouble, like I said, but it could be pretty bad though. It almost would be better if I were in some trouble. No, unfortunately it seems a little girl named Tammy Crammer went missing. Last I heard, which was as of this morning, she still wasn't accounted for. You know her?"

"No. Not a Tammy. I know a couple other Crammers, but not Tammy. Listen, I gotta work. Can I get you something when I come back?

"Um, yeah. Beer and a menu? IPA?"

She nodded her gorgeous redhead at me went off to help other customers. When she came back about a minute later, she dropped off the beer, put her elbows on the bar, leaned into me, and rested her chin on her hands. A lesser man would have never been able to look her in the eyes. I was mostly successful and received a mischievous grin as a reward for my struggle.

"So, come on. Let's hear it Mister. Missing girl? What do you have to do with that? What did the police want?"

"Me personally? Nothing really. It seems Tammy doesn't live all that far away. Just over the top of the mountain that I'm on. They wanted to know if I'd seen her, Officer Greene thought that there was a chance she might have made her way down to my place. He asked if I'd keep an eye out. This morning Officer Thompson came by to tell me she was still missing and they wanted to take me up on an earlier offer I made. I said that I could look around in the woods for her. So I did, and spent the morning hiking in this crappy weather."

"Ohh wow that does sound serious. But. But if she's only been gone since late last night? I mean, ya think there's some foul play or something at hand? Couldn't she just be at a friend's house? When I was a little girl I snuck out all the time."

"Well, I think that's what everyone is hoping for. For all I know she may have been found already. The most recent news I have was from pretty early this morning. However, at the time Officer Greene seemed to be taking it seriously enough. When we talked last night he let it slip that there had been a couple of other people who could have went missing lately. He's worried that there might actually be something going on, or at the very least there might be some dangerous animals out in the woods. He even mentioned something about the, um, scary man. Nope. Hold on, that ain't right. The um... I mean the terror man, that's what he said, Terror Man. Told me kids..."

I was instantly cut off.

"You just *HUSH*, you." Gwen blurted out excitedly in such a way that she even surprised herself. She covered her mouth in embarrassment and then let loose an angelic little laugh.

I just looked at her waiting for some type of explanation. She rolled her eyes at me and sighed.

"Sorry." She said. When I didn't reply or say anything she continued. "Oh, it's nothing. Just reacted out of habit. Automatic, like saying 'bless you' after a sneeze. Just part of a silly children's game. See, you're not supposed to say his name, that's all. Wow. I haven't thought about any of that since I was in middle school. My friends scared me pretty badly with that back then. Jerks."

Gwen leaned in and continued in a silly spooky voice. "*If you say his name, he comes looking for you, then you'll be the one with terror in your eyes.* Dumb, I know. Listen. Gotta go again, I'll be back. I'm almost finished for tonight!"

I called out after her as she walked away.

"Actually Gwen," I pointed to a stack of menus just out of my reach behind the bar. "Could you just, um, hand me one of those."

She stopped and walked back towards me with exaggerated faux annoyance. She didn't grab a menu but instead took a half sheet of stained and torn colored paper that was sitting on the bar and slid it towards me.

"Just order an appetizer from the happy hour menu Kent. You don't want to ruin your appetite".

"Um, what? I'm actually pretty hungry. Really, I could use the calories after the morning I had." I replied being confused.

"Listen Kent, while we're out having dinner tonight, I don't want you to be sitting there playing with your food and watching me eat for the both of us 'cause you ain't hungry." She paused letting that sink in. When I didn't immediately respond she continued. "What's the matter Kent, you *WERE* going to ask me out to dinner tonight, weren't ya?"

With that she turned and rushed off again to help someone else.

I was dumbfounded. I didn't even get a chance to reply. I never got picked up by women like that. Even more so, I was never picked up by extremely attractive women like that. I instinctively looked around for third party verification. Did anyone else hear the same thing I did? The couple to my right were deep in discussion and if they had heard anything they weren't going to share their thoughts with me. When I looked to the left, the old man who was intently peeling the label off his beer bottle looked over and up at me.

"Damn, son."

That was all he said. "Damn, son" and with a tight lipped smile and a head nod he went back to his beer. I just quietly chuckled in satisfaction to myself. I couldn't believe the amazing turn the day had taken. I looked down the bar at Gwen. She was asking everyone if they minded closing out their tabs before the shift change. When she glanced down to me, I'm pretty sure she actually blushed a little before she quickly looking away.

After a couple minutes she came back with another beer and a bill.

"I'm closing your tab out Kent. So, anyway, I'm basically finished here. I've got about ten or fifteen more minutes' worth of stuff I gotta do in the back before I can leave though. Afterwards, I'd like to go home, shower, and change. I can be back here at five. What'd ya say? Wait for me?"

"Yeah. Um, of course." I immediately replied. "I'll be sitting right here."

"Great Kent, I'll be back for that," she tapped on the tab, "and then I'll see you at five!"

I looked down at my watch. It was four o'clock. The thought occurred to me that there was no way she could finish her job, go home, get ready, and be back by five o'clock, but I didn't care. I knew I would've waited for her until well after last call.

The tab she had given me had one item on it which carried a $3.99 total. 'HH NACHOS'.

The beer had been comped again and she put in a food order for me that I didn't even have a chance to ask for. I wasn't quite sure how to handle the tip since we were going out on a date so I stuck a ten dollar bill in the folder and hoped it wasn't a faux pas by being too little or too much. With a small wave and a smile she grabbed my bill without looking and made her way towards the back of the restaurant.

Two new bartenders took the place of the two that left. Though I didn't pay them any mind, except for asking for a water with my next beer. Drinking too much while talking to a bartender at a bar is one thing. Drinking too much on a date is entirely another. A couple minutes later, a plate piled high with nachos, melted cheese, black beans, jalapeños, and sour cream was put down in front of me.

Time passed while I carefully pulled out one nacho at a time in between sips of beer. Halfway through the plate Mr. "Damn, son," the man sitting next to me, spoke up again.

"You know, I've been thinking about something ya said." He paused to drink some of his beer. He didn't bother to turn his head, but instead looked at me through the mirror we were both sitting in front of.

I stopped chewing in mid-crunch when I realized that his comment was directed at me. I looked over and waited for him to continue, wondering what sparked his interest.

He was an old man, but he still looked healthy. Guessing, I'd say he was comfortably into his retirement. Maybe in his seventies. His face was clean shaven except for a neatly trimmed mustache which had the same mousy grey brown tint as his close cropped hair. His clothes were old and worn in, but clean, in good repair, and well fitted. He wore a pair of large rimmed eyeglasses that went out of fashion at least ten years before.

Eventually, he turned and gave me a thoughtful look.

"I was thinking about when Ms. Gwendolyn surprised herself with her little reaction to you talking about the Terror Man. You see, it stood out to me 'cause I was thinking that I've been hearing more about that ole story these past six months or so than I've heard about it in the last ten years altogether. Ohh, I guess that had to have been since the winter my dear Gladys passed on, God bless her. Now that was a bad and cold year that was. Anywho, like I was saying, I ain't heard about it this much in a long time. Here at the bar. Over yonder at the grocery store. Sitting around the VFW. That's not to say that everyone's been talking about it every chance they got or what not, but rather it's been ten years since I've heard this much chattering 'bout the story. Though, I guess it could be that I just wasn't paying attention before. Baader-Meinhof phenomenon and all. Dunno."

At the time I didn't know what phenomenon he was talking about so I ignored that part.

"Hmm." I replied. "From what I understand, kids just like to scare themselves with those stories. Maybe it's just a passing trend or fad. You know, telling creepy tales and daring one another to go out at night. Prove how brave they are. I remember doing something like that myself. It was Bloody Mary for us. Say her name three times in front of a mirror in a dark room and she appears to kill you. Same deal I'm guessing."

"Yeah, if I think back far enough that's 'bout how I remember growing up too. My parents told us stories to scare us, 'cause their parents told 'em. Us kids told 'em to our friends then after a while they had kids too. Course, way back in my day it wasn't the Terror Man we talked about, it was the Tiermenschen." He said the last word with solid thick German inflection. "Let me see… I guess it were about fifty years or so ago when I noticed these here yokels and rednecks started messing up the right way to say it, which's how we ended up with that Terror Man nonsense."

He shook his head a little in resignation.

"Huh. That makes sense. I was wondering about that name. The Terror Man sounded, well it sounded kind of silly to me."

"Well, that's one way of putting it. You said it bit nicer than I would've. In my humble opinion some folks round here are just a bit stupid, those that ain't stupid, well there's a good chance they're lazy. But to be fair, that ain't everyone. No, not everyone. Not everyone indeed. Anyway, I'm Henry. Henry Armitage."

I quickly wiped my hand off on the crumpled napkin I had, and then again on my pants leg making sure there was no lingering nacho cheese oil on my fingers. I reached over and shook his hand. For an older fellow his grip was still strong and his skin felt like sandstone.

"Nice to meet you, my name is Kent Williams."

"Mr. Williams." He replied with a nod.

I waited for him to continue. Although I wasn't overly interested in his story, I had been making myself nervous thinking about how easily I could screw up my date with Gwendy. Having always had the most success making a good impression when I was relaxed and being myself, I worried that if I spent my time fixating on the date I'd mess something up. Learning a few things from an old guy was just what I needed to pass the time. Besides, while I might not have heard of the Terror Man, there was something about other name that rang a bell. Since I grew up in the area I figured that maybe it was a tale someone had told me once, and that was at least a little interesting.

The bustle in the dark bar continued to grow, and so did the noise level. The chill outside was non-existent inside and the room had a taken on a cheery warm feeling as customers downed drink after drink.

After about a minute of silence from my neighbor I asked, "So. You were saying?"

He looked at me confused at first, as if I pulled him from someplace far away.

"Oh? What was I saying? Oh yeah, I was saying that folks around here don't take time to learn anything anymore. They go fiddling around with words, making new ones, changing them. I mean, where the hell does someone get the word si-goggled to mean out of square or crooked? People say that around here. They truly do. Even worse is that we're losing the meaning of other completely fine words as time moves on. I'm not even talking about innocent linguistic drift or slang. People changing word's meaning to suit specific purposes at the cost of honesty and accuracy. Orwellian I tell you. It's like no one finds any value in what came before, just twistin' things to suit their immediate needs. But... Well. Well, I guess I shouldn't get too worked up. That's happened everywhere and during every time. Ain't it? That's all I was saying, just a running commentary on the zeitgeist. If you know what I mean?"

"Spirit of the day. Yeah, I understand. Actually though, I was wondering about what you first were talking about. About the Terror Man, or um, what did you call it?"

"Oh, I guess I called it the Tiermenschen. 'Cause that's what we kids knew it as."

"The Tiermenschen, huh. Thanks. The first I heard of it was last night, and with the way Gwen just reacted, well I gotta say I'm just a little curious. What stories have you heard?"

He looked down towards his label-less and nearly empty beer bottle, but not really at it. He seemed to be collecting his thoughts. Before he said anything, the big rough looking bartender who dropped off my food came back to us. I was doing OK, but I pointed to Henry's beer and then to me. He acknowledged my order and a few seconds later Henry had a fresh beer bottle in front of him.

He looked up at the bartender, who flicked his head over towards me. When Henry turned to face me again I just shrugged.

"Looked like you were running low."

"That I was, thank you kindly." He downed the remaining brew in his original bottle and slid it forward to the far edge of the bar. He then sat up a little straighter and focused on me.

"So, where was I? The Tiermenschen. Let me see." He paused in thought again. "I'm guessing you're not from here, are ya?"

"Yeah. You could say that. I'm not really."

"Then I will. You ain't from around here." Henry smiled at his little joke. "Anyway, ya seem to already know that it's one of our local monster stories. The real old timers and those who keep to themselves out in the hills would call it a haint story. Haint is just another word for haunt. Out here in the mountains, or Appalachia as you might call it, we have plenty of those. Stories that is. Scary stories. Scary stories that went back generations, or even longer. Well, that particular story is just another one of those that's been used to scare kids since people were having kids around here. Hell, my grandfather even claims to have shot at it once, if you can believe that."

I just sat there and nodded to let him know I was following.

"Anyway, it's a simple story really. One that goes sumthing like there's a spirit or monster of some sorts that lives in the forest. Some say it'll kill you if you don't sacrifice your livestock or your children or whatever to it. Or maybe it'll kill you anyway just 'cause it hates you for being alive. Heard it that way too. Never heard of that not saying its name business Gwen mentioned though. Must be something new someone came up with. Otherwise I don't know anything more than that 'cause that's about all that there is to it. Folks just tell about it from time to time, tall tales of who saw what and where. Though as I told you, it's been awhile since I've heard so many people bringing it back up. Could be there is a mountain lion or something else back in the woods stirring up people's imagination. Or not. Don't know. Like you said, could be a fad. What's old is what's new again. You know what I mean? Everything is circular, and comes back around in its own time. Have you seen these girls wearing those bell bottom trousers and flower print skirts like Dick Nixon was still in the White House? Have you? Never reckoned that God awful style coming back."

Henry had looked off into the bar mirror shaking his head again, although that time he was doing it with a smile on his face. Likely imagining girls in flower print skirts.

I joined him with a grin and a nod. "So what's the, ah, name mean? Sounds, what umm, German?"

"Tiermenschen. Oh, it's a German word alright, and we can probably assume it was the Germans who named it too. Some of the first folks who originally settled here were from Germany. The Fatherland. Deutschland. Though not as many chose these hills here as they did in, say, Pennsylvania. You might know those Germans as the Pennsylvania Dutch. Deutschland. Dutch land. Dutch. Pennsylvania Dutch. See what I'm saying about lazy? Too lazy to learn. Too lazy to think. In the end it all just leads to confusion."

He paused for a moment to scrape at the label on his bottle with his well-trimmed fingernail. After he successfully removed a small piece, he put the scrap on top of the neat little pile that he had been building. When he was finished he went on.

"If I'm to be fair though, I understand that sometimes things just change. For example, this town, Bucksburg. I believe it's been called Bucksburg for at least a hundred and fifty or two hundred years now. However, you know some time ago I read it was originally called Buchenberg. After a town in Germany. Like I was just telling you, this here area was settled by German immigrants, but the rest of the state, well it was predominantly the Scot Irish who came here. Now those men and women, they originally came from the plantation of Ulster. I guess I probably could have just said Ireland. Anyway, they decided to leave their hardships behind on that emerald isle, so they came here. Now you take one of those fellows. Why they wouldn't recognize some German name, mostly being English or Irish Gaelic speakers and all. But a Buck. That's a word they'd recognize. At some point the name probably just slowly changed to something that made more sense to them and sounded more like English. Buchenberg to Bucksburg. Guess if it happened back then, well then, it's always happened. Dunno. Maybe I'm just feeling like I'm a part of the past these days, and when people lose touch with the past, they forget why things are important. Maybe I'm just a worried fer myself. I can accept it. I just don't have to like it."

The conversation had taken a sad turn, and I hoped I could save it by shifting the subject.

"I agree and I know what you're saying. I wonder though, do you know why just this little area was settled by the Germans?" I asked with actual curiosity.

He scratched his chin and thought on my question.

"I might have known at one point, if I did, I forgot. I don't rightly know Kent. Anyway. I guess it's possible they just liked the lay of the land."

"Hmm. That would make sense, it is beautiful country." I smiled back. "Going back to that haint story, what does Tiermenschen mean?"

"That, I do remember. First it's a proper noun. The name of our local creature, but it also means something once you translate it. The word means animal man or men or people. Animal something, for sure. Maybe, I don't recall exactly."

"Animal Man, huh." I said to him. The name made me think of my front door. While thinking about it, I found myself scratching my chin mimicking Henry. It made us both look like a couple of wise old men. "Sort of like a Bigfoot type creature then?"

Only sitting in a bar, drinking beers, and talking to an old timer about monsters could it have happened to me, but right then and there a Bigfoot in my front yard made a lot of sense. The depictions on TV always made him out to be pretty huge and strong enough to beat a dent into my door. Briefly I thought maybe that was what woke me.

"Huh? Bigfoot. Oh yes. Yes." He said absentmindedly. "Wait no. No. Not at all. Completely wrong type creature. You see Bigfoot is like a, dunno, big gorilla or a Neanderthal or the likes. The Swamp Ape or the Yeti, all the same thing. A man, but more wild, like an animal. From what I understand, Tiermenschen ain't that way. From the ways I hear it, it's an animal man. An animal that walks like a man. And also not just a wolf man, or an ape man, or even a bear man, see? 'Cause it ain't just one. Different people who say they'd seen it come back with different descriptions. Like it changes when it wants. Of course, I don't believe any of it and saying all that out loud, well, it sounds all kinds of silly if you ask me."

He took a swig of beer and removed the last of the bottle label before continuing. I leaned in a little, to hear a little more clearly, as something boisterous happened at the front of the bar.

"Silly or no, my grandfather, when he described it in his stories, stories where he claimed to have shot the beast. Or at it. He told us both versions over the years, and boy did he like to share that one. Let me tell you, it was one of his favorite stories, especially at night around the fireplace when we were all just starting to drift off. Now he would tell all kinds of whoppers to us kids, and like the little fools we were, we'd believe him. Although, my favorite stories he told were always of the faery court. The Sidhe. Elves. Goblins. The Seelie court. Faery hills and what lies beneath, red caps, changelings, and trolls. The magic they had over us mortals. Oberon and Titania if you're into the whole Billy Shakespeare thing. Some of those tales of faery spells would get awfully dark and scary. Couldn't trust your own eyes. He'd get us all worked up, not being able to sleep, and then just let my parents deal with all the repercussions. He always got a kick out of that. Sleepless nights let me tell you..."

"What did your grandfather say the Terror Man creature thing looked like?" I introjected into a brief lull in his cadence. It took him a second or two to refocus but it got Henry back on track.

"Oh, well let's see, I guess he told us it was tall and thin. Its knees bent all wrong, it's back arched oddly. It was, uncanny, he would say. Not like anything else he'd ever seen. Uncanny. The defining feature though, was the boney goat head it had. You see, grandpaw saw it as a goat, but I've heard others tell of it as if it were a dog or wolf. Different people. Different animals. Body is usually the same though. Thin, boney, and starving like. Different heads on the same scarecrow. But, you know stories. Everyone tells 'em differently."

When he said scarecrow, I instantly thought back to my first drive back from the bar and what I saw in the road that night. The buck that stared me down. At that moment, once again, I couldn't really remember many details about it. Only how it made me feel. Just that was enough to give me goosebumps.

"Ever hear of a deer head on it?" I, maybe too excitedly, asked Henry.

"On what? Oh. On the Tiermenschen? Why certainly. Well. Maybe. Why do ya ask? Think maybe you've seen it too?" He started laughing to the point he started coughing and had to stop. "I don't want to cast shadows on my grandpaw's integrity, but it's usually the back country boys who say they've seen it. If you ain't familiar, they're not the most reliable lot on accounts of the quality and quantity of the shine they were known to partake in. Nowadays from what I hear it's pain pills and Mountain Dew, but for their minds, the outcome is just the same."

"No, of course not." I said in an attempt to cover my embarrassment. For a second, I got a little wrapped up in the moment. I knew I had taken all the creature talk a bit too seriously, and had to readjust my skeptic hat. Truthfully, I didn't believe in any of that crap. Sure, I thought there might still be cryptids waiting to be discovered in the Amazon, or in Africa, and definitely deep in the ocean. West Virginia, well, I thought that is an entirely different story. Might be a bug or two left undiscovered, but there's too many people and not enough land to hide something as large as a Bigfoot. At the time, for whatever the reason, I had all but forgotten my morning in the woods.

"Well, that's good. Don't be goin' down that rabbit hole."

"No. You're right. I was just making conversation that's all. I didn't expect anything I saw to turn out to be some Nazi monster." I laughed.

Henry paused before he turned to look me right in the eye.

"Listen. I got no love for any of them bastards who shot at my paw, but you do a disservice to those Germans over here and over there who ain't Nazis. Don't be lazy with words. They ain't one in the same. It's like how everybody is calling everyone else a Nazi or a fascist these days, just wrong. But I understand your joke and that it was a joke. So no harm done." He paused in thought before taking a swig from his bottle. "German. Hmmm. Here's a little something you may wanna think about. Maybe at some time there really was someone or something out there in them woods. Something for them German settlers to be scared of. Scared enough that we're still telling their stories. Maybe a vengeful Indian, or an insane woodsman, or hell, even a particularly mean bear. Just because it had a German name don't mean it had to sail over here on ship. In fact, sitting here I'm just now working up a theory our local woodland stalker stories could be actually just somebody else's stories with a new name. That's not to say there ain't enough unique stories out there or enough things out there to have stories told about them, but here's one for you to try on. Now I'd say what I was just describing to you sounds a little like something else I once heard tell about. Something called a Bubak. Now a Bubak is an old Czech folk legend, a creature that lures people to it by crying like a baby, but get this, it looks all skinny, like a scarecrow. Sound familiar? Scarecrow? Thin arms and legs?"

He waited until I replied, "Uh huh. Yeah. The Terror Man."

"Oh wait, just thought of another, this one is even better. Tell me what you think 'bout this one." He smiled in excitement. "There's a thing some people call a Wendigo. See them Algonquian Indians, who were a Native American tribe if you didn't know, well they lived not too far away from here. Not here, here, mind you. This was Shawnee land during the time I'm talking about, which was long before the white man came. Way before the Germans I was talking about."

Henry stopped to take another pull from his beer. When he finished he looked lost so I help him out again.

"Indians. Winnebago. Around these parts."

"Son, how slow are you? Winnebago? Really? I said Wendigo. Wendigo. You try it now. Go on."

"Um. OK. Wendigo."

"See, that weren't so hard. Wendigo. As I was saying, them Algonquin Indians told stories about what happens to a man that picks up the taste for human meat. Long pig it's sometimes been called by us in the West. You see, they thought that when someone becomes a cannibal, a demon possesses them and turns that person into a monster. When they tell their stories, about that monster they say the Wendigo looks emaciated. Starving like. Skinny. Scarecrow like. Top it off, they tell of it having a deer head on its shoulders! What do you think about that then!"

Laughing quietly. He seemed proud of himself. "Then again, maybe all three are out there have separate and distinct origins… you know, if you believe in that sort of thing."

"I'm guessing that you must be some kind of scholar, right? Teacher? Expert in folklore?"

He shook his head. "Naw. Me? Not at all. Just an old diesel mechanic. I've learned what I could, when I could, from who I could. Just been around a long enough time and listened long enough to what people have been saying. The Bubak creature I mentioned, well, knew a Czech years ago when I was in the Marines. For Czechs, the Bubak is essentially their bogeyman. The Wendigo? Well."

Henry started laughing to himself again.

"Funny thing about knowing 'bout that one and I'm almost too embarrassed to admit it. I learned more about it later, but I first heard of it… Well… See, couple of years ago my grandson spent a bit of his summer vacation here with us. He left some of his books, his Monster Manuals, in the John." He paused. "You ever hear of Dungeons an Dragons?"

I affirmatively nodded with a knowing smile on my face.

"Well. You can see where this is going. I like to take my time in the morning, and as I said them books were there. Now don't judge me like that. You can only read the back of the shampoo bottle so many times. You know what I'm saying Kent?"

I interrupted him with a slap on his shoulder and an honest laugh. I heard enough.

From there he found a way to segue our conversation to the diesel engines he kept running for over thirty years. Before I knew it forty minutes had flown by while we had talked about cars, metalwork, mining, and a slew of other topics. Then Henry had to leave. He paid his bill, we shook hands, and I wished him well as he left. I had a great time speaking with him.

Once alone again in the crowded bar I looked down at my watch, and saw it was five after five. I smiled to myself knowingly. I knew there was no way a woman could do everything Gwen had to finish, and still get ready to go out, all within an hour. I didn't care though, I expected her to be at least forty five minutes late.

As soon as I looked back up from my watch, the smaller of the two bartenders was in front of me with my bill. I gave him a kind of "what the heck" expression as I hadn't asked to pay.

"Gwen didn't want to come back into the bar tonight, she's waiting for you out front."

It wasn't the last time I was wrong.

"Oh, wow. Thank you."

I immediately turned and looked towards the front window but didn't see her. He glanced as well, and then shook his head at me.

"No. She just gave me a call from next door. If I were you, well, let's not go there. But, best not keep her waiting." He smiled again before he walked away to help someone else.

I laid some money on the bar and hastily headed towards the exit.

As soon as the door opened I was greeted by significantly cooler air than expected. I could tell that there would be frost that night. The sky, while not cloudy, wasn't exactly clear. Above me, stars could be seen peeking through a few breaks in the clouds and haze. There was also a modest breeze coming down the hill that added to the chill. Gone were the fog and mists from the morning. Having thought about the morning my mind quickly turned to Tammy. I hoped wherever she was, she wasn't out in that cold.

I quickly scanned up and down the sidewalk, which was well lit by the sickly monotone orange light from the sodium vapor lamps that lined Main Street. While there were a handful of people about, I didn't see Gwen among them. I was told that she called from next door so I walked downhill towards the antique store, which seemed more likely than the bank in the other direction. Before I got near the entrance Gwen stepped out.

She was an absolute vision to behold.

Her shoulder length red hair was down and perfectly framed her face. Dark smoky eye makeup accented her eyes as the dark red lipstick did the same for her lips. She wore a black skirt that was short enough that it would have been nearly inappropriate in a lot of places and below that she wore a pair of well-polished cowboy boots. Lastly, barely keeping her warm, she had on a faded jean jacket buttoned all the way up.

I believe my ogling was the response she was hoping for because she blushed and did a cute thing where she bit her lower lip and her waist did a little half twist.

After I got an eye full she said, "Stop standing around and get over here. It's like you've never seen a strong, intelligent, but yet strikingly beautiful woman, before."

"Wait? What?" I asked as I looked over my shoulder. "Is there one behind me?"

"Oh shut up you jerk!"

I started walking towards her. "I have to say, I think I might be a little underdressed for this outing. Um. Sorry."

"Oh, I wouldn't say that. Out classed, definitely. Underdressed, no. You look fine Kent." She said in a playful manner. "That is unless you're taking me out someplace really nice. Is that it, are you flying me to Paris? I've always wanted to go to Paris! And me without my passport."

In the joke there was the very real question of where *WAS* I going to take her. The way she asked me out I just assumed she would direct the rest of our plans, if I really were in charge of our dining, I was at a loss. The only place in town I'd eaten at was the Inn, and I didn't have to know much to know that it wasn't a good option. Nervousness began creeping in.

"Well, I, um."

"Relax Romeo. I have a suggestion. Its right down the road and you're dressed fine for it. Again, not as fine as I am, but that be hard for you regardless of how much time you had to get ready."

She waved at me to follow and we started walking down the sidewalk. As we made our way down the hill, she was close enough that we lightly brushed into each other a couple times more than could have been purely accidental.

After four blocks and being nearly at the edge of town, we made a left, walked another block, and then ducked behind a tiny run down office building. It's not the type of place I would've ever expected to find a restaurant. I looked up at the sign and stopped. The place was called "The Tokyo Rose." Gwen followed my lead, stopping a step or two later. When she turned back to face me I gave her a quizzical look.

"You don't like Asian fusion?" She asked with an insecure expression on her alluring face.

"No. I like Asian food just fine. Back home I head to Chinatown all the time. I am just wondering, well... I'm not quite sure what to think of the name. What kind of place are you taking me to?"

"Ugh. I was hoping you wouldn't notice." She sighed. "It's a silly little thing. Don't worry about it."

I stood my ground for long enough that she felt she needed to continue.

"Look Kent. My friend, Samantha, opened this restaurant after finishing culinary school. Her mom loaned her all the money to open it. Her mom's name is Rose. Sammy loves Japanese culture and food. She just put two and two together. Probably heard it somewhere before. Listen, she's a great chef and a good friend, but... Well, she loves everything Japanese. Like that anime and manga stuff, but history... it isn't really her thing. World War Two is so far into ancient history for her it might as well just be a myth."

I laughed at her a little. "Yeah but, try telling that to the fifty plus million dead..."

"Did I also mention she is stubborn?" Again Gwen sighed. "Look Kent, I'm not disagreeing with you. More than a handful of people have talked to her about it. However, as she likes to point out, she DID already have the sign made. Listen, do me a favor, and don't bring it up. She's having a hard time, and if something doesn't change soon this place won't be open by summer. Besides having a name that'll anger pretty much any vet, of which this town has many, Bucksburg is also not really the hottest spot for an Asian fusion restaurant. No matter how good the food is, this is meat and potatoes country. Come on Kent, be a sport."

It didn't take much for me to give in.

"No problem, as long as it wasn't named in malice, I don't have any problems."

"Thank you. I'm sure you'll love the food, and Sammy is great. She'll take care of us. Plus, since it's not popular, we can talk without a bunch of nosy busy bodies trying to eavesdrop on us. Come on. Let's go in, I'm FREEZING."

As a sign of agreement, I walked up and opened the door for Gwen.

As soon as I stepped foot inside I was assailed by an amazing aroma that was so vastly different from the ubiquitous strip mall type Chinese food restaurants I was familiar with. The scents of garlic, ginger, seafood, and sake wafted through the air. Those wonderful smells instantly brought my attention back to how hungry I was.

The floorplan inside was similar to that of The Inn. It was long and narrow, but that was the only comparison between the two. Where the bar I had just left was dark and subdued, the Tokyo Rose was gaudy and brightly lit. One wall contained a giant backlit photo of the Tokyo skyline. Smaller photos of Asian landscapes were spaced evenly along all the remaining walls. Gold, red, and white paint were applied liberally everywhere else. Deep booths lined the long wall filling most of the room. What was left was just enough of a walkway to make it to the kitchen. Each table had a live lucky bamboo plant in a glass bowl as a centerpiece.

The whole place dripped of tackiness but also of comfort.

There were only two other patrons in the restaurant besides us, a middle aged couple who sat silently near the front slurping noodles from oversized bowls with their forks. They paid us no mind. The food they had looked as good as the place smelled.

While I oriented myself a smiling, stocky, woman, with short spiky blond hair and dark roots, ran up to us and gave Gwen a huge bear hug. The ladies almost tumbled over from the impact. Even though she was at least six inches shorter than my date, the hugger was able to plant her feet, lean back, and lift Gwen off of the ground. Once she was put back down and let go, playfully Gwen pushed the woman an arm's length away. When she was sure there wouldn't be a second assault, Gwendy took the time to fling her hair back behind her ear and adjust her clothes. After she was sure everything was put back in order, we were introduced.

"Kent, this is a good friend of mine. Sammy. Sammy this is, also a friend. Kent. I was wondering if we could get a table in the back"

"A friend? Your FRIEND. A friend named Kent? In the back of the restaurant? Alone? All alone back there?" She said to Gwen with a sly grin and raised eyebrows. "Um. Of course! Sit anywhere you like. I'll be back with some menus."

Sammy gave us a mischievous smirk as Gwen grabbed my hand and led me to the furthest booth in the restaurant. We slid in opposite from each other, and she just sat there smiling at me. I assumed it was a reaction to her energetic friend, but I had high hopes that it was because I was there.

In a blink of an eye Sammy was back with menus and glasses of water. She looked between the two of us a couple of times, all the while rocking back and forth on the balls of her feet. She beamed at Gwen and said "I'll be back in a little while, yous twos. So cute. So cute."

With that, in a flash, she was gone again but for her lingering giggles. Gwen sighed heavily, shaking her head.

"Don't mind her. She's this way with everyone. So?" Gwen asked. "What do you think?"

I flipped through menu. It wasn't so much a Japanese restaurant as much as it had dishes from all over Asia and if there was any fusion in it, it was in the Americanized Chinese dishes. I saw carryout staples such as Egg Foo Young and General Tso's, but also Pad Thai from Thailand, Bibimbap from Korea, and Pho from Vietnam. The Japanese dishes that immediately stood out were the Ramen and Udon. Everything was listed together mixed under broad categories such as "Rice," "Noodles," and "Seafood." Honestly, the menu was a mess.

"Seems extensive." I replied. "I'm sure I'll enjoy something from here. Though, I couldn't really complain even if I wanted. I couldn't have offered to take you anyplace else. The only restaurant I've been to in town has been The Inn."

"And I'm so, let me stress this again, I'm so very glad to be away from there tonight. Believe me. I've really been putting in the hours for a while now. I'm just happy to be anyplace else." Then with a warm, inviting smile she added "Plus it's nice ta see you in some literally different light."

My face turned a little red, blushing, and I was left speechless.

"Lighten up Kent. I didn't say the bright lighting in here was doin' ya any favors. Relax. The hard part is over. Now all you have to do is be yourself and have as much fun as we do when I'm slinging beers at you."

Gwen's focus shifted, and I glanced over my shoulder to see what she was looking at. Sammy was standing a few feet away. Not obviously listening, but rather being overly attentive. Gwen suggested that we order so Sammy wouldn't hover around waiting. We put in an order for a couple appetizers, some sake, and a pair of entrees. Too much food, but there was so much to try.

Once Sammy left, we both kind of just looked at each other until it grew a little awkward. I used the opportunity.

"So yesterday, you said next time we talked you would tell me a little more about yourself. Let's start with why all the extra shifts?"

She paused and became slightly more serious.

"Damn Kent, ya sure know how to get to the point, don't cha?" She scrunched up her face like a cute little mouse. "Wow, ok. Where to start?"

"I personally, like starting at the beginning, but listen, if you don't want to tell me I don't mind. I thought it was an innocent enough place to open, but we can skip it. I got other questions. Let's see, hmm.

Where do you see yourself in fifteen years, or what is your greatest weakness?"

"Monaco, doing the international spy thing, and being far too perfect in an imperfect world, but I think that's enough of the interview. I'll answer the first question, but to answer it I kind of really have to explain a lot. The trick for me is how to tell ya without ya runnin' outta here." She paused with a hopeful smile on her face, sighed deep, and shook her head defeatedly. Some of the confidence and control I was used to seeing from her slipped away. "I'm working the extra shifts because otherwise I'd be home with my mom and dad and mom's getting on my very last nerves. I need the money so I can move out and get a place of my own. I had to move in with my parents this winter, ready for date no-no number one, because I broke up with my longtime boyfriend and moved out of his apartment. When I say long time, I mean, long time. Like since high school. I haven't been on a date since the breakup, so technically that makes you a rebound. So there you have it."

It was a lot to take in and she spit it out so fast that I didn't have a reply ready. About all I could do was force a weak smile and take a sip of water to give myself additional time.

"Damn it. I knew I should have waited. I sound desperate? Don't I? Maybe pathetic? I'm sorry. Look Kent, I'm fine, I ain't looking for a rebound guy. Damn. Not that you'd be a rebound guy in any sense other than technically this is a rebound date, but don't worry about it.

If that's all I wanted, a rebound, I could find a rebound. Believe me, in a town like this? Not a problem, not for me, the guys here drool over me. I ain't bragging it's just true. That's why I wanted to go out with you. You're not from around here."

I hadn't heard the word "rebound" so much outside of a basketball game.

"Ouch" I said, only half joking. "So you needed to freshen up the genetic stock, huh? Or maybe it's an Officer and a Gentleman type deal?"

"Ohh damn it all to hell." She said flustered. "That came out so wrong. So very wrong. Let me start again."

I wasn't insulted, and even if I were she was hot enough for me to put up with a slight that mild.

"Hear me out Kent, when I first met you, I was just looking forward to talkin' to someone different. Hearing somethin' new. Anything new. I listen to the same shit day in and day out at The Inn. I talk to the same crowd day in and day out. It's almost the same day, day in and day out. You get the picture. Almost all my friends went away to college while I stayed here with the deadbeat ex. When my friends graduated, none of them came back. Well, one. Sammy. The people I knew that didn't go away, well, they all started having families and we just grew apart. I grew apart from my ex too. Near the end we barely spoke and we didn't even sleep in the same room. Though I promise I won't talk 'bout him anymore. I just want you to know where I'm at. I guess my main point is that a new face was refreshing. You could have been the biggest asshole in the county and I would have still talked to you for at least a bit, just to break up my day. The more I talked to you, once you got out of your shell, you were a lot of fun. I wasn't trying to sound superficial or like I needed anything from you. I just want to have a nice night out. Can we still do that?"

How could I have disagreed with that plea? With a little more daring than I usually have, I reached across the table and took Gwen's hand.

"Of course."

Sammy came by with our sake and giggled when she saw me holding Gwen's hand, which I promptly stopped doing causing both girls to laugh.

From then on we had a great time that night. We finished our meal and just stayed in our booth talking. A few other couples came in, but the place never filled up so I never felt like we needed to go. Sammy brought us a few additional carafes of sake and the hours sped by. At some point Gwen slouched into her seat, kicked off her boots, and propped her feet up on my side of the booth. I got comfortable doing the same. I never had so much fun on a date before.

Eventually, we saw one of the staff start mopping up. I gave Gwen a mournful look, and she nodded. When I reached for my wallet, she laughed.

"I'm not going to be beholdin' to you Kent, not tonight. I paid the bill when you went to the restroom."

On the way out the door Sammy gave us both hugs. I received an additional smack on my butt as I walked by. She gave Gwen an approving nod.

The world was dark and cold past the threshold. Gwen immediately wrapped her arms around herself and then nuzzled up against my side for warmth. I was still blissfully warm from the date and the sake. I wanted nothing more than to just stay there with Gwen, but I knew we needed to go.

I walked Gwen back to Main Street and then to her Jeep several blocks further up. We stood outside of her old blue Wrangler taking turns looking at each other and then at our feet. Anxiety crept over me. I knew I had to kiss her goodnight. I wanted to kiss her goodnight. I was pretty sure she was standing there waiting for me to kiss her goodnight. Eventually, I leaned in and so did she. The kiss was everything I thought it would be. I pulled her close and she hugged me tighter. Our feet got a little tangled and we had to stop before we lost our balance. She put her head on my chest for a second to catch her breath before stepping back and looking me in the eye.

"Am I going to see you again soon?"

"As soon as I can." I replied.

"When might that be? And before you answer, I think you can tell that I don't like to play games."

I frowned. I thought about the upcoming day and my commitment to Johnny. The following week at work I was booked and really couldn't have taken off without repercussions. I didn't know what to do because I couldn't stand the idea of going until Friday without seeing her again.

"I have a meeting tomorrow at noon that shouldn't take too long, which honestly, I could probably blow off. Otherwise nothing else until I have to head back. I could swing by The Inn?"

"Well, I'm not going in there on my day off, especially with you. The gossips around here would just love that. Don't pout, Kent. I'm only a little embarrassed of you." She teased. "We could do something else though, if you'd like? Who has meeting on Sunday, if ya don't mind me asking."

I gave her a much abbreviated version of Johnny and the rifle. Inadvertently, it might have been the best thing I could have done to impress her. She looked up at me with a mix of appreciation and interest.

"Aww, you're so kind. That's so sweet. Stupid too. Very stupid. But so kind… and so so stupid" She told me shaking her head before stretching up and quickly kissing me again. "I'm coming with. Meet me in front of the Tokyo Rose at 11:45. Don't be late and don't you *DARE* stand me up."

With that she ran around the side of her Jeep and got in. I stood there and waved once as she drove away. I was on cloud nine. The walk back to my car and the drive home was a blur to me. Nothing else that weekend existed, only the date. Only Gwen.

That was until I parked in front of my house and saw three large crows fly away as I got out.

"One for sorrow, two for mirth, three for a funeral…"

There were only three that day, so I stopped the old nursery rhyme right there. I refused to read into it. Even before I started the rhyme I wondered why I even noticed the animals at all. Why it bothered me. Birds. In the woods. I hardly ever saw birds. Earlier that day I did. Then I remembered the sparrow that bashed itself to death against the side of a tree. Fleeing from something. Remembering gave me chills, but that was all. I let the feeling go and it slipped away.

For the first night since arriving on Thursday, I slept soundly.

Andy was silent

Kent took a deep breath while organizing his thoughts. The silence drew Andy's attention and he shuffled about on his seat.

Andy didn't say anything, but he was tempted to. He wanted to make some type of crack about sleeping and how nice it would be to be doing so. He wanted to remind Kent that he was married, and that he was collecting a lot of dirt the way he was gushing over Gwen. Andy also missed being the center of attention, a place he wasn't for most of the evening, but he wasn't going to admit that to himself. He was also feeling a mixture of being too tired to care about the end of the story and too interested to interrupt. Being silent and patient was an odd state of being for him and he was having a hard time accepting it. Andy squirmed on his log a little more before just giving in to the silence.

Instead of speaking out, he reached down and pushed the logs at his feet the remainder of the way into the fire. The fuel they had dragged from the forest was nearly depleted so he grabbed whatever other small pieces around his seat he could reach and tossed those into the flames as well. Almost immediately the fire responded by growing bright and hot. Andy rocked the log he sat on a few inches closer to the warming flames.

The early morning had grown frigid. Kent hadn't moved his seat, but at some point during his tale he inched as close to the edge as he could. His ungloved hands never left the rifle he cradled.

The sky took on the initial visible signs of the coming dawn, although for the three men it would have been very difficult, if not impossible to discern through the thick evergreen cover. Any real light was still an hour away. It would be even longer still until the sun could actually be seen from the valley floor, but a hint of indigo was beginning to form on the edge of the black starless sky.

Professor West continued to sit patiently. A very slight, almost unnoticeable, complacent grin rested on his lips.

After a few seconds of silence, Kent continued.

James 2:19

The sun was out and shining brightly when I woke, real piercing sunshine, and not just daytime. The weather outside matched my cheery mood. The sky was an amazing rich dark blue spotted with enormous puffy white clouds that swiftly raced across the horizon with the wind. Nearly ten hours of uninterrupted sleep blessed me that night and it felt wonderful. Restful sleep, paired with the anticipation of seeing Gwen a few hours later, left me ecstatic. With a light step and a smile I rushed around the house getting ready. I wasn't going to be late. Nothing else was on my mind, not even going to Johnny's. Giving him the Pontificio had only become a means to seeing Gwendy again.

I was smitten.

I showered, got ready, and deemed myself as good looking as I could be. After all, though as nontraditional as it was, dropping off a gun was going to be our second official date. I headed out the door with the rifle, still wrapped in its blanket, and the box of shells I had for it.

When I got to the bottom of the porch stairs, the first and only negative thought that morning crossed my mind. I wanted to fire the weapon before I gave it back, but I also remembered that the Crammer's might have been searching my property for Tammy. I hoped to god that she had been found by then, but I didn't know one way or the other. I didn't want to shoot unsafely.

While considering my options I unwrapped the rifle on the hood of my car and looked down at it.

Once again I felt a real and physical connection with history. A connection with each of the men who held, relied on, and fought with the weapon. It almost called out to me when I ran my fingers over the stamped image of the Crossed Keys. There was something else as well, but I couldn't put my finger on it at the time.

I had begun to regret my decision, parting with the Remington, but after telling Gwen and to a lesser degree, Johnny, I couldn't go back on my word. With my course set I was determined to still shoot it once or twice.

Being on the side of a mountain, I knew that if I just shot uphill it would be nearly as good as shooting into an embankment. I picked a spot where I could see nearly 100 yards up the hill before the trees completely obscured my view. I placed a cardboard box about fifteen yards from where I'd be shooting. After loudly calling out a few times and hearing no response I figured I was good. From where I was shooting my voice would have carried further through the trees than my bullets.

I went back to the car and took hold of the weapon. Before loading it, I put it up against my shoulder, and tried it on for size. Although heavy, once again I was surprised at how well it felt compared to how unbalanced it looked. It wasn't as comfortable as a modern firearm, in fact it was nowhere near that, but still it impressed me as to how practical it actually was. I understood why so many variants of it were sold.

Like all roll block rifles, I first had to pull back the hammer and lock it into place. Next, I pulled back and rotated the rolling block to expose the empty chamber. From the hand I was holding the rifle in I took a round and slowly slid it into the chamber with my right hand. I noticed I was trembling a little. How many other men throughout the century went through the same ritual? I rotated the block back into place and took aim while pulling the butt tight into my shoulder. I leaned into the rifle.

With a deep breath I pulled the trigger.

Then I pulled it some more.

I had to stop and double check that there really wasn't a safety hidden somewhere. I tried again, this time really squeezing the trigger. Finally, after a ridiculous amount of pressure, at least 15 pounds or so, the hammer flew forward and the powder exploded inside the shell.

My first thought, pain. Pain in my shoulder and pain in my ears. In my hurry I completely forgot any safety equipment for my vision and hearing.

My initial view after the shot was of nothing but huge clouds of unwholesome grey and white smoke from the black powder cartridge. Between the smoke and the shock I didn't see where the bullet had struck, but I could see I didn't hit my target.

I repeated the steps with second round. Again the firearm barked out a nasty growling report. That follow-up shot seemed twice as loud to me and really left my ears ringing. I was prepared for the recoil, but even with the weight of the rifle to help dampen the blow, the large shells still kicked heftily. Again I missed the box but the churned up earth about a foot above my target showed me I was close.

I wanted to shoot more, but not without ear protection. I already had done enough damage to my hearing, but I also didn't want to be late for Gwen. The thought of unlocking the house, going down to the basement, digging out my earplugs, relocking the house, coming back outside, all seemed like too much of a chore to get done in time. It was about then that I realized that Johnny still couldn't legally own the gun, and that I might as well keep it with me until it was sold. Since that was the case, I could shoot the rest of the rounds later.

Knowing that I was running out of time I rewrapped the rifle in the old blanket and tossed the bundle into the backseat of my car. I wasted no time getting moving. Once off my dirt access road I raced towards Bucksburg with all the speed I could safely muster. As I got to the restaurant I saw Gwen's Jeep pulling in at the same time. We both arrived five minutes early. Once out of our vehicles we awkwardly approached one another. Gwen, as usual looked stunning, this time in form fitting jeans and a large oversized jacket. Although the aviator glasses she wore looked great on her, I instantly missed seeing her eyes.

We neared each other and I was unnecessarily filled with doubt. What was the protocol for a second date? A hug? Lean in for a kiss? A handshake was out, that much I was certain. When in reach she opened her arms and immediately I went in for a hug which was rewarded with a light kiss on my cheek.

"Punctual." She said, glancing down and tapping at her watch-less wrist. "I like that. A fine trait for man."

"After the warning you gave last night, I wasn't about to risk revealing my naturally tardy self to you just yet."

"Is that so, what else are you hiding from me?" She joked.

I shrugged with a grin. "Only time will tell."

I suggested that we continue our banter inside my car, since it was a still a little too chilly outside with the wind. In reality I just wanted to get Johnny out of the way to selfishly have Gwen all to myself. I figured that if I were able to free enough of the afternoon we might be able to head up to Morgantown or over to Charlottesville. Places I was familiar with and places where she wouldn't be subjected to her regular customers watching us to satisfy their small town gossip needs. However, both excursions were far enough away that just getting there and back would eat up a good portion of the day. Going to either was doable but would require keeping our visit with Johnny as short as possible. Something I planned on doing.

She hopped into my car, checking it out as she strapped herself in. I shifted into reverse, backed up about three feet then stopped. I looked up and down the road. It wasn't before then that I realized I wasn't even sure how to get to Johnny's. From our conversations I gathered he still lived in the same house I had visited as an eight year old, but I didn't remember what it took to actually get there.

Embarrassingly I explained my conundrum to Gwen which absolutely made her morning. It gave her ammunition to pick on me mercilessly. She didn't have a clue as to where Johnny lived but using a few landmarks I remembered, many of which weren't there any longer, Gwen was able to guide me close enough that I could find the rest of the way to his house on the far outskirts of town.

It's kind of funny. One of the goals I had since that first visit back was to find that one part of the county that hadn't changed through the years. I finally found that on Johnny's street. The trailer park may have been a slightly worse for wear but was otherwise identical to how I remembered it.

Although, calling it a park was a bit of a stretch. It only consisted of five isolated trailers on a cul-de-sac. Actually, a calling it a cul-de-sac was also a stretch as it was just a muddy gravel driveway that dead ended at Johnny's place. There were two trailers on each side of the drive with a fairly generous thirty to forty yards between each. Straight ahead, at the end, was the light blue trailer Johnny had lived in since he was born. Behind that was a pronounced drop off and a clearing through the trees for power lines.

From the street, it was clear that all the trailers but one were in pretty bad shape. Just as I remembered. Trash and junk were piled high everywhere in the front yards. Faded paint. Broken fences. A boarded up window or three. At least four abandoned cars could be seen. Mountain Dew and beer cans littered the yards. That description fit all the homes except for one. Not Johnny's but one of the two directly next to his. It was in perfect shape and surrounded with a freshly painted white picket fence. Hedges lined the building and a freshly swept field stone sidewalk ran up to the front door. The well maintained trailer made all the others homes look even worse than they might not have otherwise.

I was happy to see a beat up purple truck parked sideways in front of Johnny's trailer, he might have been hungover, but seeing his vehicle was a good sign he wasn't out somewhere. I pulled in next to it. Gwen gave me the "what the heck did you get me into look," I shrugged and we both got out of my car.

The approach leading up to the front door was a small set of unpainted wooden stairs with a tiny platform at the top which was barely large enough for one person to stand upon. As we climbed the steps, I noticed that some of the boards were recently replaced. Replacing steps wasn't the type of work that Johnny would have paid for. He had been using some of the handyman skills he learned from his job to fix up his place. I was happy for him. It was a good sign that he was planning for the future.

Although it accomplished nothing, I opened the glassless and screen-less storm door and loudly knocked on the door behind it.

We waited.

I knocked again. Harder.

We awaited again.

"Hey Johnny. It's me, Kent. Open up!" I yelled between additional knocks.

"Maybe he isn't home?" Gwen suggested looking up at me with her big questioning eyes.

Seeing her beautiful face I had no patience for a hungover drunk. I really pounded on the door.

"No, he's home. His truck is here. I'm pretty sure he doesn't have another vehicle. He said he was going out last night. He's hungover or passed out is my guess."

"I don't know, Kent." Gwen replied with some doubt. "For the last couple months he's been pretty tame, well, at least at The Inn. We haven't had ta eighty-six him in a long time."

She took a couple steps down the stairs, leaned over, and tried to peer into a front window with no real success. I pounded on the door a couple more times.

"Well, I guess that's that. He's not answering." I told Gwen. "I think we're done here. So, I have some ideas for today..."

She cut me off.

"A quitter, huh?" She asked with an exaggerated frown on her face. "That, I did not expect from you. That's a black mark, Kent. Let's try not to accumulate too many more of those today, OK? I think you need to hold them horses and let's see what we can see before giving up so soon."

She was looking at the front of the trailer while backpedaling, trying to determine the best window for a view inside. It didn't take her long to realize that short of collecting some junk to stand on there weren't really any good options.

"I'm goin' a run 'round back." She decided and started into a relaxed jog with a happy expression on her face.

"Gwen, wait!" I yelled trying to stop her. "There's no reason for that. We tried. I can always come back another time."

"Nope. Can't hear you." Was all she said as she ducked behind the corner of the building.

In frustration I pounded on the door yet again. Over the roof I heard her call out "hello?" and lightly rap on the back door. That made me smile, like he'd hear her gentle taps instead of my loud bangs. Then again, I thought heck, maybe the sound of a familiar bartender could rouse him.

I waited. Nothing. Then everything changed.

About ten seconds after her last knock I heard a blood curdling scream. A horror movie scream queen scream, but worse because I could tell it was real. Without hesitation I leapt down the stairs in a single stride and then ran towards the corner that Gwen disappeared behind. As I reached the edge of the house Gwen came around the corner, slammed into me, and grabbed onto my jacket. She held on with all her strength while half crying and half trying to say something.

I was looking over her shoulder, not knowing what to expect, or what might come from the other side the building. I held her close until her fear drove me to action. I gently pushed her away from, and then behind, me.

"What's wrong?" I asked, with whatever confidence and strength I could muster. I stared off to where she had run from. "What did you see?"

She pulled back even further from me and stood up straight, wiped her eye with one hand, and flicked back her hair with the other. She stared at me and then slightly down to the ground.

Quietly but clearly and with complete control over her voice she said "Down the hill. In the rocks. Johnny is dead."

"Stay here." I told her as I rushed behind the house.

The back yard had more junk strewn about it than did the front. I recognized at least one piece of rusted metal that was there decades before. Johnny and I had played on it. From the yard it was hard to see down the hill as it was covered in thorny bushes and weeds. I couldn't make out anything. Gwen probably had a better angle from the stairs that led up to the back door. Instead of heading that way, I cautiously pushed through what almost looked like a trail. After about six feet of brush, the ground dropped away into a rock and boulder covered field. Power lines ran above me.

Johnny's parents never liked us back there. Between the hundreds of discarded and broken beer bottles and the eastern diamondback rattlers who made it their home, the area wasn't a safe place for a kid. It wasn't a safe place for anyone.

Once I pushed through to the edge of the brush it only took a second to scan the area. There was Johnny Smalls. Twenty feet down the hill from me. Face up, eyes open, and lying on a jagged pile of two hundred pound hunks of stone. Blood had oozed from the back of his head, onto the rocks, and congealed into a thick black and red stain. Even more blood had pooled on his left side, where there was something odd about his shape and the way he laid.

Understanding what I saw took time. When I finally put together what was in front of me, it was something I've never forgotten. His left arm was missing, ending at his shoulder behind a torn sleeve. It was just gone, not rolled up under him, or broken, or twisted. Gone. In his remaining, outstretched, dead, right hand he was clutching a large screwdriver.

His pale face was not one of peace. Fear and shock dominated his lifeless expression.

Once I realized his arm was gone and I was sure that it was him, I turned away and walked back through the brush. There wasn't any help anyone could offer. He was gone.

The horror of seeing a corpse was one thing, but the surprise I felt at my own sorrow was another. I'd experienced loss before. My father. Some of my friends. Some distant family. With those losses my morning was deep, but it was mostly focused inward. I was sorry for myself. My loneliness. With Johnny it was a loss for what might have been. He was a man who had pulled himself out of a self-destructive hole and for what purpose?

I didn't know why it had to happen to him, but I knew whatever it was it wasn't pleasant.

I went back around the house knowing I needed to find someplace from where I could call the police. When I returned to the front yard I saw Gwen walking back from the nearest trailer, the nice one. We met in the middle, halfway between the two trailers, and without asking she told me that the police were on their way.

I held out my arms to her, but she hesitated approaching me and looked down and off to the side. I took a step forward instead and hugged her firmly. We stood that way for some time.

The small community around us gradually came alive as the news spread. Children first, followed closely by a collection of adults, all of whom began coming out their trailers. A dozen or more people eventually made their way out onto the street. Hushed conversations were accented with explosive disbelief and profanity. A pair of teenage boys ran back to see the body for themselves and quickly returned to confirm Johnny's demise to the assembled crowd. When a small group approached us I held out my hand to keep them at bay. We walked backwards to keep our distance. I lead Gwen to my car and we both got in. Silently we sat there, deep in our own thoughts. Gwen eventually reached over and grabbed my hand.

As we watched the scene through the closed car windows, more and more denizens of the tiny neighborhood made their way to behind Johnny's house. I thought about the possibility of the crime scene being trampled over, but I didn't have it in me to stop the onlookers. Later I found out that the lady from the well cared for trailer was sort of the unofficial mayor of the park and she had kept the crowd under control.

Fifteen minutes after being called, the first police car arrived speeding down the gravel driveway with sirens and lights on. Officers I didn't recognize got out, were swamped by children pointing, and then jogged off towards the body. A minute later an ambulance arrived. Five minutes after that, another pair of police cruisers pulled in as well.

I figured it was about time I approached someone to give my statement to.

The first cop I walked up to told me to back off and yelled to his partner to get out the yellow tape.

"This one is for real," I overheard.

While I stood there trying to forget the look on Johnny's face, yet one more squad car pulled up. Officer Greene got out of the passenger's seat. I signaled him with a wave and when he noticed me he did a double take. After a moment's hesitation he walked over.

"Stay where you are Kent. Let me get a handle on this circus. I'll speak with you in," he paused looking around. "Maybe ten minutes."

I nodded.

The first officers to arrive on the scene made their way to Greene, and gave him a series of quick but hushed reports. He responded with agitated pointing. I began to gather that he was in more of a leadership position than I originally knew. He wasn't happy with how things were being handled.

"Don't screw this up." I heard him say through clenched teeth. I glanced back at Gwen, who was looking up at me through the window. No longer vulnerable, that had only lasted a minute, her face was somber but in control. We made eye contact and she acknowledged me with a nod. We hadn't said a word since before we sat in the car.

Fifteen minutes later Officer Greene came back.

"Mr. Williams, what are you doing here?" I noticed I was no longer Kent to him. "Did you know the deceased or maybe someone else in the park?"

Silently Gwen came up beside me and slid her arm in behind mine. Greene let slip a mildly surprised expression flash briefly across his face.

"Yes, I knew Johnny. Not well, but I knew him. We were the ones who found the body."

"Wait! What? You telling me that you found the body? Anyone here speak with you, no?" He shook his head disappointed before yelling. "Derrick, get your sorry ass over here, right now!"

Officer Greene yelled the last part which instantly encouraged a young cop to run over to us. He was one of those who arrived in the first cars to the scene. Greene continued in his regular subdued tone once the officer arrived.

"Why did you tell me the Harris boy made the discovery when this man just told me that he found the deceased?"

"Well, um. Ya see, they was in the front yard, and Frank Harris was in the back. You know, standing next to it, it was kind of crazy what with Mrs. Amanda yelling at him to get up away from it and all and she was the one to call 9-1-1, I just thought..."

"Jesus. Alright, get back to what I told you to do and think, really really think, about why I'm going to tear into your ass when we debrief. Do we have an understanding?"

He mumbled something that was most likely "yes sir" and hustled off back behind the house.

Officer Greene then turned slowly and started making his way in the same direction urging us to follow. He returned to our conversation once we were all moving.

"Now, it was you found the body? I think maybe you can guess what my next question is going to be..." He paused, his speech and his walk, all the while still not facing us.

I started with my classic silence killing "um" but Gwen jumped right in.

"What were we doing here?"

"Exactly." And with that he started walking again. We followed.

Gwen nodded to me, and I took over.

"Well, I ran into Johnny outside of The Inn last night. He had to get back to work so we didn't have much time to talk. I told him if he wanted I could stop by today. Gwen asked to come along so we did, stop by, that is. After banging on the front door, we tried the back door. That's when we saw his body."

Green stopped and turned to faced us.

"Now, maybe this next part will be important, maybe it won't be import. But Mr. Williams, I gotta ask myself and in turn ask you, why would a town drunk, convicted drug user, petty criminal, and general pariah want to speak with a vacationer from the city?"

I should have been thinking of myself at the moment. However, my first reaction was to address how Officer Greene was besmirching the dead man I that was once, albeit a long time ago, a friend of mine.

"You know he's been clean for a while and he got a job that he was doing well at. I don't think it's right the way you categorized..."

I was cut off by a gentle hand on my shoulder. The officer's hand. He slowly nodded in reluctant agreement with me.

"Fine, fine, that's fair enough. Maybe I misspoke. Maybe. I still want to know why you were here."

I told him how he spotted me in the bar months before. How I grew up in the town. How we were fairly close as children. I left out the guns partially because I didn't want to add complexity to our relationship, but mainly out of brevity.

"You think maybe there is a reason you didn't tell me you were once a local when we talked the other night?"

"No. No reason, it didn't really come up, although you may recall I started to mention it. There were more important topics to talk about that night, with Tammy." I saw the officer cringe a little at the name but he was otherwise unresponsive so I continued. "My family moved away when I was eight or nine or something. A kid. Didn't think it mattered. That was twenty or more years ago and I hadn't been back since last fall."

"Maybe it doesn't. We will see. You two, hold up right here." He stopped us and walked a few feet over to a uniformed officer. They spoke to each other in hushed tones. I couldn't make out a word, but the cop sprinted off to his car and got on the radio when they were finished.

Gwen and I were still a dozen feet from the hastily put up yellow tape that was blocking off the backyard, and we were at least dozen feet even further from where there was even a chance at seeing the body, but Gwen had already started hanging back.

I looked around and tried to get a feeling of what was going on. The whole area was full of activity. Two officers were speaking with neighbors and otherwise just keeping people away. A portly gentleman with an ugly tie was being assisted down the small but steep hill behind the house by two more cops. I thought maybe he was a medical examiner or a paramedic or something. I saw a couple more police searching around under the power lines and in the stone field while a few more were walking through the nearby woods. I could hear someone moving around in the trailer as well.

When Greene came back to us he wore an annoyed but quizzical expression on his face.

"So, from what I understand you two were in town last night? Maybe on a date?"

I looked over at Gwen. We didn't say anything about dinner to Greene. She looked angry but before she reacted Greene continued.

"You both were seen walking out of that new high end Chinese place. Pretty late actually. Didn't seem all that important, until now."

My first thought was that maybe Officer Thompson or someone else saw us walking back to our cars. Maybe she drove by or something? I couldn't think of any other reason someone would take note of us. Whatever it was, none of it really mattered, as there wasn't any reason to deny it.

"That's correct, we had dinner last night. We were out until, I don't know when, it was late when I got home. Maybe midnight."

"Not when *WE* got home? You separated afterwards? Alright. Alright. Don't give me that look. I'm just trying to get everything straight. Ya see, we had a noise complaint called in for this trailer after dark. It was about six PM last night. That's generally a little early for noise complaints in this town. Seems the late Mr. Smalls was heard yelling loud enough that Mrs. Amanda over there, his neighbor, called us. You may not know, but generally she takes care of things around here by herself. Something about last night, something made her maybe think twice about dealing with Mr. Smalls on her own, so she got us involved. By the time an officer got here it was all quiet. When no one answered the door he did a quick walk around and then left. I guess maybe now we know why it was so quiet. Well, maybe. Anyway, I just wanted to know where you two were at the time, is all."

"Wait, do you think that..." Gwen started angrily before I cut her off by holding up my hand.

"Officer Greene," I said calmly, "Gwen and I were together from at least five o'clock until after eleven. There are multiple people who can confirm we never left town during that time. If you think we can be of any additional help, I'd be glad to assist. However, if your questions continue in the direction I think you are implying, our cooperation will be in the presence of an attorney."

"Do what you gotta do boy," he said with some ferocity before catching himself. When he spoke again, it was back to the calm buddy like manner that I had become familiar with. "Sorry about that, it's been a long hard couple of days and I've had some bad experiences with people lawyering up just to make my job harder. Expensive waste of talent the way I see it. No, I don't think my questions will continue in that direction. Hell, I'm no coroner, and even I can see that his body has been there for a long while. Probably since around 6:00. Once I get a better time of death, well, then maybe we won't need to talk no more about this. Maybe."

After the way he quickly changed his attitude and calmed down, I didn't assume anything about him again. At some point he had been acting, but I wasn't sure when he was or wasn't.

"Look, I really do want to help you but we had nothing to do with this."

"I'm apt to believe you. His head on that rock killed him. Looks crushed. Likely fell down drunk. Fell down hard. Blood tests will determine what he had in him. Limited blood around the arm means it likely came off after death. My guess, animals. Wild dogs or coyote.

Bear maybe. Hell, a mountain lion might even be a remote possibility. Listen, this is ongoing, I just wanted you to know…"

He stopped as a police officer, the one he just chastised, came jogging back to us.

"Found some thin', Chief, found some thin'," he called still several yards away and out of breath.

"Thank the Lord" Greene said more to himself than anyone else. When the officer stopped he continued. "I was worried one of these kids around here would find what was left of that arm."

"Ohh, I didn't find no arm."

"What? That's what I asked you to find!"

"No, I found Duke. Widow Murphy's dog, Duke." He paused waiting for praise or at least recognition from Greene. "You know. The Great Dane? Hell boss, she's called three or four times a day for nearly a week now."

"For the love of God, no, I don't know and right now I don't care. Call animal control and have them catch it. If you get the time, notify Mrs. Murphy, but damn it Derrick. Focus on what's important. Wait, unless you think the dog was responsible for the arm?"

"No. No I don't think it ate the arm, and I don't think I need to call animal control neither. It's over there."

The young officer pointed towards the tree line on the other side of the power lines. At first I didn't see anything, and had to look back at where the cop was pointing a couple times. Then I saw it. Greene must have seen it at the same time because his body tensed. Gwen gasped a few seconds later.

"What in the world?" He asked in disbelief, then almost immediately afterwards he faced us. "I don't see any reason to keep you two any longer. If we have any further questions, I'll swing by or have someone else do so."

He put his hands on both of use and gave us a gentle nudge towards my car before turning back to the other officer.

What we saw in those trees was a massive grey dog, about the size of a deer, ten to twelve feet off the ground. It was hanging by a front leg which was held up by a broken tree branch that was pushed through the dog between the muscle, tendons, and bone. The animal was gutted, its intestines and organs spilling out, and it was missing its lower jaw.

It swayed gently in the breeze.

I put my arm around Gwen and guided her back to my car.

We didn't say a word to each other until we were back on the paved road. I wanted to take her hand, pat her leg, or rub her shoulder. Heck I wanted to hug her if I could have done so while driving. Any type of physical comfort I could offer, but I wasn't sure how she'd take it. Her face was blank and unreadable. So, instead I tried talking.

"I'm so sorry about today, Gwen. I really really am. I'll take you back to your car. I hope you'll be ok."

She stayed silent, so I didn't bother continuing. About five minutes later she spoke up.

"Don't take this the wrong way. I mean, don't expect anything. Really, just take what I'm going to ask you at face value. I don't want to go home. Can we go back to your place?"

"Um? Yeah sure. Whatever you want?" I said questioningly.

She forced a weak smile at me.

"You're not getting lucky Kent, OK. That's all I'm saying." She sighed heavily. "It's going to take me a while to clear my head. I don't want to go home and have to explain to my mom why I'm back so early. I don't want to go to the bar. I don't want to visit Sammy. I don't want to be alone. I just want to try and forget that awful, that god awful, sight. I don't know if I can, but I wanna try to go back to how I felt this morning."

"No. I understand. I was happy this morning too. No worries. I'll be my normal gentlemanly self. We can watch a movie. Something funny. Sound good?"

I figured I have to leave a voicemail for my boss. Maybe tell her the truth, maybe tell her I had the flu or something. Stomach issues are always a good excuse. No matter what, I wasn't going to go back to D.C. that night. I didn't want to look like I skipped town in case the police came by, but more importantly I wasn't going to rush Gwen out of my house just so I could drive back for job.

Gwen smiled again and nodded her head. She then scrunched up and pulled her knees to her chest. She looked even younger than she was and more vulnerable than I ever imagined she could. For a split second I was pissed off at Johnny for dying like that, for being laid out bare and dead to the world for us to see. For hurting Gwen.

But it wasn't his fault. Or was it? The cop said that he probably fell down drunk and hit his head. But if he had went back to work at four by six or seven he wouldn't have had the time to drink enough to get that wrecked. What about the screw driver that was clutched in his hand? What the hell happened to his arm? Why would an animal chew off just an arm? Didn't I read that predators eat the head first or something? What about the yelling the neighbors heard?

Gwen stopped me before I went too far down that rabbit hole. She must have seen the confusion and frustration on my face. She put her hand over mine on the stick shift.

"Hey, they'll figure out what happened. I'm sorry about your friend."

"Thanks, yeah, you're right. I'm sure they'll piece it together. Friend though? Yeah, he once was. And might have been again. Seemed like he was getting his life together. But what am I saying? You probably knew him better than I did."

"That's sad but probably true. Even sadder is that we probably knew him better than most. He didn't really have any friends that I saw, or at least he didn't bring any to the bar. He was getting better though, working for Patrick. The two of them would come in after work and both would take it easier than they did when alone. But I didn't really know him and I saw him nearly every day. Not the way you must have known him. To Johnny I was just a smiling beer delivery system with a nice set of tits." She laughed out loud at herself. Then she changed the subject. "Say, you have anything to eat at your place?"

In fact, I didn't. So I pulled into the strip mall where I shopped. We ordered two pizzas from a carryout place and while they baked we went into the grocery store and loaded up on movie watching junk food. Chips, dips, popcorn, soda, candy, a six pack of beer, and a bottle of wine. After we collected the pies it was back to my place.

An overcast sky that matched our miserable moods had replaced the cold bright sky from the morning by the time I pulled up to the house. The grey weather had become an unfortunately familiar scene. I realized that while my chat with Greene had turned somewhat confrontational, I chastised myself for not asking about Tammy. I half expected to see her family walking around in the woods still looking for her. Although I wasn't proud of myself for doing so, I pushed those thoughts out of my mind. I didn't want any additional concern to show on my face and I didn't want Gwen to have any more depressing thoughts. She didn't need anything else to bring her down that day and I certainly didn't want to be associated with tragedy in her mind.

As I parked we were pleasantly chatting. I was telling her not to expect too much from my humble home away from home.

"Not bad, Kent. Not too bad at all." She said with a mischievous grin after taking in the front of the house. "Not what I expected, it's a lot more... I dunno, cute than I thought it be. For a big city boy like yourself I thought it be all fancy steel and concrete. Jacuzzi. Odd angles. Metro...politian."

"Easy there. I bought the place used remember? Plus, I'm from Washington D.C., not Miami. Give me a break." I took a second and joined her looking up at the house, dented door and all, with pride. "You know, I like it. I very much like it here. So Gwen, you be nice."

She laughed at me.

"I do too, though you need to grow a pair and stop being so sensitive. Come on, let's go inside, the 'za is getting cold and is probably soggy by now."

"Cold maybe, but soggy only because you wanted so many toppings on yours. My cheese and mushroom will be fine." I said knowingly while Gwen rolled her eyes.

We went inside. She didn't say anything else about the house but she did look around with an approving expression on her face. I broke out some plates and put away what needed to be refrigerated.

"Start on the pizza. I'll be right back." I said as I quickly ascended the stairs two at a time. I got out of my pants and shirt, that while comfortable enough, weren't quite right for relaxing on the sofa. I put on some jogging pants and large tee shirt. Then I found a pair of pajama pants and a couple of baggy shirts for Gwen to choose from and went back downstairs.

"I changed into something more comfortable, wink wink nudge nudge".

"I don't think you are using that line correctly." She laughed at me. "But you do look comfortable. You look like a slob. But a comfortable slob."

"I brought some down for you too if you'd like. I don't know how well you can relax in those skin tight jeans you've got on. If you're interested, you can change in the bathroom or upstairs. Or not at all, just thought I'd offer."

Gwen put down her slice of pizza, which was basically only crust by then, and grabbed the clothes I held out to her. Two steps later she was closing the bathroom door.

"I have to say Kent, you sure do know how to dress a lady. You one of those big city fashion designers?" She accused me through the door.

"Jesus, I told you. I'm only from D.C.! But if you don't like what I've got, you don't have to wear it, I just thought you'd want to change."

"Oh, you'd love that. Me coming back out with nothing on." She joked. Yes I would've loved that, but I didn't feel like it was the time to flirt too heavily.

"Anyway," I slowly replied. I heard her chuckle through the door before I continued. "I'll pick out a movie, I don't have any DVDs or a player here, but I did bring up most my tape collection."

I walked over to the shelf I had recently repaired and started going through the twenty or thirty tapes I had on hand. I started looking for something funny and lighthearted. My first pick was *The Goonies*. Everyone loves *The Goonies*. Then I remembered that the kids find Chester Copperpot dead. I wasn't sure how that would play out but put it off to the side anyway. *Better Off Dead*, skip. *Ghostbusters*, skip. *Caddyshack*. Classic and only one person dies. *Ferris Bueller's Day Off*, in "keep" the pile. *This is Spinal Tap*, heck yeah.

I figured Gwen would have to like at least one of the four films I picked.

As soon as I stood up and turned around, tapes in hand, Gwen opened the bathroom door. I'm sure my jaw dropped a little. In fact I was lucky I was able to maintain my balance. She had changed into my old green and yellow college sweatshirt. It was loose and hung heavily on her, with the neck hole showing quite a bit of her collarbone and shoulder. The fabric draped over her figure softly highlighting her chest. The shirt went way below her waist line. I couldn't tell from beneath the sweatshirt but she must have tightened the pajama bottoms drawstring to their limits. The pants legs completely covered her small feet.

I don't think she had any idea how attractive she looked styled out in those comfy clothes. She was hotter at that moment than she was on our date the night before.

"What?" She asked. "Why are you looking at me like that? What's wrong?"

She turned around and I caught a glimpse of the hiked up bottoms accenting, well, her bottom. A second later she faced me again.

I replied. "Nothing. I was just wondering if you wanted to watch any of these. Each one guaranteed to put a smile on your face."

I held them out, two in each hand so she could see the covers.

"A personal guarantee, huh? In that case, yes."

"OK, which one?"

"All of them. Let's go left to right."

With that she took the pizza box and the bottle of wine over to the coffee table and plopped down on the sofa. She grabbed the blanket from the back of the chair and made herself comfortable. I put *Caddyshack* in, hit play, and joined her.

The next several hours were amazing. We laughed through *Caddyshack*, both of us quoting the movie before the characters said their lines. "Excuse me if I'm wrong Sandy, but if I kill all the golfers, they're going to lock me up and throw away the key." Halfway through *Ferris Bueller's Day Off* she threw a pillow up against me and laid on it. Her arm rested on my leg. Part of me felt like I was a kid again, nervous and excited. It brought back memories of watching movies with my high school girlfriend in her family's basement. The other part of me experienced a comfortableness and confidence I never had back then. A sense of belonging. After a while I put my arm around her, she accepted it without apparent notice. After that, even my anxiousness transitioned into pleasant familiarity. *Spinal Tap* came and went, Gwen almost spit out a sip of wine at "green globule."

By the time we put *The Goonies* on, it had grown dark and rainy outside. While it wasn't late I was worrying about the end of the evening. When the last movie finished, what then? I guessed I'd have to drive her home, it be after ten o'clock. I wished I had five or even six movies in my hands. I realized I could have always suggested we watch another but I was worried that any change, any new plans, or anything that disturbed the ordered and the blissful house of cards we built would bring it all crashing down. We both were hiding from the gruesome scene we witnessed and I guiltily loved it. With nothing else to do I resigned myself to accepting whatever fate handed me after the pirate ship sailed off and the credits rolled.

Gwen was all but practically curled up on my lap, and the Fratellis were just about to pick up Chunk from the side of the road, "I like the dark. I love the dark. But I hate nature. I hate nature," when I felt something change. At first I thought it was just disappointment or worry about the evening ending, or maybe missing work, or that I was coming to terms with Johnny's death. It wasn't any of those, but rather something else. The uneasy feeling grew in the pit of my stomach with each passing moment.

Unease then transitioned itself into anxiety. Gwen stiffened and then half sat up.

"Kent?" She asked.

I didn't have a reply for her. I moved to the edge of the sofa and she grabbed my arm.

"I'm scared Kent, what's going on?" She quietly pleaded.

"I'm not sure. I feel it too." I whispered, too afraid to make much noise.

340

She shook her head, in disbelief, unsure. Nothing was any different, the light rain pattered outside against to roof and windows. The TV continued to play. Nothing was out of the ordinary.

As my fear grew, so did the dark memories that pushed themselves to the forefront of my mind. Again I saw the bird killing itself, fleeing. I felt its struggle end as it rushed up the hill head first into that oak. I remembered the shape in the woods, in the mists, and again on the road. The deep terror it caused in me. I remembered hiding under my covers as a child, feeling the same anguish and hopelessness smothering me. I smelled again the odor of rot, death, and burnt sink.

Then I realized the last wasn't a memory. The stench in the air was real.

As it was in the woods and in my car, all I wanted to do was flee. To run. To abandon everything. I was a rabbit caught out in the open, hawk above me, fox behind me. I needed to get out of there. Out of the house. But I couldn't that night. There was nowhere else to run, not with Gwen with me. Her being by my side was the resolve I needed to stay put. Only a small amount of discipline, to be sure, but I found what I needed nonetheless. I couldn't leave her.

I stood up and sidestepped to the back of the couch and over to the coffee table. I reached back and slid my hand under the toppled pile of mail and grabbed the Springfield pistol I hid there the afternoon before. Since I didn't see anything to be afraid of, I didn't know if it be helpful, but at least I felt a little less helpless.

Gwen was as close to breaking as I was, I could see the terror welling up in her eyes. Madness bubbling through to the surface, but I also saw her control. For her, I forced a look of confidence into my face, despite having none within me.

The real courage I needed I didn't have, so I faked it the best I could. I walked up to the window that looked out into the front yard. Darkness. Nothing but a wall of black. Nothing but a pitch dark stormy night. I took a step over and rested my hand on the doorknob and hesitated. The fear and the stink, they had to be just in our minds I told myself. We were rational adults, what could be out there? With a quick twist of my wrist and a pull I yanked open the door.

Gwen gasped and I fully expected to face some unimaginable horror. Some upcoming doom waiting for us on the porch.

Instead we found nothing. The same dreary rainy scene I saw from the window greeted me at the front door. The feeling was still there, maybe even more so, but there was nothing I could see. I solidly closed the door and walked back to where Gwen was alertly perched on the edge of the sofa. Neither of us said anything, while I scanned the room. We both knew something was wrong.

On the TV, Chunk was being interrogated by the Fratellis. I started to reach for the remote to stop the movie. The noise, it was too much. I needed to focus on whatever terrible sensation was affecting us.

Before I was able to grab the controller, the motion detector light came on outside. Both of us raised our heads towards the window but otherwise were as still as statues.

Seconds stretched by, feeling like hours. From our position by the sofa, nothing out of the window was visible except the faint impression of the distant tree line lit by the lone floodlight. Details were obscured by the light but steady rain and the mist.

Then we saw it.

The doorknob shook, just a little. Then a moment later it turned.

I held my breath as I watched the door get pushed open, inch by slow inch. It stopped less than a quarter of the way through its arc. I couldn't see what was outside. The fear that ripped through me felt like it was enough to stop my heart. My stomach sank and I felt light headed. My vision twisted and blurred. The urge to run, to get away, was all consuming but at that point I couldn't move. I was frozen in place. I found myself trying to scream but all that came out of my mouth was a faint wheezing exhale.

Just below the door handle, something pushed its way into the house. Purposefully. Slowly.

The dark shape grew as more and more of the nightmare made its way in. At first I couldn't tell what it was I was seeing. The details didn't make sense. As it revealed itself I was horrified to make out something that looked like a large and partially decomposed horse head with a long matted mane hanging behind. Once past the door, the head turned, scanned the room until it saw us, and then stopped. Large sections of skinless muscle and bone were visible next to the rain soaked black fur that covered the remainder of the head. An animated rotting horse skull itself was unnatural, but that creature, that thing, was even more perverted. It wasn't a whole skull, but rather it was a collection of parts. Its lower jaw, stuffed with sharp predatory teeth, was mismatched from the rest of the head. Too many teeth. Extra teeth. Extra rows of teeth, like a shark. The outermost jutting jaw looked added on, parts of it from multiple wolves or very large dogs. Broken but fused together. Hunks of dead but still moving sinew, tendons, and torn flesh held together the collection of bones, muscle, and teeth.

I remembered Duke the dog, hanging from the tree. Jawless.

The head, never breaking its sideways stare at us, slowly rose until it was stopped by the top of the door frame. When the creature reached that height a grotesque knotted leg and cloven hoof pushed its way across the threshold and forced the door the remaining way open until it stopped against the wall with a thud.

What stood in front of us defied any sane description. Dripping wet pieces of man and animal were lashed and tied together with twice living meat and cobbled into a huge lanky roughly humanoid shape. Antlers built into a mostly hollow ribcage, the cavity filled with human and animal skulls in varying states of decay. A hip bone used as a shoulder joint. A patchwork of hairy tuffs from multiple animals stuck out from crevasses where skin was attached to supplement its form. It was huge. Even partially desiccated, the thing must have weighed over three hundred and fifty pounds.

Then I saw it.

There on the creature, the terror man, the Tiermenschen, I saw its left arm. A human hand was cupped around the elbow of the monster, fingers pushed into the dry flesh and bone. The wrist and the rest of the arm lead up to the shoulder. Pink and blue flesh mottled with purple and black rot bound to the side of the creature's long arm. Incorporated into and added to its structure. It was Johnny's missing limb.

While my eyes told me what I was seeing was real and was in front of us, the beast didn't feel like it could exist to me. Rather it was a nightmare made from hate, and fear, and evil. Such was its existence that the very light in the room seemed to be swallowed by it.

It was concepts, and abstractions, and emotions all tied to our world with living tissue. Something like Frankenstein's monster or a flesh golem. Where Hebrew lore described golems as mindless automatons, the Tiermenschen faced us down with intelligence. Its mismatched dead yellow milky eyes stared at us, through us, deep into our souls with thoughtful understanding. When it realized we were unable to run, we watched leathery corded muscles contract around the face pulling what passed for cheeks into a crude animalistic smile, an evil imitation of joy and humor. Small bits of flesh, too dried or decayed to flex, fell from its maw. Without breaking its eye contact with us, and almost as an afterthought, it flicked out with one extended arm and smashed the table near the doorway. The table held one of the two lights in the room that were on. The bulb broke as the lamp hit the floor casting us further into shadow.

Something about it felt ancient to me. Like it didn't see our lives as anything other than a brief flash in its long history. Beyond my terror, and almost worse, was that it made me feel so woefully insignificant that I knew I was absolutely nothing in its presence.

I also knew I was dead. I knew we were dead. There was no plan I could make, no movement or attack that would save us. What was logic, reasoning, or action when faced with pure emotional horror? It was hopelessness incarnate. Any helpful thoughts that may have formed had shattered against the wall of terror in front of me. My mind was consumed by the walking embodiment of festering fear that came through the door. Even if I weren't terrified, how could I ever fight something of that size and shape.

The television, unaware of the nightmare we faced, continued to play. Chunk had just spilled his guts to his kidnappers and confessed to all his sins. He was then introduced to Sloth.

Chunk screamed through the small TV speaker.

His fear was weak, artificial, and pathetic compared to ours, but his cry was still loud in the otherwise silent room. With that change in the volume Gwen, who still had her hand on my leg, dug her nails through the soft fabric of my pants and into my skin. The pain and the reminder of Gwen's presence was what I needed. What we needed.

I forcefully told myself that I wasn't a lamb waiting to be butchered. I was a man with his god given right to self-defense. I was an armed man. I had a chance.

Gwen fought through the fear that paralyzed us and gave me the strength I needed to do the same.

I raised my arm.

I exhaled, concentrated, and then pushed my thumb down on the safety of the Springfield.

Align the front sight post, squeeze the trigger.

Front sight post, squeeze.

Front sight post, squeeze.

I mechanically repeated the process and kept firing. The violence of the shells exploding was enough to break Gwen from her death trance as well. She got up and stood behind me as I emptied the last five rounds into the Tiermenschen.

With each trigger pull I saw the bullet's effects. Bone and rotten meat burst out from the new cavities that erupted from the beast. Ripples of shock moved outward from the point of impact. However, where I would expect puffs of blood from any living creature, my shots produced only clouds of dust.

Each bullet found its home in the center mass of the monster.

Each bullet inflicted damage. Mortal damage on any living thing.

Each bullet didn't appear to cause the creature in front of me any pain or do anything to even move it.

The slide locked back.

The smile across its hideous face grew larger until the equine jaw opened wide in an almost human silent laugh.

A saying I had heard years before popped into my head from out of nowhere. *"A sidearm is only good for fighting your way back to the rifle that you should have never put down in the first place."* I understood that saying completely at that moment.

"Gwen" I yelled as I pushed her in the right direction. "Down the stairs!"

For us it was only a few steps to the cellar entrance, far closer than the twenty or so feet from the front door the thing would have to cross. I knew we would make it.

A second later I wasn't so sure. With a single bound, far more agile and faster than I would have expected from something so huge, it covered half the distance to us. In another second it would have been upon us if it didn't stumble on Gwen's wine bottle which had fallen off the table. Even with that fortunate help we barely made it to the stairs.

I slammed shut the basement door behind us and immediately I threw my back against it. While it wasn't some cheap modern hollow core door, it wasn't built to stop anything of that size or strength. Before I got a chance to reflect on how bad off we were, below me Gwen was heading back up the stairs with a six foot tall step ladder.

With her quick thinking we jammed the ladder against the door and the opposite wall. It was only in place for a second when I began to see the door being tested. First by the turning of the knob and then when I saw the door flex, pushing the ladder legs into the drywall. We were far from safe.

I leapt down the stairs and tossed my skis, the nearest items to me, up the stairs. Then I grabbed a wooden book shelf and threw that up as far as I could. A broken lamp. A box of paint brushes and tools. Anything to slow it down. I hoped that if we could tangle it in junk, we could make a run for it by going out one of the windows. It was far too large to follow that way and by the time it circled around the front of the house we'd have a head start. Not much of one, but I was grasping at any chance we had.

I oddly remember at the time thinking about how throwing ourselves into action allowed us to force through the nightmarish horror we felt. We were still terrified, but that was really only fear, and not hopelessness, and that was something.

With a loud crash the door gave as the ladder was pushed halfway through a wall and fell free. It lasted in place for less than a minute. Instead of barging down, I saw the monster's head slowly emerge, once again close to the floor, peering down the stairs. I remembered I led us into the basement for guns. As I turned around to grab one, there was Gwen, feeding one last shell into the Remington 870 shotgun.

I don't know where I was able to find it with all the horror and fear inside me, but I was able to give her a weak smile when I realized how much courage and fortitude she had in her.

I accepted the offered gun and pointed to the window with my free hand.

"When it's committed to the stairs, get out, and run. *NOT* into the woods. Down the road." I knew I didn't have to tell her not to stop. We were both barefooted, and I didn't have my car keys. Running would be hard on the gravel, and the thing was fast, but we were past the point of simply giving up and dying. We would at least run.

Just like Johnny had run.

She hesitated at first like maybe she wanted to say something. Maybe she realized that I wouldn't have time to do the same after giving her a head start. Instead of speaking she forced a smile then went to the window. The pane opened with a squeak. It would be slow getting out, but she could make it.

When I turned back around the Terror Man had started its decent out of the shadows at the top of the stairs, head first and on all fours. Its wiry legs and arms, much longer than any natural beast, twisted at unnatural angles. In that orientation the demon looked more like a spider than any of its component creatures. It carefully stepped to avoid the clutter I used to block its advance. I watched it see Gwen by the open window then quicken its attempt over the bookshelf and fallen ladder. I'd have to slow it down more.

"GO! NOW!" I screamed without looking back.

I pulled the trigger and a blast of lead shot carved a small fist size hole into its shoulder. The wound was shallow, but at that distance even birdshot could cause serious damage. The monster faltered and slightly lost balance. The shot had stopped its advance.

Having just that smallest taste of hope I racked the action, aimed, and pulled the trigger again. The damage my second shot inflicted was much like the first. Lead shot ricocheted around basement, some biting into my arms and face. As fast as I could I fired twice more, unable to miss at that distance. Plastic ejected shells bounced on the ground at my feet, silently for all I knew. With each shot my ears experienced some of the worst pain I'd ever had. The ringing was constant.

With one shot left, it was clear I wasn't going to permanently stop the monster with the weapons I had. Maybe with a M2 Ma Deuce, or some other big bore, or squad automatic weapon, bullets could have chipped away at it enough to render its physical form useless or cause it to flee. However, to it, my shots didn't amount to much.

I imagined how it would use my dead body for parts to repair the minor damage I had inflicted on it.

I backed up to the window, wanting to draw it further into the room, to give Gwendy a few more seconds after I was dispatched. The creature advanced, stepping through the shelves of the busted bookcase, down to the basement floor. Slowly it unbent and stood up to its full ceiling high stature. It tilted its rotting horse head to maintain eye contact with me. I was unable to look away. The creature's dead cloudy eye penetrated deep inside my soul. Holding onto my sanity I fought hard to push it out of my mind, to not sink any further into the terror it was drowning me in.

I thought of Gwen. Of her running for her life down the road. I tried to get angry. It was over a mile to the public road and then her only chance was flagging down one the rare trucks driving that time of night. It would have been at least five miles of running before she'd find someone's home. Thinking of her running, with that monstrosity gaining on her, was what I used to steel my mind.

I knew I couldn't stop it from killing me, not with one shot left, but I thought maybe I could slow it down. For Gwen I had to try. I lowered my point of aim and squeezed off the last shell. At ten feet away the beast's knee blew out and nearly detached. It would have fallen over if it hadn't stabilized itself by reaching up and grabbing one of the exposed floor joists above. After the shot I uselessly threw the empty gun at it as hard as I could before I grabbed a shovel from the corner behind me.

I waited for it to attack.

Instead of rushing in, it disappointingly shook its head at me in a disturbingly human like manner. Then it smiled a toothy menacing grin. It let go of the ceiling and fully rested its weight back on the damaged leg. The knee held. I had failed Gwen.

Just as I began to wish I used the last shell on myself I saw it flinch, and cock its head sideways. I braced myself for whatever would come. Instead of attacking, it turned, and with two bounds it loudly pushed through the clutter. With that the Terror Man was back up the stairs. I heard its long claws and hoofed feet scratching and pounding the floor above me as it dashed on all fours across the living room. I didn't know what to think. Did Gwen come in back to find my keys? Did it hear her running? Was it worried she would get away? I glanced out the high basement window and was able to make out distant moving lights on the tree line. Someone was coming down the driveway.

I couldn't will myself to directly follow the beast back up the stairs, so instead I wiggled my way out the same window Gwen exited and onto the muddy wet ground outside. I pulled myself up. My whole body was trembling from fear and mental exhaustion. I didn't want to come face to face with the living corpse coming around the corner so I moved away from the house before heading to the front yard. To where the lights were coming from.

Then, once I made it out far enough, I saw a police car. Outside of the car I saw someone shining a flashlight at Gwen who was animatedly yelling and pointing back towards the house.

As soon as I saw the two, the police officer must have seen the creature. I couldn't actually see it from where I was, the house blocked it from my view, however by their reactions they were looking right at it. The officer took a couple steps backwards which put her into the path of the headlights. I could see it was Officer Thompson visiting again. She kept back pedaling until she hit the front of her cruiser and was only barely able to stop herself from falling over the hood. Once she righted herself she waved back to Gwen yelling something I couldn't make out. They were only thirty or forty yards away from me but it would take hours for my hearing to return to normal. I started heading towards them in a hesitant and careful jog.

Gwen then got into the back seat of the police vehicle. My heart sank a little. I thought that if she had got in the front, there was a chance she could have driven away. Although in hindsight it might have been the better choice since there was no telling if Thompson left the keys in the ignition. The back seat was reinforced to carry prisoners.

Meanwhile, the Officer had drawn her service weapon, a Beretta 92. She shored up her stance in a single well practiced and fluid movement, leaned in, and started emptying her magazine. One quickly measured shot at a time she fired at the beast. On anything alive, a well-placed 9mm round is just as lethal as any. On that thing, and I hoped otherwise, I knew that her handgun rounds were even less effectual than the ones in my forty-five had been.

She had fired at least eight or nine rounds and I still couldn't see the Terror Man. Then, in the blink of an eye, it was there in front of her. It closed the last fifteen yards visible to me in less than a second. Even with the shot out knee it stood tall and reached down with one of its huge hobbled together hands. It's long clawed fingers wrapped around the top of Nancy Thompson's head. I heard her scream as she continued rapidly firing into the monster's chest. With nothing more than what looked like a dismissive wave of its arm, the monster flung the policewoman off into the darkness. I couldn't see where she landed.

The Terror Man turned its attention towards the car.

I stopped in my tracks.

I didn't know what to do. I didn't know what I COULD do. All I had was the very real knowledge and understanding that the beast wasn't going to let any of us make it out alive. We were going to disappear into the woods, our bodies used to piece together, repair, and to strengthen that horror that was standing in front of me. I was trapped again within my fear and doubt.

The Tiermenschen started pounding on the cruiser door, striking wildly. The window broke almost immediately, but the perforated steel sheet on the inside was holding. The barrier was designed to keep violent drunks and handcuffed felons inside the vehicle. I didn't know how long it would last keeping something like that creature out. Gwen was screaming at the top of her lungs.

Blow after blow shook the car, even with my damaged hearing the sound of twisting and fatiguing metal could be heard over Gwen's cries. I knew I had to do something, but I was paralyzed. Then shots started firing again.

Pop. Pop. Pop.

Pop. Pop. Pop.

I heard a small caliber pistol ring out. Muzzle flashes from the brush let me know that Officer Thompson was still alive and still fighting. The evil entity stopped its brutal assault on the car. It glanced to where the shots were coming from, and then it turned and stared directly at me. I was still deep in the shadows but it looked unerringly at me. Again it's intelligence shown through its rough animalistic form. With centuries of experience it knew that none of us had a chance. It had hunted those ancient mountains long before my time on earth. It would catch us one by one when we lost hope again and ran. It couldn't afford to have any of us reach safety. This time too much had happened. We'd remember something, point to the evidence, and maybe we'd help others remember. It didn't want us to be hunting it. The demon had to finish us off.

Slowly it turned its back on me. It knew I was harmless, especially unarmed.

Purposefully it began a slow walk into the bushes to put an end to Officer Nancy Thompson's annoyance. Something about its certainty, its absolute knowledge that our fate was sealed, pushed me back into action. I couldn't stand there watching a good cop get ripped to shreds, she didn't deserve that. Gwen and I didn't deserve that.

I restarted my slow jog up the slight hill to the driveway. I still didn't know what I could do, but I knew I couldn't do it from where I was. I looked around for something to use as a weapon. A rock. A piece of wood. Anything. Then it occurred to me.

Ten feet away in the backseat of my car was the Remington M1868.

The Pontifico.

Its action would be slow in my unskilled hands, but I figured I might be able to get off two shots before I resorted to using it as a club. Two shots were better than nothing. I opened the back door nearest to me, putting the car between me and my monstrous adversary. I hoped the barrier would be enough to buy me the time needed to do some real damage with the nearly fifty caliber lead slug I was about to fire. A bullet with even more energy than the shot gun shells I fired earlier. I opened the box of ammo, spilled most, but still managed to clutch two rounds in my trembling right hand.

With my left hand, from under the blankets where it had laid covered, I pulled free the old rifle.

As soon as my hand touched it, I heard an unearthly snarl bark out from the beast. It was the first sound I heard it make that night with its decaying vocal cords. A sound so hideous and corrupt I could never fully describe it. Shivers ran down my spine at the unnaturally dischorded noise. My knees buckled and I nearly fell. I looked up just in time see the Terror Man howl out again, filled with hatred and anger. Its arms flailed and lashed out towards the sky in protest with rage and hostility.

When it finished, it turned to face me yet again.

I focused on my task. The roll block was still open. I slid the shell into place, and threw the block forward.

I shouldered the weapon and looked up.

I was almost too late. The thing was coming at me on all fours with impossible speed.

Without thinking about what I was doing, I offered the shortest, most sincere prayer I ever made.

"God, help us."

Then I pulled the trigger.

The massive kick to my shoulder was expected.

Where I anticipated another deafening boom, something else happened.

It was the loudest sound I'd ever heard. It was the most beautiful sound I'd ever heard. Its majesty shook me to my very soul.

Instead of an explosion, I was greeted by a note. Or a chord. Or every note ever played combined in perfect harmony as the perfect chord. It was a flawless silver bell ringing out. It was a choir. It was a Les Paul playing a power chord through a Marshall stack. It was all of those and nothing even close. It was the most loving, beautiful, and powerful sound in creation.

It was a sound I'd never heard before or since.

The muzzle flash that accompanied the ring was no less impressive. A golden sphere of pure caring, warmth, and belonging. The light was like a thousand fiery suns. I was blinded but could see everything with perfect clarity.

The bullet, a forceful, mighty, and glowing white light, streaked through the night. Time almost stood still as I was able to watch the shot fly true towards its target.

Even the rain drops stopped and hovered in the air.

The round found home and struck the undead evil creature directly in the upper chest. Chunks of seared and smoldering rotting material flew off in grotesque arcs. A melon sized cavity was blasted violently through the monster. Every seam holding the demon together flashed with black smoke and bright white fire.

The terror man was running full speed at me when it was hit. The mechanical force from the projectile didn't completely stop the monster's forward momentum. As it tumbled, as it slowed and fell to the ground, it came apart. The impossibly old darkness that bound its flesh together, the power which held the demon to our plane, was torn from its physical form. The dark essence that gave life to its animated corpses was utterly destroyed. Hunks of rotting tissue littered the ground around my car, but nothing remained of the twisted intelligence that controlled it.

I was filled with wonder and joy. Despite the horror I had faced I'd never felt so perfectly loved and calm. I just stood in blissful awe.

Eventually a noise casually drew my attention back to the police car. Gwen had bent back the corner of the twisted metal that had protected her. The door had only been seconds away from failing under the beast's assault. I looked over and saw her arm reach around to unlock the car from the outside. Seconds later she was running towards me.

As she approached she didn't slow. When we collided she wrapped her arms around my neck and forcefully kissed me.

Without breaking contact I gently laid the rifle back down on the seat, knowing with absolute certainty we were safe. Sitting in the car the whole weapon seemed to glow. Especially the Papal Seal. In the darkness the engraving of the Crossed Keys of Saint Peter was plainly visible.

With my arms free I squeezed Gwen back as hard as I could.

Slowly the golden light which had filled the surrounding forest and yard receded. We separated enough to catch our breath. Gwen started to gently weep in joy on my shoulder, but that only lasted a moment. She pulled back just enough from me and looked me in the eyes while wiping tears from hers.

"Kent, what was that? It was... Wonderful."

Before I could reply Officer Thompson came running up with a pronounced limp, cuts on her face, and with her left arm bleeding and hanging uselessly broken at her side. She was obviously injured but didn't seem to care.

"That sound? That light? What was it? Why am I so happy? That thing is it, is it dead? Is it gone? What happened? Are you two alright?" She asked in rapid succession.

I didn't have it in me to even begin to reply to her. The euphoria of the moment had begun to fade and with that my fatigue returned. Instead I nodded to her, leaned against the side of my car, and slid down to the muddy ground below where I sat exhausted. Thompson accepted my reply for what it was and looked over to Gwen.

"How about you Teresa? Do you need help? Are you alright?"

Gwen answered, "Yeah, I am now. Thank you Mrs. Thompson, for everything. I really am alright now."

It took me a few moments to realize that I wasn't sure who Teresa was. I glanced between the two of them confused.

"Teresa?" I asked, not even really sure I cared. "What?"

"Oh. That's me Kent." Gwen answered with a gentle laugh as she turned to face me. "My first name is Teresa, I always hated my middle name. Gwendolyn. When the other kids found out I could never get them to stop calling me it. I honestly just kind of gave up trying after Middle School. Next to no one calls me Teresa anymore."

Officer Nancy Thompson shook her head and looked at us befuddled.

"Well, I don't understand any of this. I got to report, this, whatever this is." She said hesitantly as she limped over to what was left of her patrol car.

Gwen, or Teresa as we all call her now, slid down next to me on the ground. She wrapped her arm around mine, put her head on my shoulder, and we both spent the next half an hour there together in the mud.

Dew points, temperature, and relative humidity

The campfire was nearly out. Only the smallest flames remained dancing on the darkening coals. The campers could barely see each other across the dying fire. The canopy above was still overwhelmingly black.

Kent had finished his story and sat waiting.

Andy reacted first with a resentful outburst.

"Great fucking story Kent. Real great." Andy stated exasperated. "You had me going for a bit. Almost pulled the wool over my eyes. Yep, you nearly got me, but if I'd known you'd be feeding me horseshit all night long I'd have gone to sleep hours ago. Thanks a lot for that. Oh, and thanks again for telling me the truth, asshole. I guess I should be happy that I at least *SAW* the rifle this time. I'll ask your wife what the real fucking story is. At least I know Teresa won't tell me a fabricated pile of shit like that. Especially now that I got some leverage on her too. Going to start calling her Gwen. See how she likes that.

That is, unless that was just bullshit too? Did she really go by Gwen? You know, I don't know what to believe after that. You know what, screw you Kent. What do you think about all this shit, Professor?"

Andy briefly looked over at their guest for support, although he wasn't finished berating Kent for wasting his time. The more he thought about the story the more Andy got mad. Halfway through Kent's description of the monster attack, Andy had made up his mind that Kent was pulling his leg and decided the whole tale was just some long drawn out ghost story. For Andy, demons and holy magic rifles that shot heavenly bullets were just too much to accept as reality.

After his brief glance towards Herb, but before starting back up again on Kent, Andy had to do a double take. There was something not quite right about the professor's face. Andy couldn't seem to focus his eyes on him. He was kind of blurry. He looked away and everything else seemed fine, but when he turned back to the professor his body almost seemed like a photo that was doubly exposed. He saw the professor, but something else as well.

"Hey? What the..." Andy started to say as he rubbed his eyes. However, Kent cut him off firmly.

"*YES* professor, what *DID* you think about the ending?" He asked quietly but forcibly.

West didn't reply. Instead he hissed out a curse that damned
something that sounded like "lamb king" and slowly rose. Kent
followed suit by also standing while keeping the muzzle of the rifle
pointed towards the professor.

"Actually, don't answer that." Kent said. "I have a better question for
you, since I think we only really have time for just this one. Herb, how
is it that in this cold air, I haven't once seen your breath tonight?"

Andy looked at Kent.

"What? Wait? What the fuck?"

When Andy turned back to West, he no longer saw a double image.
Instead, as the glamour fully dropped away, he was able to see through
the professor's face that was rapidly fading out. He was able to see
clearly what was behind the facade. For the first time all night Andy
realized his eyes had been lying to him, his vision placed under some
Unseelie spell. Andy had never been so scared in his life.

Instead of an awkward and cold professor, what he saw was taunt grey
green skin over a mostly human face. The thing sharing their fire was
shorter than the man it had pretended to be. The North Face
windbreaker and pants the professor had been wearing were still there
on the creature, real in every regard, but tattered and filthy. Its
wickedly wide mouth was filled with hundreds of tiny sharp needle like
teeth. Its eyes too big, fiery red, with slits like a cat. Its nose long,

hooked, and pointed. The rough sewn cap on its head, stained black, brown, and coppery red with old blood was pulled down loose over its ears. Long hooked black fingernails adorned both of its four fingered hands.

With an angry laughing cackle and unreal speed the creature leapt across the fire pit directly at Kent. Andy fell backwards off his log screaming out a high pitched cry in terror.

With the thing still in midair, for a split second, there was a faint sound of a click and the last whispered syllables of a prayer.

The clearing filled with golden bright light, and the sound of a powerful and beautiful silver bell rang out into the early morning.

About this book

Writing this book has been one of those projects that I never seemed to get finished. It kind of started about fifteen or so years ago, before I ever considered telling a story, when I learned of the existence of the Pontificio. I remember that I emailed a friend a link to the rifle with a note that said, *"If I needed to fight a vampire, this is what I'd want."*

Years later, after reading a popular urban fantasy novel, I started imagining a story about an everyday guy faced with something truly evil and what it would take to fight it. Not a magician, not a Navy SEAL, not a hero. Just a regular dude. Something more "realistic". At that point I remembered the M1868 Papal States Remington. From there things just kind of just clicked.

I didn't know how to write a book, maybe I still don't, but I figured I could give it a try. So I did. For several years, on my train ride to and from work, I would reread a little of what I wrote, edit a little, and if there were time, write a page or two more. The project kept my mind off my commute, which I loathed, and it gave me someplace else to be.

First on a Galaxy Note 1, then a Google Nexus 7, and then finally on two different NVidia Shield Tablets I slowly touch screen typed my way through this. For over 5 years, with more than a few extended breaks, I opened up Google Docs and hammered away until I "finished" writing. At which point I realized how much work it still needed. For example, at one point the book was 29,000 words longer then it is now (without any real changes to the narrative). So it sat, defeated. Then a friend published a collection of his short stories, and that re-motivated me. Whenever I had the time, I'd pick it up again. I spent a few more years re-reading, re-writing, and re-editing everything over and over again. Maybe once or twice a year I'd read it again with pen in hand. Sort of like sanding, I worked on the rough spots with finer and finer sandpaper... err... edits.

Until now. At this point I'm considering this book finished. No more sanding for me. It is what is it, and what it is, is done. Now maybe I can begin working on something else.

- Old Man Ski

Made in the USA
Middletown, DE
24 December 2020